FAITH

CHRIS PARKER

FAITH

THE FINAL CHAPTER IN THE MARCUS KLINE TRILOGY.

CHRIS PARKER

Urbane
PUBLICATIONS

urbanepublications.com

First published in Great Britain in 2018
by Urbane Publications Ltd
Suite 3, Brown Europe House, 33/34 Gleaming Wood Drive,
Chatham, Kent ME5 8RZ
Copyright © Chris Parker, 2018

A CIP catalogue record for this book is available
from the British Library.

ISBN 978-1-911583-78-3
MOBI 978-1-911583-79-0

Design and Typeset by Michelle Morgan

Cover by Ben Thomas

Printed and bound by 4edge Limited, UK

URBANE
urbanepublications.com

For Peter and Mike

- and with gratitude to all the other men and women who do
the same challenging and much-needed work.

FAITH: *noun*

Complete trust or confidence in someone or something.

'It is not enough to ask a question
you have to seek the answer.
It is not enough to hold a belief
you must challenge it constantly.
It is not enough to lay claim to faith
you need to exercise it openly in the face of adversity.'

Epiah Khan

PART ONE
FRAGMENTS

CHAPTER 1

There is a difference between sure and certain.

Sure is more certain than reasonable doubt and less certain than certain.

That's how it is in our so-called justice system. That's the very thin dividing line. Move just a fraction of one percent in one direction and you're sure. Be persuaded a fraction of one percent in the other direction and you have reasonable doubt.

It's important because if the jury is less than sure, you're innocent. If they are sure, you're guilty.

We don't hold trials to create or establish justice. We hold them to provide theatre and provocation and justification. Trials are gladiatorial. The weapons of choice are words, gestures and stories – especially stories. It's all about influence and nothing to do with truth. It's all about who is the most convincing.

Which person do you believe?

Which person do you trust?

It's all about who gets inside your mind, who takes control of your emotions and decision-making.

They are going to send a barrister against me. It will be a man. He'll stink of confidence.

He'll be deaf to possibility.

Wrapped in arrogance.

Helpless.

He will be that way because you can't imagine what you don't know, what you don't believe is possible.

And whatever they think, they don't know me. So they can't imagine what I'm going to do to them. They can't even begin to imagine it. Instead of imagination, they have faith. They have faith in their own experience and ability. They have faith in what they call the system.

It's misplaced.

And the worst thing you can do with faith is to misplace it. That's worse than losing it. And it's far, far worse than having none.

Most people, of course, wouldn't understand that. Most people need faith just to get by. It gives them hope. It creates meaning. Sometimes, when they've reached the point of confusing faith with certainty, when they are more than just sure, it makes them brave. That's usually when they get killed. Or when they start killing. It's when they are certain they can step off a cliff and fly, that they will live forever, change the world.

Defeat me.

When faith is that misplaced, the outcome is inevitable.

Absolute destruction.

Inside and out.

If you think I'm wrong – if you're not quite sure – just watch what happens. Stay safe on the sidelines and watch what I do with them. Watch it all from the security of your seat. Watch and decide who is in control. Who has the power. Who wins. Watch it to the very end and then, when there's nothing left, you judge.

Go on.

I dare you.

CHAPTER 2

MONDAY - TRIAL DAY 1

'All rise!'

Anne-Marie Wells jumped to her feet faster than everyone else in the packed courtroom. She coughed nervously, covered her mouth with her hand, and kept her gaze low. She didn't want to look at anyone. She didn't want anyone to look at her. And she certainly didn't want to be heard.

Right now the only thing Anne-Marie Wells knew for certain was that she was incapable of giving testimony, of talking out loud in this place. Above all things she wanted to sit there in silence and be ignored.

Anne-Marie straightened her fingers. Her nail varnish was light pink - not quite skin tone and shinier. She had studied it several times already since entering the courtroom. Her nails were covered perfectly.

The Clerk's voice thudded into her consciousness for a second time. She guessed he was responding to something the Judge must have said. She realised she hadn't actually seen or heard the Judge enter and take his seat. She realised everyone else had sat down again. She didn't have time to join them.

'My Lord, today's case is the Crown versus Anne-Marie Wells.'

The words exploded in her chest and gut. She rocked in place, vaguely aware of the seat pressing against the back of her legs. She gasped, gulped in air, was forced to look.

The Judge was ready for her, his eyes unblinking and penetrating. She knew them, just as she knew his voice.

'Anne-Marie Wells welcome to my courtroom, my centre of justice. I won't ask how you plead because I know how you do. I have heard you plead. Remember? Of course you do, impossible to forget. I have heard you plead and I have heard you do other, more intimate things, too. That was the case, wasn't it? Inescapably so.'

'Yes.' The answer escaped her. Quiet, but loud enough for all to hear.

'The case today is inescapable, too, because the truth is inside you, swirling and swelling and soon to come out. Isn't it?'

'It...it can't. It mustn't.'

'Who are you talking to now, Anne-Marie?'

'Myself. Myself. I can't. I mustn't. Not again. Not ever. It must be a secret. You promised it would be a secret.'

'The best secrets are meant to be shared. The best place to share such secrets is here. Now. This is the place where intimacies are revealed, either by accident or design. Sometimes willingly, sometimes forced. It's why you are standing there now.'

The Judge leaned back in his chair.

'You know as well as I that the more you try to resist, the more you will begin the process of remembering and recreating and moving, from the inside to the out, opening to the inevitability of what is happening, like the currents drawing the tide, making it swell, unstoppable...'

'No, please!' Anne-Marie heard his words as she once had before; felt them affecting her in exactly the same way. She tried to shut them out, but his voice was irresistible.

'That's right!' He said. 'Feel how your heart rate is increasing. Feel how your blood is flowing faster. Feel the tension and how your skin is already tingling. Feel how the inside is already affecting the out. That's it! Your body is preparing you when it spasms like that. It knows how to do this so well. And it has been waiting for you to release again, building secretly, so that here now you can show us all. Show everyone present! And as you do this, know forever that I can see you Anne-Marie Wells. Inside and out.'

'Please! No! Please, not again!' Anne-Marie pressed her fingers tight into her palms, hoping the pain from her shiny pink nails would break through the trance.

It was hopeless.

She felt a part of her brain in the back of her head, the same part he had influenced once before, urging her to surrender.

'I am guilty!' She gasped. 'I am. I admit it! Please, I'm guilty so punish me a different way. Please! Don't make me!'

'You will orgasm now,' the Judge commanded. 'More powerfully than before. You will let everyone see and hear! This is my courtroom!'

'No!' Anne-Marie felt her body begin to tremble, her blood pulsing. 'No!'

'That's what you said before. This time it's taking you there more quickly. We are all, indeed, going to know. And when you orgasm you know what to shout, you know what you want us all to hear.'

'Oh God, no!'

Just as before she could feel his words touching her, penetrating her. The sensations rushed through faster than she had ever experienced.

'Do it and tell them all!'

'No! Please! No!'

'Do it now!' The Judge leaned forwards, slamming his palms down hard. 'Now!' He left his mouth open. She could see his tongue. She squeezed her eyes shut.

'Tell them!' The Judge roared. 'Tell them now!'

Her orgasm overwhelmed her, blinding her to any sense of time or place. She heard herself scream his name.

'Ethan!' She repeated it again and again. 'Ethan! Ethan!'

Then her body exploded.

CHAPTER 3

MONDAY - TRIAL DAY 1
4.25am

Anne-Marie Wells sat bolt upright in her bed as the nightmare forced her awake. Her right hand was clutching at her chest. Her heart was thudding against her breastbone as if trying to escape. Tears were flowing down her cheeks, mixing with her sweat. The words of Ethan Hall echoed in her mind. She bit back the urge to scream with rage.

The dream had made her orgasm again, just as it had last night and the night before. He had been reappearing in her dreams, repeating the abuse, increasingly as the trial drew closer.

Ethan Hall.

The master hypnotist. The great manipulator and destroyer of lives. The man she had first seen preparing to kill her husband, Marcus Kline.

Ethan Hall.

Worse than the worst form of cancer.

Anne-Marie knew that for certain. Despite Marcus's best efforts to save her, she had been dying of ovarian cancer when she had opened the door and looked into Ethan Hall's penetrating eyes. He had hypnotised her effortlessly and deeply. She remembered vaguely images of green fields, of feeling she had left her body behind, that the cancer was disappearing – dissolving - as his words moved through her.

She remembered more clearly what happened next. She had no

doubt that was his intention.

'You have to show me your bedroom,' he had said, before walking her to the stairs.

She had led the way, then laid down on the bed - *this* bed - because he ordered her to. The hypnotic trance he had created pinned her in place. She felt her body betray her as his words invaded deep inside, making her orgasm against her will time after time.

Ethan Hall raped her without once touching her physically.

He raped her after saving her life.

And she had told no one. She never would. It was the only certainty left in her life. He had created a secret that held her prisoner more completely than any cancerous cells ever could.

Now her illness was in remission – 'Miraculous', her doctors called it – and she hated herself and her life almost as much as she hated Ethan Hall.

Worse than the worst form of cancer.

Anne-Marie looked to her left. Marcus wasn't there. Again. Third night in a row she had woken from her recurring nightmare to find herself alone.

Not so long ago, before Ethan's arrest, before his visit, Marcus was always close by, ready to hold and comfort her whenever the cancer-dreams attacked. It was, she reflected, just as well he had been unable to sleep of late; the only thing that could make this dream worse, would be having Marcus next to her when she woke. Her very sanity depended on no one ever discovering her secret.

Anne-Marie forced herself out of the bed and crossed to the window that looked out over the rear garden and the valley beyond. He was standing in the middle of the lawn with his back to the house, just as he had been on the two previous nights. Tonight he was looking at the earth rather than the stars.

She had wanted to move out of this rented house, but had forced herself to stay. She wanted to burn the bed, but how would she possibly have explained that to Marcus?

'Ethan is driving us apart,' she whispered, 'just when we most need to be together.'

She turned away from the window. The bed dominated the room. Anne-Marie looked at the bedside clock with its illuminated hands.

4.30am.

Six hours before the trial of Ethan Hall began.

Anne-Marie shivered.

CHAPTER 4

MONDAY - TRIAL DAY 1
4.31am

Marcus Kline was oblivious to the bitter January chill, to the silence in the garden and the valley, to the darkness.

'Perhaps we do live in a world of ghosts.' His wife had said to him only hours after his best friend DCI Peter Jones had informed them of Ethan Hall's arrest. 'And, if we do, perhaps they see us as the otherworldly beings.'

A world of ghosts.

It felt increasingly as if she was right. Only the ghosts weren't spiritual entities. They were memories; fragments of the past with lives of their own. Fragments that could whisper or shout, influence your behaviour, blind you to things happening right in front of your eyes. Fragments that reached out, morphing subtly as they shaped the present.

Marcus Kline could remember the time when he had believed himself to be the most powerful communicator alive, when his consultancy, **Influence**, had been in demand from leaders across the globe. But since he had become a victim of Ethan Hall and lurched terrifyingly close to a complete breakdown, that success had evaporated and the associated memories had all but disappeared over the horizon of his mind. In the forefront now were powerful, pressing images of how easily Ethan Hall had won their battle of words, of the scalpel in Ethan's hand pressing against the skin just above his temple, of his wife's cancer.

No matter how much Marcus wanted to believe his use of hypnosis and trance-states had played a pivotal role in Anne-Marie's incredible recovery, he simply couldn't. The cancer, combined with a mind-numbing fear of losing his wife, had proven too much for him. He had failed the most important task he had ever undertaken. He was at once overjoyed at Anne-Marie's return to health and deeply ashamed of his inability to help her.

And in a few, short hours the trial of Ethan Hall, his nemesis, would begin. Soon the two would be face to face for the first time since Ethan had almost killed him.

Marcus reached into his jeans pocket and took out his mobile phone. He needed to listen to Peter Jones's voice message again. He had received it eight hours earlier. He had replayed it five times already. He pressed the phone to his ear as the familiar voice sounded.

'I hope you are both doing your best to relax today, and that you get a good night's sleep. If you are going to think about anything, remember what you saw and heard when we went to court last month to watch a trial in progress. You've been there, seen it and heard it now, so you know what to expect in terms of procedure and attitude. The only difference, as we've talked about, is that this is a much more high-profile trial than the one we visited. There'll be a lot of media attention. You can expect them to focus on you and Ethan Hall equally. So use all your skills and experience to present yourself well; at all costs avoid getting drawn into any sort of confrontation with the press. Or with Ethan. Especially with him.'

'When you are in the witness box listen carefully to each question you are asked and answer only that. Answer precisely, simply, and say nothing more than is required. If anyone can separate the question from the questioner, it's you my friend.

Whatever you think about yourself currently, I still regard you as the best in the world at what you do. It's crucial, though, that you avoid a communication battle with Ethan in court. It's what he'll want. It's what he'll expect. We can't play into his hands.'

'Leave the winning up to Mike. It's his world. You just do everything in your power to distance yourself from the memories of what Ethan has done and deal with the present in as clean and simple a manner as possible. You can do this Marcus. Trust me. Trust yourself. Find some way to cocoon yourself from the past and from your feelings towards Ethan. This time you'll influence best by not taking the lead.'

'And remember what Imran, the owner of the curry house says. Everything passes. Even this. When all is said and done, Ethan Hall is just a piece of shit so let's flush him away and move on. There are much better things to focus on in life. Right? Be brave.'

Marcus kept the phone to his ear for a few seconds, listened to the click as the call ended, listened to the silence as if there were a few final words he had missed. There was nothing. Just as there had been nothing the five times before. He returned the phone to his pocket.

Distance yourself from the memories.

He knew how. He'd helped countless other people change their relationship with past events. Only this time it was different. The memories he needed to escape from felt as if they were imprinted in the front of his brain, as if they were attached to a seemingly innocent range of objects and places he encountered every day.

Cocoon yourself.

Daren't even try. Right now it was impossible to differentiate a cocoon from a prison cell. He felt too isolated and trapped to even consider another form of separation. Not every cocoon protects and releases life, he told himself. Some became finely woven coffins. Some things just don't pass through easily. Some things stick and stay. And then eventually, unable to process, unable to make a clean start, the organism dies.

Marcus Kline inhaled deeply, letting the winter air chill his lungs. He wondered if Ethan Hall was having a good night's sleep. He wondered who else was awake thinking about what the day would bring.

He glanced back at the house and decided to stay out a while longer. There was no point trying to go to sleep now. And besides, for some reason, the house felt colder than the winter air.

CHAPTER 5

MONDAY - TRIAL DAY 1
5.15am

Mike Coopland QC hadn't slept all night. He hadn't even tried. Instead he had walked up and down his large, south-facing lounge rehearsing his opening speech, letting his mind race from one aspect of the case to another, connecting the dots.

He had made his first cup of coffee half an hour ago. Now he was on his second. He'd pour the third at 5.30. On trial day the caffeine barely affected his system; he was too adrenalised for that. Three strong early morning coffees were simply part of his pre-trial routine. Just like staying awake all night and prowling the lounge. Like having a single slice of toast for breakfast instead of his usual porridge. Like making sure he arrived at court ninety minutes before the trial was due to start. The pre-trial routine was an essential part of his success. It meant he was ready before everyone else. It put him several steps ahead before the race to battle even started.

Mike stopped pacing, drank a mouthful of coffee, and looked at the framed photo taken on the day he had been appointed a Queen's Counsel; the day he taken silk. His wife, Gemma, was standing on his right. His two daughters, Sally and Joanne, were on his left. He was standing there, arms reaching out around them all, proud as punch, a huge self-satisfied smile on his face.

The photo had been taken twelve years ago. He could remember it as if it were yesterday. Twelve years of prosecuting and defending some of the most challenging cases seemed to have gone by in a flash. But even with twelve year's experience trial day still made him tremble with adrenalin, still made his mind race.

Mike found it irresistible. Confidence came with the adrenalin. Confidence spiced by the memories of his rare defeats – and just how painful they had been. He was, he knew, part of the best legal system in the world. Its combative nature brought out the best in all concerned. No one wanted to lose. For all sorts of reasons.

'Imagine trying to explain to the world that to be a great silk you have to be an addict.' Mike looked at his younger self, still holding on to the bodybuilder's physique even though he had stopped training a few months before the photo was taken. 'Wouldn't that shock and confuse more than a few people?'

He finished his coffee and turned away from the photograph, his mind switching back to his courtroom narrative. He ran through the content and the style, the sequencing, the key messages he needed to share to the jury and the facts he could offer to support his version of events.

As he taught less experienced barristers, to convince a jury you not only had to tell the most plausible story, you had to be the most believable and engaging storyteller. You also had to know how to turn the jury against your opposition.

When all was said and done, people were influenced by other people far more than they were by so-called facts.

Mike had known that forever.

Now he was a master at telling a good story whilst making jurors like him and dislike anyone who tried to tell a different version. And, no matter how concerned Peter Jones was about Ethan's ability to influence or, even, hypnotise people around him, Mike's storytelling experience coupled with the way he would ensure Ethan was presented to the court should make it a slam dunk.

'And that's why this particular trial is going to be - '

'- Who are you talking to?'

Mike spun round. Joanne was standing in the frame of the open door. Her long auburn hair was tousled. Sixteen years old. Precocious. Argumentative. Demanding to be treated as an adult every time she didn't get her own way. Still wearing Mickey Mouse pyjamas.

'I was running through my opening speech, getting myself ready. What are you doing up so early?'

'Couldn't sleep. Came downstairs for a glass of water. Mr Tomkins says revision and rehearsal the night before a test only get in the way of a good performance. He says if you've prepared properly the best thing to do is forget about it and make sure you have a good night's sleep.'

'And when, pray, did Mr Tomkins ever try a case in Crown Court?'

Joanne shrugged. 'He's been in charge of Upper School for ever, he's helped thousands of kids do well in their exams. He must know something. He says last minute revision only affects the short-term memory, and proper revision means that you get things fixed in your long-term memory.'

'Perhaps I should see if I can arrange a lesson with Mr Tomkins?'

'Don't see the point.'

'Oh?'

'You're not the learning type.' Another shrug. 'I mean, you must have been once. You must have been good at it then. But you're too fixed now. I think the rut's too deep for even Mr Tompkins to get you out of.'

'Thank you for the vote of confidence.'

'Just keeping it real.'

'Real, young lady, is the – '

'- Best story, best told. I know. You've told us a million times. That's my point. I've never heard you say anything different.'

'That's because it's true.'

'You don't deal only in the truth. You've told us that, too. You said you also have to make people believe you. You're a good belief-sharer. And you wouldn't be so successful at that if the jury saw you in your dressing gown talking to yourself in the dark.'

'Once you have created a system that works for you, it makes sense to keep using it. I'm sure Mr Tompkins must have told you something about that?'

'Fair point.' At least this time he earned the briefest of nods. 'But a good learner would have worked out how to streamline their preparation after all these years. They wouldn't just stick automatically to the same old thing time after time. That's more like superstition than professional practice. Anyway, I'm going back to bed. Hope you slay 'em.'

Mike heard her bare feet on the first steps of the staircase. He realised he was open-mouthed. For the first time ever his pre-trial routine had been disrupted and demolished. Suddenly, the adrenalin wasn't filling him with confidence. He took a large swallow of his coffee and pulled a face. It was cold.

CHAPTER 6

MONDAY - TRIAL DAY 1
5.32am

Naseem Akhtar kept his head low as he walked, even though the city streets were almost empty, even though his baseball cap was pulled down over his forehead. Even though it was still dark.

You can't be too careful.

The thought made him shiver more than the cold. Even though it had been several months now, his mind was still flooded with the unfairness and horror of it all, with the loss and terrifying realisations that had ripped every one of his taken-for-granted beliefs apart.

Media stories don't have to be true – they just have to newsworthy.

And if the story plays into existing bias and hatred it will be accepted gratefully by those who long for just one more excuse to vent their vitriol and spite.

On one level Naseem had known that forever. You couldn't grow up as an Asian in Britain and not experience racism. But he had never let it stop him and he had always believed he could prove his value through his efforts and achievements.

Until five months ago life had been going according to plan. He had been enjoying a growing reputation as a successful local businessman and philanthropist. He had only ever been presented in the press as a role model. His family lacked for nothing. He was on the way up and he thanked God on a daily basis.

Then all hell had broken loose. A major police investigation – named Operation Sandcastle – resulted in the arrests of thirteen men in the East Midlands accused of grooming, assaulting and raping dozens of teenage girls. Naseem's cousin and former business partner, Raj, had been identified as the leader of the thirteen and charged with numerous counts of sexual assault.

Naseem and his extended family had been shocked beyond words. They had struggled to believe it was true. Even the fact that Raj had misappropriated funds from the business prior to his acrimonious split, didn't mean he was automatically capable of such awful things. There were, after all, levels of badness, and mishandling money was nothing like child abuse.

The situation was made worse by the constant press harassment.

Reporters were camped outside their house, waiting for Naseem at work, trying to ambush him at the gym, desperate for an interview or a sound bite. Anti-Muslim fervour ramped up. Naseem's six year old daughter was bullied in the school playground. When things seemed that they couldn't deteriorate any further, they did.

Unbelievably so.

Raj claimed that Naseem was the fourteenth member of the gang. For some reason, one of the other men backed him up. Naseem was immediately taken in for questioning. He screamed his innocence. The detectives were cold, suspicious and thorough. The press was loud, provocative and certain. Naseem's name, face and life story were everywhere. His lawyer suggested that Raj had been offered a deal if he named any other men involved. Naseem could only remember how close to blows the pair had come during their final business meeting.

It took eight days for the police to conclude that Naseem had no case to answer, but by then the damage had been done. In the eyes of many he was guilty by association. The newspapers asked questions about his release, repeating the phrase *due to lack of evidence* at every possible opportunity. Their coverage encouraged many to regard him as the lucky one who got away with it.

Protestors appeared outside his offices. Business slumped. When he was forced to close his social media accounts, the threats and abuse were transferred to his wife. She was accused of being complicit in his illegal activities. The pressure didn't stop. The media kept returning to the story. A public campaign calling itself *Enough is Enough!* began demanding more rigorous policing and more careful scrutiny of suspected paedophiles.

By the end of the fourth month Naseem's marriage was in bits, his business irreversibly tarnished. He left the family home at 3am on a Wednesday morning and moved into a one-bedroomed flat in the city centre. He paid the rent by cash. He grew a beard. He changed his wardrobe. He kept his passport close, having left a message for his wife saying that he was leaving the country for good and she was better off without him.

The press used his disappearance as a further sign of his guilt. His sense of isolation and loss grew. He realised he should have moved further away, but now daren't travel. He left the flat only during the early hours of the morning. Once he would have thanked God for the supermarkets that were open twenty fours a day, but he had left God behind too. He really had nothing. Apart from the need to go unnoticed.

You can't be too careful.

He caught sight of himself in a shop window as he shuffled past. He looked like an old man. He moved like one, too. Sooner or later he would have to summon up the courage to leave for good.

'But do I have the courage?' Naseem stopped and looked down at the pavement. 'If I had courage I would have killed myself by now. Given them a final story to write.'

He raised his head and set off again, moving slowly for several minutes along Maid Marian Way before turning left into Mount Street.

It was his usual route; giving him the chance for some physical activity, to breathe in what he now thought of as fresh air, purchase his required shopping and be back inside, with the door locked, before the city truly woke up.

Mount Street marked the start of the slight hill climb he had factored into his walk. Not so long ago he would have barely noticed it, now he could feel his heart quicken; funny how his physical condition had deteriorated along with everything else.

Just one more of Life's sick jokes.

'Help me! Please!'

The voice came from across the street. Naseem stopped instinctively and looked in the direction of the sound. It came from the side entrance to the multi-storey car park. He saw a figure, hooded, dressed in black, stagger against the inside of the glass-panelled doors that led to the lifts and stairway.

'I'm dying! Save me!'

The figure pulled at the door, but collapsed before it was more than half open. Naseem was already hurrying across the road, faster than he'd moved in weeks. He was inside within seconds. The figure was unmoving, head slumped, back against the wall, legs outstretched and lifeless. Naseem dropped to his knees.

'Can you hear me? It's going to be OK. Can you hear me?'

The figure groaned. Naseem raised the head gently, easing back the hood. Pale blue eyes stared back at him. The tip of a pink tongue licked thin lips. The mouth curled into a snarl.

The figure's right hand punched violently into Naseem's throat.

The blow was excruciating, knocking him back, sending waves of pain and panic shooting through his system. As Naseem's shoulders hit the floor the figure pulled his legs up underneath his body and drove forwards.

A knife flashed as he continued his attack with three, rapid thrusts. Naseem screamed once before he lost consciousness.

The figure finished his work with the knife, wiped it clean on Naseem's coat, and rose to his feet. Then he took out a mobile phone.

CHAPTER 7

MONDAY - TRIAL DAY 1
9.10am

Mike Coopland was cursing under his breath as he strode forcefully through Nottingham's Crown Court building towards the large robing room in which he and his colleagues changed into their barrister's garb.

He was ten minutes behind schedule. That had never happened before. Trials began at 10.30am and he always arrived at 9am. Today his pre-trial routine was going to hell and back. Today he was not, as Joanne would have said, keeping it real. Because, apart from telling the best stories, real meant doing those things you always do, it meant sticking to the tried and tested.

The tried and tested.

Usually that phrase brought a smile to his lips. Not now, though. Now he didn't have time to enjoy any clever wordplay. He was ten minutes behind schedule. That meant everything from now until the trial began was out of sync. That was enough to make any man curse.

'I've always fucking hated Hilary!' He breathed. 'The worst fucking term of the lot – and the coldest!'

Hilary was the name given to the legal time period running from January to April. Mike had suffered his only two legal defeats during Hilary. One had been a fifty-fifty pick 'em type of fight. In the other he'd been the clear favourite. Until a police cock-up had taken his feet from under him.

'I'm not having a hat-trick of losses!' He reminded himself. 'And definitely not with this one.'

Mike stormed into the robing room. Without hesitation he opened the travel case he'd been carrying and took out his barrister's robes. He took off the soft collar from the pure white shirt he was wearing and replaced it with a starched, winged version. Next he put on the bands, two white oblong pieces of cloth tied at the neck, the formal neckwear of his profession. The traditional long sleeved waistcoat followed and then the silk gown. Only then did he pause. The room was unexpectedly empty so he allowed himself a breath before opening the purpose-built wig tin. His wig was his pride and joy.

'You battle-scarred beauty,' he whispered as he put it on. 'Here we go again.'

Mike checked himself in one of the full-length mirrors. He was dressed for battle.

'Ready, Hilary or not!'

He nodded and straightened automatically. The wig did it every time. It changed him, brought out the fighter, the hero, the protector. He didn't need a mask and a cape. Once the wig went on, even Superman would have been stupid to face him.

Five minutes after entering the robing room Mike Coopland was on his way to the barrister's canteen. He was no longer rushing. He was occupying the centre of the corridor. He let those walking towards him separate on either side of his twenty stone bulk. He kept his eyes fixed straight ahead. He left behind all the thoughts that had kept him awake throughout the night.

There were a dozen other barristers in the canteen when Mike entered; all engaged in the pre-trial mind games that were such an essential part of their work. Some feigned confidence, sitting back, sipping their coffee as if they didn't have a care in the world. Others were making carefully planned points to their opposite number. Two were talking loudly with their Junior, the barrister they had chosen to be their right-hand, about the cast-iron certainty of their case.

Usually Mike would have been joining in, doing whatever he could to gain the first psychological advantage.

Not today though.

Today, for the first time ever, he was about to begin prosecuting a case with no equally qualified professional present to defend against him.

His mind tried to remind him that his pre-trial routine was missing another link. He willed the intrusion back into the robing room with all his other misgivings and doubts. Then he poured himself a black coffee and took a drink. It was hot. Thank God.

'One final caffeine kick and then into the arena we go.'

Mike spun round. Brian Kaffee was standing behind him. Grey haired, short and lean, five years older than Mike, he peered up over his round, gold rimmed glasses.

'Caesar, those about to die salute you,' he said, tapping his chest with his left palm.

Mike scowled. 'I'm not about to be thrown to the lions thank you very much. I'm at the top of the food chain as you know full well, and as you're my Junior for this one that means you are, too. And, for the sake of historical accuracy, gladiators almost certainly didn't say that before the fighting started. It's an example of what Trump has taught us all to call fake news.'

'OK. I'll accept the history lesson.' Brian nodded. 'But the point still remains, if you can get enough people using your words - '

' - You've told the winning story.'

'Exactly. And we know what the winning story earns us.'

'In this case, a guilty verdict.' It was Mike's turn to nod. 'Followed by a very long time in prison for Mr Ethan Hall.'

Brian considered briefly. 'I still can't get my head around it.'

'Neither could Ethan's first victims.'

'Very funny.'

'I'm just warming up.'

'Good to know. There'd be cause for serious concern if that's you at your best.'

Mike raised an eyebrow.

Brian went on quickly. 'I can't get my head around the fact that he is actually going to defend himself. At first I thought he was bluffing. When it became clear he wasn't I thought that at some point he'd realise it was suicidal and seek professional help. Amateurs lose to professionals. And the best professionals crush first-timers. That's the rule in everything. How stupid do you have to be to throw away your only chance of saving your freedom?'

'It's arrogance, not stupidity. He thinks he'll be able to get inside the jury's minds, trance them out and get them to think and do whatever he wants. At least, that's what Peter believes.'

'If that was true it would mean that any decent hypnotherapist with no experience in trial law and courtroom strategy could give a silk a run for their money. And that's obviously bollocks.'

'Obviously.' Mike swallowed. 'Ever been to a hypnotherapist?'

'Not personally. Helen took James once in the run-up to his 'A' levels. He was getting anxious, couldn't revise, couldn't sleep, started saying that he wasn't even going to sit the damn things. I knew it was going to be a waste of time and money, but Helen said we had to try everything and she'd got this recommendation so off they went.'

'Any good?'

'Of course not. James said the guy tried to hypnotise him, kept telling him he was sinking into a deep sleep. James wasn't having any of it. He told me he just closed his eyes and played along until the time was up.'

'So what happened with his exams?'

'It was all fine in the end. A storm in a teacup. I think James was so embarrassed at having to go to the hypnotherapist it made him get his act into gear. That same night he started revising and then slept like a baby. In the end he got better grades than predicted. Shows you what schools know.'

'Mmm.' Mike swallowed again. 'Let's just remember that, even though Ethan's a beginner, we're bringing our 'A' game. We have a responsibility to win this and I don't want anyone in that courtroom – judge, jury, audience or media – to have any doubts about his guilt. Clear?

'Yes sir.'

'Are we clear?'

'Crystal.'

'And you can handle the truth, right?'

'Absolutely.'

The two men smiled.

Brian said, 'That's still the worst impersonation of Jack Nicholson I've ever heard. It doesn't matter how many times you do it, you don't get any better.'

'And you look less like Tom Cruise with every day that passes - and you didn't look like him to start with.'

'Can't argue with that. This is what the real Kaffee looks like I'm afraid.'

'An amazing brain behind a tragic face.' Mike patted Brian's shoulder with his large left hand. 'Trust me when I say I'd rather have you and your amazing brain with me right now than Tom Cruise and his.' He paused. 'Although at least the fictional Lieutenant Kaffee was able to call Colonel Jessop as a witness.'

'True. The film wouldn't have been the same without those two going at it.' Brian frowned. 'In our case, though, the fact that Ethan is defending himself does mean you can't call him as a witness. The law really is crystal on this one. So no matter how much you want to, we're not going to get our Cruise-Nicholson moment. Which is a real shame.'

'I'm not so sure. You see, I've been thinking about it, too.'

'Oh?'

'I think if a man is arrogant enough to defend himself, he's arrogant enough to believe he'll cope well in the witness box. I think such a man might not even need too much encouragement.'

'You think he'll choose to offer himself as a witness?'

'I think he might be desperate to. And if he isn't now, he might be persuaded to feel that way.'

'Sounds like you have a plan.'

'I have several.'

'So you might actually get round to the code red question?'

'You're god damn right I might! That's why I'm leading this prosecution, why I'm society's protector. You see Kaffee in places you don't talk about at parties, you want me on that wall! You *need* me on that wall!'

This time they broke into laughter. They both knew it was more of a protective measure than anything else.

Sometimes, Mike considered, the most important mind games you played in the moments before you went into court were with yourself.

CHAPTER 8

MONDAY - TRIAL DAY 1
10.14am

Detective Chief Inspector Peter Jones was feeling as calm as was humanly possible.

Considering.

Sitting alone in the Crown Court building in a room he had requisitioned to serve as both police waiting room and a store for exhibits, he let his mind review it all one last time.

He had read and reread all of the relevant files. He had cleared his diary, provisionally at least, to give himself the best chance of being available every day until a verdict was reached. He had tried every way he knew to share with Mike Coopland his insights into the threat posed by Ethan Hall. He had spent dozens of hours quietly reviewing every aspect of the investigation and eventual arrest.

Every detail was clear and recorded.

At least, every detail they had.

It was the missing details that were fraying the edges of his calmness. The missing details from the missing hours. The unaccounted time between Ethan Hall's escape from hospital and his subsequent arrest. There were just too many hours when, according to their records, Ethan Hall did absolutely nothing at all. And to Peter Jones's way of thinking that didn't make any sense. Ethan Hall was a class A predator. A shark. And sharks didn't stop moving just because they were out of sight. So the questions were simple.

Where did he go?

What did he do?

Simple questions his team had still not been able to answer, despite their ongoing investigation.

Now, even though it felt as if there was still unfinished business, it was time to step back and let Mike take the lead. Now his role was to support the barrister as best he could. From past experience he knew that meant providing answers, ideas and reminders only when asked. When a trial began Mike demanded the spotlight. Which was ideal as far as Peter was concerned, even though he did torment his friend about it relentlessly.

'You are the world's biggest Diva!' He had once proclaimed. 'God forbid, if you could sing like Mariah Carey you'd have an entourage twice the size and make more demands than a terrorist group who'd kidnapped the American President.'

'And I'd ban you from all my shows,' Mike replied.

'Wouldn't need to. It's all I can do to cope with the courtroom performances.'

Which was an absolute lie. Peter had long been an admirer of Mike's creative and charismatic delivery. He had seen it be the deciding factor in more than one trial.

'We can't guarantee justice,' Peter mused, ' but we do go after it with everything in our power.'

His words triggered a memory of Calvin Brent; of a conversation they had shared several months before.

'Detective Chief Inspector,' the drug baron had said in his loud, mocking voice, 'I am a law-abiding businessman who contributes to society by meeting the needs of my local community. So why don't you stop wasting time and money and leave me alone?'

Brent, known on the streets as The Numbers Man, had leaned forward across his heavy mahogany desk. 'Besides, you can't ever catch a big fish with a small fishing rod.'

'What's that supposed to mean exactly?' Peter kept his face expressionless.

He had tried for many years to end this man's criminal reign, but no one had ever been brave enough to testify against him and Brent had always ensured he was far removed from the action.

'It means you're not equipped to fish in the deepest waters. You should stay in the shallows, picking up what you can, convincing all the good tax payers of Nottingham that you are in control and keeping them safe.'

'I catch everything I go after,' Peter said grimly. 'Besides, sometimes the biggest fish are so sure of their invulnerability they swim where they shouldn't and find themselves beached. We all know what happens to a fish out of water.'

'The trick is to always be clear which way the current is flowing.' Brent sat back. 'Anyway, to return to your original reason for being here, let me say again I have never met or, indeed, communicated in any way with Ethan Hall. The fact that one of my occasional employees, Matthew Lawson, had dealings with him has nothing to do with me. The fact that he was then taken prisoner by Hall suggests they had problems of their own. I, obviously, know nothing about that. As an upstanding member of the community, I assure you I would tell you if I did.'

'Forgive me if I don't find that at all reassuring.'

'Of course. I'm famous for my forgiveness. You know that.' The Numbers Man bared his teeth.

Peter left without saying another word. Two days later a package had been delivered to his home address. It contained a copy of Moby Dick. He gave it pride of place on his bookshelf.

Now Peter looked round the small room he was sitting in. 'Ahab, you should have killed that fucking whale for sure,' he muttered.

'And you should never have let it drag you down.'

Peter stood up and stretched, forcing Calvin Brent from his consciousness. Here and now, in the real world, the trial was all that mattered.

His mobile phone began ringing at precisely the same moment Detective Sergeant Kevin McNeill knocked on the door and entered the room.

'No need to answer that Boss!' McNeill raised his right hand as if stopping traffic. 'Whatever it is, it's not as important as this!'

Peter hesitated briefly and let his anger show. 'I'll be the judge of that.' For all sorts of very good reasons his DS had never before come close to giving him an instruction. Which was reason enough to ignore the phone. 'You'd better hope you're right.'

'Yes Boss.' It was McNeill's turn to hesitate.

Peter watched him realise the risk he was taking. The ringing stopped. 'It's too late to turn back now, Kevin. You've placed your bet so roll the dice.'

'Yeah. Of course.' McNeill wiped his mouth with the back of his left hand. 'There's been a murder. Body found at 5.56am this morning. The entrance to Mount Street car park. Multiple stab wounds to the lower abdomen. And a sheet of A4 pinned to his chest with the word *Paedo* written on it.'

'What have we got, someone who doesn't know how to spell long words or someone who's just saving ink?'

'Might be a frugal, illiterate butcher.'

'A butcher?'

'Yeah. The victim's bollocks were cut off and left on the paper.'

'Dear God! Do we know who the dead man is?

'A local businessman – ex-businessman I should say. He lost everything fairly recently. His name's Naseem Akhtar. He was investigated as part of Operation Sandcastle.'

'I remember. He had a family member who was the ringleader of the gang. Akhtar, though, was freed without charge. He disappeared off the grid sometime after that.'

'The thing is the killer posted a photo of the body on all the usual social media.'

'Fucking technology! I keep telling you we'd be better off without it!'

'That's as might be Boss, but the really bad news is - '

'- You don't think what you've just shared is bad news?'

'Yeah, it's bad. It's just that this is worse.'

'Excellent. Go on.'

'He gave the picture a headline – a call to arms – and a hashtag. He wrote, *Reclaim our streets*. Hashtag *Pass it on*. It's gone viral. Thousands of responses already, most of them cheering their support.'

'Bollocks!'

'Anyway you look at it Boss.' McNeill raised an eyebrow.

'Yeah, fair point,' Peter chuckled. 'Who's the lucky sod who's drawn this one?'

'DCI Anderson.'

'Let's hope he can sort it quickly. As it stands the press are going to have a field day, what with Ethan Hall in here and a lunatic paedophile killer out there.'

'You never know, it might distract from the trial; ease our pressure a bit.'

'Doubt it. To be honest with you, even though it seems clearly disconnected, I can't help but wonder about the timing of it all.'

'It can't be anything to do with Hall.'

'That would be the logical conclusion.'

'But?'

'But sometimes gut instinct trumps logical conclusion, and this just feels wrong in my gut.'

'I keep telling you, you're eating too many curries.'

'Let's hope that's what it is. Anyway, it's not our case so let's focus on what we're here to do.' Peter looked at his watch. 'Because if all is going to schedule our main attraction should be making his way into Court Number 1 right now.'

'Here we go then,' Kevin sighed and shook his head. 'Ladies and gentlemen, for the first time ever, a murderous hypnosis weirdo meets men in wigs. All fucking rise.'

CHAPTER 9

MONDAY - TRIAL DAY 1
10.30am

Ethan Hall saw every detail of the courtroom in one casual turn of his head. He started with the shimmer of past events, the flickering colours of decisions, lies and emotions clinging to corners and crevices.

'The residue of conflict,' he whispered so quietly the two security guards he was handcuffed to failed to notice. He smiled at their lack of awareness, letting his eyes capture the members of the media sitting in the slightly removed front row and the eighty or more members of the public sitting behind them.

Many were looking back at him. The journalists were conditioned to be coldly curious, to demonstrate to each other just how professionally detached they were. He took each one in turn, reading them as if they were a newspaper headline.

The others he corralled together in his mind.

The herd.

He saw a mixture of hatred, confusion and disbelief rising from them. He watched it colour the air like a delicate cloud and through it he saw their eyes widen, their breath and shoulders rising.

'Mine already.' The whisper moistened his mouth and lips, the wetness on his tongue obvious as a waterfall.

The big man came to him next. He had refused to turn, the breadth of his back magnified by the ceremonial robes.

They are going to send a barrister against me. It will be a man. He'll stink of confidence.

The presumption echoed in his mind. He had been right, of course, but there was something more. This man feigned confidence, using his experience, size and reputation to intimidate and disguise. Ethan saw the uncertainty he was trying to hide, a pulsing blood-red knot threatening to twist and pull at his stomach. If it took control, Ethan realised, it would drag him to his knees.

'You are right. I am that different,' Ethan's lips curled. 'I will bring you down.'

This time the guards thought they heard something. They glanced at him and then at each other before shifting their attention to the Court Clerk and, beyond him, the Judge robed in scarlet and ermine. Ethan felt the two, burly men stiffen slightly as if standing to attention.

The Clerk ignored them. He spoke clearly and confidently.

'Are you Ethan Hall?'

Ethan noticed how he dropped his inflection, turning the question into something closer to a command. Obviously ex-military, still thinking he was on the parade ground.

'Yes.' Ethan dipped his shoulders and sagged just a little.

The Clerk nodded curtly. 'You may be seated.'

Ethan slumped.

The big man rose. He spoke to the Judge. 'May it please your Lordship I appear in the case on behalf of the prosecution together with my learned friend, Mr Brian Kaffee. The defendant, Mr Ethan Hall, has chosen to represent himself.'

Ethan didn't bother looking at the barrister's helper, Junior Counsel as he was properly termed. He knew everything about that man's role. He had done his research a long time ago. The truth was he knew more about a criminal trial before a High Court

Judge than any of them could imagine.

Instead of imagination, they have faith...faith in what they call the system.

Junior Counsel was there to guide and support. Despite his pristine black jacket and pinstriped trousers, he was nothing more than a glorified golf caddy, a man walking in the shadows, carrying the load for the high-profile player. He was a man to be dealt with later. If necessary.

Ethan saw the Judge glance in his direction. He kept his own gaze low, enjoying the pretence of being lost in his own thoughts, cowed by the situation.

The Judge moved on quickly, speaking directly to the big man, Mike Coopland QC.

'What preliminary issues are there in the case that we need to deal with?'

The answer was immediate and, to Ethan's ears, clearly rehearsed.

'Perhaps the first is whether the defendant should, in the particular circumstances of this case, remain in handcuffs throughout. I anticipate the defendant will have something to say about that. As indeed he might about my application to have him screened from the jury.'

Ethan listened to the words with interest. Coopland spoke from deep in his belly. It was exaggerated; a performance voice. Ethan was sure that even Marcus Kline would have recognised the boy inside the big man.

'Mr Hall,' the Judge's tone was procedural, 'are there any preliminary issues you would like to raise?'

Ethan looked up. 'My Lord, I concede the handcuffs, but would like therefore to be allowed to sit on Counsel's Row.'

The Judge did his best to remain expressionless. Coopland's

shoulders rose fractionally. The response was as scripted as the rest.

'We will deal with applications now, in order,' the Judge said. 'So, Mr Coopland, given that Mr Hall is willing to concede the issue of handcuffs, let's address your request to have him screened in the dock which, of course, is completely at odds with his request to sit where Defence Counsel usually does.'

The big man stood. 'My Lord, we want Mr Hall in the dock because these are charges of murder and this is where the defendant usually sits. The dock provides security and in this case, bearing in mind the factual circumstances surrounding the deaths and Mr Hall's unique and potent ability to manipulate and influence the minds of others, I believe strongly that additional security in the form of screening is required. The risk that Mr Hall poses to the jury needs to be minimised as much as possible. Obviously we cannot prevent him from talking to the jury, but a screen would prevent him from being able to look at them directly. Allowing him to do so - and especially from a position as close as Counsel's Row – would be to risk their wellbeing as well as the integrity of these proceedings.'

The Judge nodded curtly. 'Mr Hall?'

Ethan looked up at the ceiling as if briefly composing his thoughts. 'My Lord, it is true to say that I do indeed have a unique skill set. I have been gifted – although, given the nature of my current situation, it feels easier at this moment to say cursed – with the ability to understand others in ways that very few people ever have. This understanding enables me to change the lives and circumstances of those in need in the most powerful and positive of ways. This, as I am sure will become clear in the coming days, is what I have dedicated myself to. I am not a perfect human being. I have made mistakes. As we all have. However, I pose no threat to the jury or indeed anyone else who will appear in this courtroom.'

'Beyond that, I would make two further points. Firstly, if you screen me from view you are implying my guilt and, inevitably, biasing the jury against me. Having chosen to defend myself I did hope I would be allowed the courtesy of presenting myself in some form of equal manner to Mr Coopland. Although, of course, I do accept that these,' Ethan raised his hands and tugged gently at the handcuffs, 'are the inescapable burden of my status and impact negatively on my claim for equality.'

'Secondly I believe, as no doubt we all do, that the English justice system is the finest in the world. Here, now, is the place where facts truly speak louder than words.'

'Mr Coopland cannot surely be suggesting that in this, the most serious of circumstances where life-changing decisions are made, words and looks and gestures are more influential than the actual facts of the matter?'

'If that were so, it would seem Mr Coopland is arguing that justice is determined by who can tell the best story in the most persuasive way. I would certainly hope that is neither his belief nor his experience. As the defendant I need to know that I am trusting my future on the truth of facts, not the quality of a performance piece.'

Ethan took a half step back and let the energy drain from his body as if, having made his first speech, he was suddenly tired and unsure. He blinked twice and licked his lips whilst pretending to await the decision.

In his mind, however, there was no question to be answered. The Judge had reached a conclusion even before he had started speaking. Ethan had seen it as clearly as a painting on a wall. For all his finery and learned language, Mr Justice Stephen Mulvenny was just a man, as open to him as any other.

So Ethan's words had never been for him; they had been aimed at the barrister, and they had struck home with expected ease. The mix of emotions he had created was playing beneath and beyond the surface of Mike Coopland's large frame. Ethan looked through the flashes of amber, green and grey as the Judge ended the charade of his consideration.

'Mr Hall, you will stay in the dock throughout the trial. No screen will be put in place, however. In that regard, I recommend that you keep your hands out of sight. That will also limit any possible jury bias. And I want to make it clear to you Mr Hall that I shall be watching you very closely throughout. If I see anything improper, anything at all with which I am concerned, I may well revisit this decision. Now, gentlemen, let's move on to jury selection.'

Ethan Hall dropped his head as if in acceptance of defeat. No one saw him smile.

CHAPTER 10

MONDAY - TRIAL DAY 1
11.23am

Marcus Kline waited for his wife to formulate her question. He watched her create and dismiss three alternatives. He saw how each challenged her in a similar way. He wondered what her secret was.

In the end she settled for the question she had asked before. 'Do you really think he's chosen to defend himself because he's too egotistical to let someone else do it for him?'

'Of course.' Marcus settled for the same answer. 'His logic will be that he can learn enough about the law to manage the requirements of the court, and that no one else will be able to get inside peoples' minds the way he can.'

'Is it what you would do in his position?'

'I would have, once upon a time. But you know what they say, feedback is the lifeblood of learning. And the feedback I've received over the last year has taught me that arrogant independence isn't the best way to go. So, no, I'd prefer to engage the expertise of someone like Mike.'

'So you definitely think he's got less chance of winning because he's doing it this way?'

'That's what the experts have told us.'

'But what do you think? What's your gut instinct? You understand him better than anyone else.'

He saw the flicker of *something* in her face, not quite a lie and not a doubt, something far more complex and painful. He knew he couldn't ask.

'My instinct is that his skill set shines most brightly in the shadows. Now he's in the spotlight he's going to find things very different and I wouldn't be at all surprised if he struggles in ways he never has before.' Marcus considered briefly. 'Actually, given Ethan's synaesthesia, I wonder if the emotional intensity of the trial will actually confuse or even blind him to some degree.'

'Because of the way he sees emotions as colours in the air?'

'Absolutely because of that. He believes his synaesthesia gives him unique insights into others. You know I don't agree. I think he's a naturally gifted influencer and hypnotist who has actively developed his skills to a world-class level.'

'Synesthetes are simply people who experience sensory stimuli in ways most of us don't; they are no more likely to be incredible communicators than the next person. When you combine the complexity of Ethan's personality with the delusions he holds about his synaesthesia, you can make a very strong argument that he's actually far more vulnerable than he realises. Especially when he's out of his environment and up against such a brilliant professional as Mike.'

'I hope that's true. He deserves to lose. He deserves to suffer.'

'I'm sure he will. Consequences are inevitable. That's the first of all rules.' He saw the flicker return.

'That man deserves the worst of all consequences.'

'Yes.' The word felt dry in his mouth. She hadn't been able to say Ethan's name for months now. He hadn't been able to tell her how terrified he was of the havoc Ethan could cause in a courtroom. He continued quickly, 'And when it's all over we can find ways to put him and his memory in our rear view mirror.'

The flicker was more obvious this time.

'I would willingly shorten my life to avoid all of this.'

They both thought of the cancer as they listened to that.

The phone rang before either could speak again. Marcus answered it.

'Hello?'

'It's Nic.'

The voice was barely recognisable. Soul-less. Like a ghost. Marcus's grip tightened on the phone. 'Nic! My God! Where are you?' He heard his mouth ask the right question despite his shock.

'Bristol. We've always been here.'

'We? Nic, who are you with?' Marcus put the phone on to loudspeaker. Anne-Marie took a step closer, her eyes widening.

'Sometimes he's here, right next to me, then he disappears and I don't see him for days. Sometimes he's less solid than others, like a shimmer. I have to chase him then, go looking for him round all the streets. He leads me a merry dance. Makes me cry. I don't know why he does that. Why come back and not stay close? Why call me here and then play hide and seek? I wondered if you could talk to him. In your professional way. He needs help. He shouldn't lead me a dance. It gets dark at night.'

Marcus couldn't help but glance at his wife. For the first time in a long time, she had clearly forgotten about herself. His mind slipped gratefully into work mode.

'Nic, who called you to Bristol? Who is leading you a merry dance?'

'Sometimes he wakes me in the middle of the night. When he knows I've seen him he goes and I have to follow. But he goes fast. And when I shout he doesn't answer.'

'Nic, what's his name?'

'It's because there aren't many cars in the dark. That's why.'

'Why is that important to him, Nic? Why does it matter that

there aren't many cars?'

'He has to be safe. Can't happen again. Can't be lost again.'

'Nic, when was he lost before?'

'For a long time. After the hot sun. He came back though. So that I could know where to find him.'

'Where in Bristol are you, Nic? Where, exactly?'

'In the street.'

'Which street?'

'Busy street. Said he'd be here.'

'Tell me the names of two shops near to you.'

'Yes.'

'Tell me the first name.'

'I've seen him! Look! Over there! I have to go!'

The phone went dead.

'Damn!' Marcus looked at Anne-Marie.

'What just happened?' She asked.

'A voice from the grave.'

'You didn't secretly think that Nic was dead, did you?'

'No. But to end a relationship without warning isn't something Nic would naturally do. And I never believed he left because he could no longer cope with Peter putting his work before his personal life.'

'Why not? That's been the reason for the break-up of Peter's previous relationships.'

'Nic was always more tolerant than the others, and in some way more needy. My assessment was that Nic had accepted the inevitable trade-off. He was prepared to love Peter more than anyone and anything, and in return Peter would love him more than anyone and anything apart from the job. Once someone accepts that sort of trade-off and commits to it, there's very little that can shake it.'

'Although some things can?'

'Yes. But they have to be very significant. A pattern interrupt of seismic proportions.'

'Such as?'

'Something so significant it cuts through existing neural pathways, creates an abrupt shift in perspective and in doing so changes emotional states and responses. Something that becomes the dominant life factor.'

'Are you going to hazard a guess as to what that might be?'

'I am, but I really hope I'm wrong.' Marcus tipped his head. 'The clue, I fear, lies in the identity of the other person; the one Nic was so focussed on.'

'But the way Nic was talking it sounded more like a vision than a real person.'

'That's the problem. I think the person was his brother, Andrew.'

'But Andrew died three years ago!'

'In a car crash. And now Nic thinks he's come back from the dead. Or that he never died. Either way, it's not at all good.'

'Are you sure?' Anne-Marie grabbed hold of Marcus's right hand with both of hers.

'It's the logical starting point,' he said. 'Andrew died in Spain, in the hot sun, in a car. Now Nic is seeing a temporary, shimmering image. As you said, it's clearly not a real person. Given that, we have to conclude he's currently delusional.'

'But he'd managed his grief as well as anyone could. He wasn't ill in any way. So why would he decide six months ago that Andrew was alive and wanted him to move to Bristol?'

'If you ask the question "How could he have been persuaded to believe that?" it's easier to arrive at an answer.' Marcus sighed. 'I think it was Ethan Hall. He could easily have got to Nic before Peter arrested him, and it's precisely the sort of torment he'd create for those he didn't want to kill.'

'Poor Nic!' Anne-Marie sobbed, her tears offering no defence against the image of Ethan Hall that was filling her mind's eye.

'Torment and secrets and isolation,' Marcus went on, 'they're his trademarks; preferable to him, I think, even than murder.'

'Whatever are we going to do?'

Marcus walked over to the window and looked out at the valley. 'Tell Peter,' he said finally. 'He has to know. He has to start a search for Nic. He isn't safe on his own.'

'But Peter's under enough pressure with the trial!'

'There isn't another option,' Marcus shrugged. Anne-Marie couldn't tell if it was with resignation or defeat. He kept his back to her, lost in his own thoughts.

'Can you help him?

'No. Not with this. Not now,' Marcus turned back to face her. 'And he wouldn't want me to. He'll want me to save all my energy for the witness box tomorrow.'

The witness box.

Anne-Marie shivered. Mike Coopland was calling her as his second witness. Ethan Hall would no doubt cross-examine her, just as he would her husband. It was a prospect that took her breath away.

'Yes. Of course,' she said. 'The witness box.'

She wiped away her tears with the back of her left hand. Her husband watched, unmoving. Once again it felt as if they were worlds apart, separated by secrets.

CHAPTER 11

MONDAY - TRIAL DAY 1
2.03pm

Stephen Mulvenny had been a High Court Judge for five years and a barrister for eleven years before that. He knew the system. He understood the people who had committed themselves to that system. He recognised the distinct challenges each new case presented for both the prosecution and the defence.

Sometimes the weight of evidence was stacked in favour of one or the other. Sometimes the charges brought seemed a step – or more – too far. Sometimes, from his experienced, objective position at the front of the courtroom, the outcome was impossible to call. A genuine 50-50 contest, a trial in which barristers' reputations could be made or lost.

Which, he wondered not for the first time, was the Crown against Ethan Hall? Was the prosecution pushing too far in seeking a murder conviction? Was that going to prove a struggle even for such an accomplished silk as Mike Coopland? Or was Ethan Hall making a fatal error in choosing to defend himself?

The latter was the logical conclusion. An absolute beginner against a world-class professional at the top of his game ought to be a no-contest. Only if the stories about Ethan Hall were true, maybe the usual odds didn't apply? Maybe there would be nothing usual about the entire process?

Mr Justice Stephen Mulvenny certainly hoped not. The system worked. It worked because there were rules and boundaries because, for all of the egos and personal agendas, everyone involved believed in the most important of all social concepts: justice.

Stephen glanced at the jury. The decisions-makers. Seven men and five women. He saw the usual mix of confidence, curiosity and concern. He promised silently that he would guide and protect them. The last thing he needed right now – the thing he would never allow – was for a so-called hypnotist to influence and disrupt the system.

Not on my watch!

Stephen sat back, bolt upright, keeping his face expressionless as Mike Coopland QC stood up and began his opening speech. He spoke with a deep, measured gravitas, his hands resting on the lectern in front of him.

'Ladies and gentlemen, the man in the dock is the most dangerous individual the world has ever seen. He is a killer who doesn't need to hold a gun. He will make you pick up that gun, press its cold, heavy barrel against your pulsing temple and pull the trigger yourself.'

'He doesn't need to push you from the top of a tall building. He will make you jump. He will make you want to jump. He will make you jump with a smile on your face, believing perhaps that you can actually fly.'

'He doesn't need a knife to plunge into your heart. He will make you take your sharpest kitchen knife, roll back your sleeves and sever the arteries in your wrists. Then, if he chooses – and, believe me, he is most likely to make this choice – he will have you sit there, unmoving on the kitchen floor, watching your blood pool around you; he will make you sit there until you lose consciousness and die.'

'Even if you knew this man was intending to scalp you, to cut off the top of your head so he could explore your brain and watch it as you died, even then this man would take away your ability to either flee or fight. Instead he would use his terrible power to make you submit quietly whilst he carried out his vile act.'

'Ladies and gentlemen, Ethan Hall, could kill any one of you – could persuade you to kill yourself – in any way of his choosing. Now, you might be asking yourselves "How can this normal-looking man possibly be so dangerous? How could he begin to do this and, even if he could, what might possibly possess him to do so?"'

'These are, indeed, reasonable and proper questions. I'm going to answer them now and as I do, and over the course of our time together, you will come to realise the terrible but inevitable truth of what I am sharing with you. The terrible truth that will mean whenever you look at Mr Ethan Hall you will see beyond the veil of normality and recognise instead the most dangerous man the world has ever seen.'

Mike paused and looked briefly in the direction of the dock. The jury followed his lead. He gave them a couple of seconds before he continued.

'How is it then that this normal-looking man can be so dangerous? How does he kill in such unusual and despicable ways? The answer to both questions is the same: he is a master hypnotist, the most powerful yet evil hypnotist alive. He has skills that are hard for the rest of us to imagine. His complete disregard for the sanctity of human life and his willingness to destroy and kill are equally difficult to imagine and even more difficult to understand.'

'When I first read this case, when I first learnt of the skills Ethan Hall possesses and the danger he presents, I found it not only hard to imagine, but implausible. However, by the end of the case, you will be left in no doubt that every word I have said is true. Ethan Hall is unique, brilliant, dangerous and evil in equal measure. And

 FAITH

yet, in another way, Ethan Hall is no different to many who have gone before him; those wicked men and women whose terrible and violent acts have been beyond our comprehension.'

Mike paused again, nodding slightly, encouraging the jurors to reflect. He watched them remember. He wondered briefly which villains they were thinking of. Then he continued.

'Our questions, created by our shock and revulsion, are actually a reflection of our normality, our respect for others, our wish that such individuals didn't exist. We ask these questions and our imaginations struggle to comprehend because we are guided by values and beliefs that make us care for others, seek loving relationships, want to make our communities safe and nurturing for all.'

'Ethan Hall seeks none of these things. In fact, he creates the very opposite. When he was free no one was safe; he had the power to invade the lives of those he murdered; they had no say in it at all.'

'The individuals you thought of a moment ago needed the obvious weapons of violence – bombs, guns, knives, fists and all the others. Ethan Hall doesn't need any of these. Instead, he uses words.'

'He has the ability to understand every single person he targets so well that he can use words as weapons; he can say whatever it takes to bend people to his will, to make them accept his desire to kill them or, even, want to kill themselves. He is a man – a unique man and therefore a challenge to our imagination – who can use words to cause the greatest of harm, who can look at another person, listen to what they say, with such acuity and accuracy he knows precisely how to get inside their mind. And, once he has penetrated, he is irresistibly destructive.'

'We all know how our communication with other people influences us. We all know how important it is.'

Mike removed his hands from the lectern for the first time. He appeared to take his gaze away from the jury, as if lost in sudden reflection. In reality he was watching them as closely as he ever had.

He divided jury members into three types. Those who made no notes at all, believing naively they could remember everything they needed to. Those who tried to note everything down not realising that, whilst they writing, they were missing important things being said. And, most importantly, those who made notes selectively; the individuals who believed they recognised something important when they heard it, the individuals who thought they knew what they were listening for.

These were the key influencers. One of them would become the jury foreman. The others would also play a pivotal role in shaping the jury's verdict. On this jury there were three. Two men and a woman. Mike guessed she would take the lead. In his experience women still had to work harder than men to achieve recognisable power. Those that did tended to know how to take control in any situation.

'We all know how words affect us,' Mike went on. 'The words others say and the words we say to ourselves. We all know how words change us physically and emotionally. Don't we?'

He gave just enough time for them all to offer their silent agreement.

'When was the last time someone said something that made you laugh? Made you feel afraid? Made you cry? Made you feel loved?' When was the last time someone said something that made you feel nervous, afraid, kept you awake at night?'

He gave that question an extra second, ensuring all of the jury members remembered and engaged. He put his hands back on the lectern.

'We have all shared these experiences, even if we don't talk about them easily. We have all shared these experiences because words affect us. Our brains have evolved for us to be influenced by the words of others. By the words we say inside our own minds.'

'Ethan Hall understands this better than anyone. He uses his understanding and his skill not to make us feel loved, or to laugh, or to feel challenged or scared, or in any of the other ways words usually influence us. He uses words to kill. Ethan Hall is the most dangerous man in the world because his weapon is communication. And, as you will soon see all too clearly, it can be the deadliest weapon of them all.'

Mike looked at each juror in turn.

He inhaled, sighing as if there was a weight on his shoulders, and then said, 'We have all heard the phrase "Sticks and stones may break my bones, but words will never hurt me." We were taught that as children. Perhaps we have even taught it to our own, even though we all know it is only half a truth. Sticks and stones can indeed break our bones. However words, as we have all experienced, can hurt us to our core.'

'Ethan Hall has taken this several terrifying steps further. Now I am going to continue answering the questions you first had by sharing with you the horrors perpetuated by this normal-looking man. This master hypnotist who lives to destroy and who uses words to kill innocent people...'

Ethan Hall ignored the jurors whenever they looked at him. If asked, they would have said he was looking at his feet or staring at the floor. They would have said that because they were as blind as the rest of the herd, because they only ever used their vertical vision.

Parents, Ethan thought dismissively, they pray for their child to be born healthy and then cripple it through their inadequate training. Born with two perfectly functioning hands, it would soon be limited to one. Born with ears that could learn to detect the slightest whisper, they would be dulled by incessant noise. Born with eyes that see far more with peripheral vision than with vertical, they would be taught to look straight ahead and focus inward, trained into tunnel vision. Parents, he thought, they cause more harm than I ever have.

Ethan was watching Mike Coopland using his peripheral vision and his special gift. He had already seen enough to know what was meant by the colour patterns emanating from the barrister, to distinguish those representing the effort of memory from those of self-satisfaction and all the rest. He was listening so intently he heard every slight syllable of doubt, every speedily covered hesitation.

Overall Ethan was quite impressed by Coopland's performance.

Impressed in the way an adult is when a child reads its first words out loud.

He had recognised with ease all of the barrister's brazen and clumsy attempts to make the jury like him, to feel they shared together an inherent sense of goodness and that he, Ethan Hall, was the outsider.

Divide and conquer.

A basic, childish ploy. Supported, of course, by repetition of what Coopland had decided were the key messages at the heart of his story and several crass attempts to lead the jurors' thoughts and emotions.

As Coopland continued speaking, Ethan watched the colours of confidence increasing around him. He watched the jury, quite literally, warming to him. It was precisely what he had expected and planned for. They were, he reminded himself, lambs playing next to a resting lion. When he was ready he would begin to destroy them.

First, though, he had someone else to address.

The larger of the two security guards, with close-cropped brown hair and a well-trimmed beard, was sitting to his right. He was over six feet tall and had, what Ethan presumed to be, the names of his children tattooed on the back of each square, powerful hand. His name was Duncan. He was clearly a bodybuilder. Ethan guessed he was built something like Coopland would have been years ago, before the fat.

Duncan had straightened and flexed subconsciously when the QC had identified Ethan as the most dangerous man in the world. His left arm especially had tightened.

His left arm.

The one with the handcuff around the wrist connecting him to Ethan.

The sensation had thrilled the synesthete. Muscle was no defence. It never had been. He had, in fact, already synced his breathing to the guard's, the muscular, inflated chest making it even easier than normal. Now he was going to start taking the lead, using subtle body movements to make Duncan copy him.

Over the coming hours he would gradually and imperceptibly increase his dominance. Before the day was over the guard would be completely under his control.

Ethan kept his head down and began by lowering his right shoulder fractionally. Duncan did the same. Ethan furrowed his brow. So did Duncan. Ethan flared his nostrils and crinkled his nose. Duncan scratched his.

In front of them, unaware of what was happening in the dock, Mike Coopland QC continued to engage and impress the jury.

CHAPTER 12

MONDAY - TRIAL DAY 1
3.29pm

Calvin Brent poured a second glass of Johnnie Walker Blue Label and handed it to his employee.

'Thanks Boss.' The heavy-set man took the glass gingerly as if scared he might drop it. 'Not 'ad this before. Really appreciate it.'

'I would hope so.' Calvin gestured towards the empty seat on the other side of his desk. 'Sit.'

The heavy-set man did as he was told, the glass cradled in his right hand. He glanced nervously at it, then at Brent, then back at the drink. He shifted awkwardly in the chair.

Calvin sipped his whisky, letting the tension grow. Just for fun. Give a gift with one hand; take comfort away with the other. He had been brought up to believe *If you can, you should.* So he never missed an opportunity. For anything. Ever. It was one of the reasons for his success.

Finally he said, 'So, Matt, the trial has begun. Right now that fat cunt Coopland will be talking his shit to the twelve good men and women of the jury. I hear he wanted them to be brought in from out of the county – Leicestershire or Northants or somewhere. He argued that locals were all too aware of Ethan Hall to be able to operate in an unbiased manner. The fat twat! Does he think the news stops twenty miles down the road?'

Calvin paused, enjoying watching Matt struggle to decide whether or not to answer. Then he went on, 'Anyway, Mulvenny was having none of it. Not that it makes any difference. The jury's fucked as soon as Ethan Hall sets about them. Aren't they?' This time he made it easy.

'Yeah Boss. Fucked.' Matt blinked and took a gulp of his drink.

'It's good, isn't it?'

'It's fuckin' great Boss.' Matt took another swallow.

'It's not meant to be rushed.'

'Sorry Boss.'

Calvin nodded once. Just enough to be seen. Just enough to be a curt acceptance. Not enough to be in any way tolerant or, God forbid, forgiving.

'If the jury's going to be fucked by Ethan Hall and there's twelve of them, what chance do you stand?'

Matt shifted again. 'It's gonna be 'ard Boss, but I'll do my best.'

'I know that. I know you're loyal and I know you'll give it everything you've got. As I've said before, I don't hold you responsible for what happened with Ethan Hall.' Calvin let his voice soften. Good leaders always pretended they cared.

'Stick and carrot,' his father had taught him. 'Never enough carrot to satisfy them, and when you use the stick hold nothing back, make sure people talk about it.'

His father had been a leader all right. He had created and grown the business; turned it into an empire. And even from prison he was helping his son expand it further. Business was better than it had ever been and the Brent name was now a significant global force.

As his father had said during Calvin's visit last week, 'No matter how many businesses Brexit fucks over, it's not going to damage ours. More and more people want to take stuff. Our market's growing, my son. And we'll grow with it.'

Calvin took another sip of his whisky. He liked the way it made Matt glance at his near-empty glass. 'No, I don't hold you responsible,' he said again. 'If anything I underestimated what Hall is capable of. I thought my plan would work. I thought we'd use him to kill that fucker Robin Campbell and then you'd literally drive him into the trap. Never crossed my mind that he'd see through it all, let alone take you fucking hostage!'

Calvin forced a smile.

It was impossible to forget the mesmerising effect of Ethan Hall's voice. Secretly, he was pleased that the hypnotist hadn't targeted him directly.

'I realise there was nothing you could have done to stop him, Matt. That's why I've kept you on, why I didn't retire you.'

'An' I'm really grateful Boss.'

'Never let it be said we don't look after our own.' Calvin smiled. 'The problem we've got, the one we still haven't been able to solve, is how to make sure we get a guilty verdict against him. My dad wants him inside. He wants to deal with him there. And I promised my dad. So how do we stop Ethan Hall from fucking with your head again when you're in the witness box, and how do we make sure the jury comes up with a guilty verdict?'

Matt shrugged. 'Maybe ya could 'elp me to just fuck off 'til the trial's over?'

Calvin shook his head. 'No. You have to be there. You're an important witness. You can tell everyone just how dangerous Hall is, how he didn't even need to tie you up, how he made you do that to yourself.'

Calvin pointed at the left side of his enforcer's head. Matt reached up instinctively, touching the place where his ear used to be.

'No,' Calvin said again, 'you have to go. The jury will look at you and be amazed that you couldn't just smash his face in. For once we have to help Coopland and Jones get what they're after.

And when the jury realises that Hall could control and damage a man like you, they'll find it even easier to believe all the other stuff they're being told.'

'But what if 'e, you know, gets in my 'ead again? Makes me say or do stuff I don' mean to.'

'Maybe that works, too? At least then the jury would see it for themselves.'

'But he'll 'ave 'ad days to get at the jury! Wha' if by then they're all under 'is control?'

'Coopland's bound to be looking out for it, he's sure to have warned Mulvenny and everyone else.'

'It's 'ard to believe it tho'. I mean, when someone tells ya wha' 'e can do, it doesn' sound real.'

'But Jones managed to catch him, didn't he? He found a way to save you and grab him at the same time.'

'But I still can't remember 'ow it 'appened Boss.'

'And I doubt that Jones would want to help us. I don't think his conscience would ever cope with that.' Calvin tapped his right forefinger on the rim of his glass. 'Thing is, we do need some expert help. No one's unbeatable, even if they think they are. It's like that fuckwit Samson who thought he could take over the city. Remember? Told us we could either work for him or fuck off somewhere else. What happened to him again?

'E went swimmin' Boss.'

'Exactly. We need to find Ethan Hall's weak spot, just like we did Samson's. And we need an expert to help us. Someone with practical experience.'

'But there's only Jones who's ever managed t'get one up on 'im.'

'True, again. So if you can't get the winner to help you, you get the best runner-up.'

'Sorry Boss, I don' understand.'

'The best runner-up. They might have lost, but they still know lots about the person who beat them. And in the meantime they might even have worked out how to win. That's what runners-up do, isn't it? They learn from their loss. They come back wiser and better next time.'

'I guess so.' Matt tried to hide his confusion by sipping at his final drops of whisky.

'You guess right.' Calvin drank too, draining his glass in one go. 'You don't have to sip it when you're celebrating,' he explained. 'Or when you're a fucking genius.'

He opened the bottle and poured them both a second large measure.

'You see, the best runner-up is in town and it won't have crossed his mind that he can be of use to us, that by actually helping us he'll be helping himself. That's what he needs to learn. That's what will persuade him.'

'Who Boss?'

'Marcus Kline. The world's so-called greatest communicator. The man who got fucked by Ethan Hall even more than you. I need to have a chat with him. Off the record, of course. Somewhere quiet. Make him understand that he needs to help us right now more than he needs to help Coopland and his best friend, Peter Jones.' Calvin took another drink. 'Marcus Kline needs to learn that it's the Brent family who can solve his problem with Ethan Hall more permanently than the court can ever can.'

'Tha's brilliant Boss!'

'Of course it is.' Calvin beamed. 'Now we need to arrange a meeting. For tonight.'

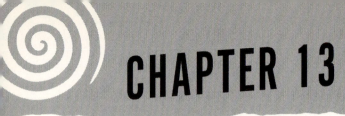

CHAPTER 13

MONDAY - TRIAL DAY 1
5.24pm

Peter Jones didn't know why Marcus Kline was suddenly so keen to meet with him. A meeting, he had insisted, not a phone call. They needed to be face-to-face.

The most logical reason, Peter decided, was last minute nerves. Mike had finished his opening speech this afternoon according to plan. That meant Marcus was in the witness box first thing tomorrow morning. And he was going to be there for some time.

Mike was questioning him first as an expert witness and then as a witness of fact.

For the first part, Marcus would be talking as the leading authority on communication, influence and the power of hypnosis. For the second part, he would be telling the jury about his direct interactions with Ethan Hall. How he had lost their battle of words, how close he had come to being scalped and killed. Mike would ask him to relive both the horror of the experience and the aftermath, when Marcus had sunk into a deep depression.

That was almost certainly not going to be the worst of it, though. When Mike had finished, Ethan Hall would have his turn. Given what had passed between the two men, Peter could understand if Marcus was in need of some final, last minute reassurance.

He pulled his car into the car park of the Travellers Rest pub. It was little more than a mile from where Marcus and Anne-Marie were living, in rented property they had moved into shortly after Ethan Hall had invaded their original home.

Marcus was waiting for him inside. He was sitting at a wooden table in the far corner of the bar, away from the businessmen, couples and young families enjoying an early dinner. There was a half-drunk pint of beer in his hand and an orange juice in front of Peter's empty chair.

'How did the day go?' Marcus asked as Peter sat down.

'Good.' The Detective Chief Inspector ignored the drink. 'Overall Mike's really pleased with how it went.'

'And Ethan Hall?"

'I haven't asked him.' Peter's smile was grim.

'You know that's not what I'm asking.'

Peter shrugged. 'He said and did very little by all accounts. Persuaded Mulvenny that the use of screens would be prejudicial, but that was to be expected. Apart from that he kept his head down.'

'That doesn't mean he was doing nothing.'

Peter shrugged again. 'Is that what we are here for, to try and second-guess what Ethan Hall might or might not have been doing whilst he sat in the dock?'

'No. That's not why we are here.'

'Then?'

Marcus let his attention be taken briefly by a couple at a table opposite. The young man was talking and the woman taking notes. It was an interview. The woman was a journalist, the man a sportsman based on the clothing and physique. It was clear he thought she was attracted to him, and that he expected her to be. Marcus guessed the man would be disappointed – angry, even – with the eventual article.

'Then?' Peter asked again.

'Then, we are here for a different reason.' Marcus looked at his friend. 'You're right, it's one I'm trying to avoid.'

'That's not like you.'

'No. And I'm sorry for asking you here and,' he gestured vaguely, 'looking for a way out.'

'So, tell me.' The DCI didn't flinch.

'I had a phone call from Nic.'

'When?'

'This morning.'

'Why?'

'He's lost. He needs help.'

'How do you know that? Did he say he was lost? Did he ask for help?'

'No. He wasn't able. That's what concerns me most.' Marcus leaned forward. 'He's in Bristol. He thinks he's been summoned there by Andrew.'

'Are you sure?'

'Absolutely.'

'Tell me what he said.'

'He was rambling. He thinks Andrew keeps appearing in front of him and then disappearing. From what I can tell he's spending his time chasing after him. Any time of the day or night he can be roaming the city looking for him. He's clearly hallucinating and in a bad way.'

'Understood.' Peter was silent for a moment. Marcus watched the DCI process the information. It was Peter's default position; whenever something bad happened in his life he let the policeman take over. Marcus had seen it numerous times before.

Finally Peter said, 'Andrew's death certainly hit him hard, but then you'd expect it to. They were close. He seemed to be over it though, as far as anyone can be in a situation like that. There was certainly nothing to suggest this type of behaviour. And he's never used drugs, so it's highly unlikely that they're the source of the problem. Yet something is. Something has clearly got into his head and shattered his normal way of operating.'

'It's what I'd call a pattern interrupt,' Marcus said. 'An event or a suggestion so powerful it's disrupts the brain's usual functioning, breaking established patterns of behaviour.'

Peter fell silent again. The realisation came quickly and he accepted it without a pause. 'So it's him,' he said softly. 'Ethan Hall. The bastard got to Nic as a way of getting at me.' He sighed. 'I always felt, once he'd escaped from hospital, that he was doing more than we ever knew. My gut just wouldn't accept that he was laying low. If we can find Nic we might get proof of that. Makes you wonder what else he did that we don't know about.'

'How are you going to find Nic?'

'I won't. I'll get McNeill on it. Firstly, he'll need to get your permission to track the call from your phone. Then he'll make a couple of calls. Pull in some favours. Once the address is identified a local officer will pay Nic a visit.'

'And then?'

'And then he'll ask all the relevant questions, make a determination of Nic's mental health, find out if Hall is involved. Obviously if he seems well enough he'll be free to go about his life as he chooses.'

'And if he says he saw Ethan?'

'I'll respond as I would with anyone else. I'll send McNeill to interview him formally. I need to stay in Nottingham, close to the trial.'

'This is Nic we are talking about.'

'I'll do what I can to make sure he gets help if he needs it. Right now though, in terms of the trial, it's even more important to know if he had any interaction with Hall.'

'Is that it?'

'Yes. Sometimes there are more important things to address than personal relationships or concerns.'

'But you two were so close.'

'Were being the operative word. As ever I couldn't make a relationship stick. Nic and I were already over. I've seen the signs before, remember?' Peter forced a dry smile. 'Nic just needed time to accept that and move on.'

'But he hadn't gone! That's the point! He was still there fighting. If we're right, Ethan Hall hypnotised him into believing Andrew was still alive and made him leave. It isn't time to give up on this relationship!'

'I can't allow myself to think about that right now. Like I said - '

' – There are more important things to address.'

'Exactly.' Peter pushed the orange juice away from him.

'And getting Ethan Hall locked up is at the top of that list?'

'It certainly is. And after him, there'll be someone else.' Peter stood up abruptly. 'I have to be going. I'm obliged to let Mike know that we met and I'll tell him what it was about. Be at your best tomorrow in the witness box. Remember what I've told you. Mike needs you to be brilliant.' He turned and left as abruptly as he had stood.

Marcus looked at his pint glass, still half-full. At the table opposite the interview had come to an end. From the shift in body language, the young man was now trying to get himself a date. If he had asked, Marcus would have told him he had no chance. The woman was as distant as a foreign land.

CHAPTER 14

MONDAY - TRIAL DAY 1
6.01pm

The car park was less than half-full and yet the owner of the large, black Mercedes had chosen to park next to Marcus's Jaguar. Marcus shook his head in quiet bewilderment.

As he opened his driver's door he heard the Mercedes passenger door window slide open.

'Mr Kline, I'd like to 'ave a word with ya.'

Marcus turned. The driver was leaning across the seat. His eyes were cold and confident. His expression implied an order rather than an invitation.

'And you are?'

'I'm just a driver. It's my Boss who'd like t'talk to ya.'

'And he is?'

'The man who sent me.'

'I see. Well, suppose you tell your Boss that I'm not available and if he wants to make an appointment he can contact me via the office?'

'That wouldn't work, Mr Kline. My Boss doesn't make appointments like normal people. And when 'e wants t'see someone, 'e does.'

'That sounds like a threat.' Marcus kept both hands on the car door, using it as a shield as much as he could.

'It's just a matter of fact. And, anyway, he wants t'see ya because he can 'elp ya with a particular problem ya've got.'

'Which is?'

'Ethan Hall.' The man tried to smile, but it showed as a smirk.

'If your Boss has information about Ethan Hall he needs to contact DCI Peter Jones. He led the investigation.'

'He knows all abowt that. He knows too what Ethan Hall is capable of in court an' e's decided you're the man to talk to, not Jones. Now, d'ya wanna make sure Hall gets convicted or not? 'Cause if ya do, ya need t'get in the car now.'

Marcus looked up at the January sky. The words came back unbidden.

'Getting Ethan Hall locked up is at the top of that list?'

'It certainly is.'

Marcus locked his Jaguar without saying another word and got into the Mercedes. It smelt new. The driver smirked again. The journey took less than twenty minutes. They pulled up outside the main entrance to the Arboretum, a park close to Nottingham city centre.

'He's in there,' the driver said. 'You'll find 'im.'

Marcus got out of the car. The passenger window slid down again.

'An' keep yo'r 'ands off yo'r phone! Don't try an' get clever! This is a private meetin'.' The window closed and the car pulled away. Marcus walked into the park, keeping both hands out of his pockets.

The man was sitting on the first bench he came to. He stood up as Marcus approached. He had a certainty about him that made the driver seem hesitant. He extended his right hand. Marcus took it; the grip was firm.

'I'm Calvin Brent. You've heard of me.'

'Yes.'

'Let's walk.' Brent didn't wait for a reply. Marcus moved with him, keeping next to his right shoulder. 'I like this place,' Brent said. 'First opened in 1852. Got eight hundred trees. Some have been here since it opened. What are the odds of that?'

'I guess they've been protected.'

Brent shook his head. 'Respected. That's what they've been. Respected and then protected. Respect always comes first. We don't look after anything we don't respect.'

'And what is it you respect?'

'The odds. The game.'

'The game, or the rules of the game?'

'They're inseparable.'

'So what happens when someone breaks the rules?'

'They're taken out of the game. What else would you expect?'

Marcus considered briefly. 'You could teach them to respect the rules, then give them another chance.'

'The fact that they don't get another chance is what teaches them.'

'And who sets the rules?'

Brent stopped walking. 'Fuck me! You're a man of the world. You know the answer to that. The person with the most power sets the rules. And they always make sure the rules suit them.'

'Sometime rules can backfire, work against the rule-makers, be responsible for things falling apart.'

'Nothing's falling apart in here. As for the rest, I'm a businessman not a fucking philosopher.' Brent started walking again. 'Now, I wanted to see you because we've had someone trying to play the game who doesn't even belong at the table. He's caused a lot of damage. You know that better than most.'

'And all being well, he'll be sentenced for it.'

'Long odds, my friend. Trials are a lottery. You pick your best team to fight your corner, but there's never any guarantee.' Brent looked at Marcus. 'You ever done any fighting?'

'Only in a boardroom.'

'Well let me tell you, in a real fight everything can be lost in a second. One unexpected blow to a vulnerable spot and it's game over. Do you understand?'

'I know change can happen quickly.'

'Yeah, course you do. Fucking change...Jesus!' Brent slowed slightly. 'Ethan Hall needs to be found guilty. Whatever it takes, the prick needs to go down. We agree on that, right?'

'It depends what you mean by whatever it takes.'

'It means that in a fight the only thing that matters is winning. In a card game you can always throw in your hand and walk away, regroup, come back and start again. A fight is different. It's life and death. There's no coming back from being dead.'

'A trial isn't about whether the defendant lives or dies. It's about justice.'

'Bollocks!' Brent spat. 'You have a choice. You can put your trust in the system and hope that it all works together nicely and Hall gets found guilty. Or you can do everything in your power to stack the deck. Because that fucker deserves to lose! And between us we can make sure that happens.'

'Why do you care? Why is Ethan Hall so important to you?'

'Because I look after my people and he took one of my employees hostage.'

Marcus smiled. 'I know what you do for a living, Mr Brent. And I'm sure you know what I do.'

'What's that got to do with it?'

'I know when I'm being lied to. Even when it's by a professional like yourself.'

'Is that a fact?' Brent's face hardened. 'Well, given what you do for a living, I'd have thought you knew the dangers of speaking out of turn, of being a smart-arse. Anyway,' he clapped a hand on Marcus's left shoulder, 'the bottom line is we both want to see Ethan Hall in prison. And I'm bothered that my employee will get turned inside out when Hall cross-examines him. For fuck's sake, he's already made him cut his own ear off.'

'I think that's a very reasonable concern.'

'Good. We agree on something.'

'Therefore?'

'Therefore, Mr Communications Specialist, we both need for my employee to hammer some big fuck-off nails in Ethan Hall's coffin! And I can't teach him how to do that.'

'And you think I can?'

'Didn't you learn something when he beat you? I'd have thought you would, because most good professionals learn from their defeats and you're supposed to be really good. In fact, you were supposed to the best weren't you?'

'Some people would have said so.'

'You would have been one of those people, right?'

Marcus felt himself blush. 'That's really not relevant.'

'You fucking hypocritical bastard!' Brent snorted. 'Why don't you just accept that you've got as much in this game as me? That we're not so different on one level? You need everyone to acknowledge that you're the best at what you do, and so do I. You need to beat all challengers, and so do I. Now what's so fucking wrong with us working together to win this game?'

'The best way I can answer that is to say we are not obvious team-mates.'

'Fair point,' Brent nodded, 'But we fought with the French to beat the Nazis and we fucking hate the Frogs.'

CHAPTER 15

MONDAY - TRIAL DAY 1
6.19pm

'Strike one for the good guys!' Brian Kaffee said raising his glass.

'Strike one,' Mike Coopland agreed, accepting the toast. 'But this is definitely my last pint. I need to get home, see the girls, have some dinner and then run through my plan for tomorrow one more time.'

'Only one?'

'Well, for only one night.' Mike took a swallow of his Italian lager. 'Tomorrow is the day we really start learning how we stand. We did well today, the jury certainly ate it up, but you know as well as I do we now need our witnesses to tell the story for us.'

'You'd expect Marcus Kline to get us off to a good start, wouldn't you?'

'I'd bloody well hope so. We go from strike one to being in deep shit if he doesn't.'

Kaffee frowned. 'Do you have any concerns?'

'There are always concerns, right?' Mike took another drink. 'Look, Kline clearly has everything we need in an expert witness. If that was all he was being and if he wasn't so personally involved in the case, I'd be as relaxed as I could be. All I'd need to do was establish his credibility, ask him the technical questions and let him enjoy being the genius at the centre of our attention. It's him also being a witness of fact that bothers me. I can't help but think that might muddy the water.'

'But he understands all of this, and he's a clever guy.'

'Of that there is no doubt. The problem is that he's got an ego and a bag full of emotions just like the rest of us. My concern is that he goes off on one when Hall cross-examines him. Remember, Hall bested him once. What happens if Kline tries to even the score?'

'You really think it could turn into some sort of duel? A trance at seven paces?' Kaffee chuckled.

'Not funny. It won't matter how well I question and how well he answers if his ego gets the better of him once Hall starts talking. For Christ's sake, if you're Hall you don't need to bother with any hypnosis, you just do whatever it takes to wind Kline up. Maybe just the fact that Kline has to sit there and answer Hall's questions, that he's got to cede authority to his attacker, that he sees Hall as being in control once again, maybe just that will be enough to make him say something stupid.'

'But Peter Jones has had some obvious conversations with him?'

'Yes. And he says that Kline understands what's needed.'

'So everything's been done that could be done – apart from you going through it all again tonight?'

'Yeah.'

'And we've both managed potentially challenging days in court a hundred times.'

'Yeah.'

'And you're on a winning streak and we're a winning team.'

'Yeah.'

'And none of this is making you feel any better, is it?'

'Nope.' Mike drained his pint glass. 'We're pushing the boat out charging Hall with the murders of three people when all we have is circumstantial evidence. If we'd played safe we would just have gone after him for the attempted murder of Kline.'

'You never play safe when you're sure you are right. Remember last year, a dead body and no obvious cause of death. No one, but no one, was thinking about a murder charge until you took the case and insisted on it. Even then, as the trial progressed, everyone kept telling you what a huge mistake you'd made.'

'You certainly did.'

'That's because I thought it was a huge mistake. It didn't stop you, though, did it? It didn't throw you out of your stride one little bit. In fact, your closing speech was the best I've heard.'

'Thanks.'

'After which the jury was out for how long?'

'Thirty minutes.'

'Exactly! It took twelve people only thirty minutes to convict a man of murder, even though the exact cause of death had never been proven. You did that! No one else could have. And you feel the same way now, about Ethan Hall, as you did then. So you are absolutely right to go for it! If you were anyone else I might indeed have urged caution. If I hadn't shared that case with you last year, I still might. Only I did. And you are who you are. So, whether we are working with circumstantial evidence or not, we have enough between us to win this thing, to get justice for the victims and Hall off the streets. Now, are you sure you don't want another pint?'

Mike sighed. 'OK. Just one more. Thanks.'

'Good man.' Kaffee finished his glass of Pinot Gris and set off for the bar, working his way through the usual after-work crowd.

Mike eased back in his chair and looked up at the ceiling. The building was a Grade II listed church. Once it had housed rites of passage. Now it was a bar offering a wide range of drinks and an all-day menu. Now stained-glass windows shone light onto Pornstar Martinis and bottles of Malbec.

And here I am, Mike thought, part of the drinking congregation.

He checked Kaffee's progress. He was already being served. He had, as ever, found a way to insert himself at the front of the queue. He was good at that. Good at pushing in without offending anybody. No doubt Marcus Kline could have explained why.

Mike tried to let the thought go. It tried to cling and spawn a hundred others. The adrenalin was twisting his stomach into knots. He hated it and loved it at the same time. He hated it because it was all consuming. He loved it for the same reason. Adrenalin was the fuel of victory.

As long as you knew how to control and use it.

He had done that well today. Of course, there had been a few fractions of a second when it had almost thrown him, but that was all they were. Fractions of a second.

Too brief for anyone to have noticed.

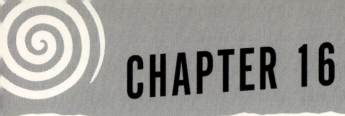

CHAPTER 16

MONDAY - TRIAL DAY 1
6.58pm

Anne-Marie Wells was struggling to concentrate on her new photographic commission. It was titled *Fractions and Fragments*. According to the brief the photo essay had to convey the story that whilst everything and everyone was merely a fraction of a fragment, combined they formed the perfect whole.

Anne-Marie had accepted the task because she had no idea how to begin or what to create. That was precisely how she liked to work. With a sense she could produce something meaningful yet with no obvious starting point. No idea of what images she might shoot.

No idea...

Anne-Marie Wells, world famous photographer known professionally by her maiden and not her married name, had always found a strange, adrenalised comfort in having no idea. Mrs Anne-Marie Kline, however, found the same scenario terrifying.

At times she felt like two different people living inside the same body.

In her experience of shooting photos around the world that was a luxury unknown to the desolate and homeless.

So Anne-Marie Wells had welcomed the task and trusted that the ideas would come. She had used her tried and tested process to encourage them. The first step was to take the key words in the brief or title quite literally and to research them, to find out different meanings and interpretations, their implications in different historical periods, in different cultures and industries.

She had researched the words fractions and fragments individually and then done the same combining them as a phrase. She had discovered that Fractions and Fragments was the name of an album produced by a Swedish punk rock band in 2000. She made other discoveries, too. Many related to various aspects of medicine, some to historical discoveries. The one that most took her attention she found in an article about the growth of the Nazi Party in the decade leading up to the start of World War II.

In 1929, she had read, the total population of Germany was 64,720,000. Nazi party membership at that time totalled 130,000 which, as the author was keen to point out, was just more than one fifth of one percent of the German population and 0.065% of the world's population. By 1938 however, the situation in Germany had changed dramatically. In the general election of that year the Nazi Party swept to power receiving 44,451,092 votes, which was 99.1% of the total vote. In 1939 Germany invaded Poland.

The article was titled The Power of One Fifth of One Percent. It was, from Anne-Marie's perspective, a clever and disturbing historical reminder that mighty oaks grow from tiny acorns. She had found it impossible to read without thinking about her cancer. Even at its worst it had been only a tiny fraction of her entire physical self. Yet it would have killed her.

If it hadn't been for Ethan Hall.

Anne-Marie stood up from the desk where she was sat making notes and walked into the kitchen. She poured herself a glass of water. Ethan Hall knew how to fragment, knew the chaos that caused, understood the pain. Ethan Hall was going to cross-examine her in the witness box. Even though there would be dozens of other people in the room, it would feel as if they were alone together again. With her terrified about the words he might say and how he might use them.

Anne-Marie put the glass down. Her throat was dry, but she couldn't drink. She wondered where Marcus was, wondered how he was. Then her mobile phone began ringing. She took it out of her pocket with a smile on her face. How often had she found herself thinking of Marcus only for him to call her at that precise moment? She knew it was only coincidence of course, but it was nice to pretend it was something more. A sign of their special connection or, at the very least, a reminder of how important he was to her.

Anne-Marie picked up her phone. Her smile was replaced by a frown. It was an unknown mobile number. She hesitated for a second and then answered the call.

'Hello?'

'Good girl.' The voice was disguised, but the words were clear enough. The words made her freeze. 'Because that's what you are, isn't it? A good girl. A good girl who knows how to do things again and again when she's told to.'

They were the same words. The words Ethan Hall had used after he had made her orgasm. The words he had used before he made her do it again.

'Please, no...'

'Please, yes. Indeed. Good girls never mean no. They only mean yes. They only mean yes again and again – and anywhere they're told to.'

Anne-Marie screamed and dropped the phone. The nightmare was no longer confined to her sleep. Sometime soon she would have to be there.

The witness box.

Her and Ethan Hall.

Separate from the rest.
Joined by their secret.
And her fear.

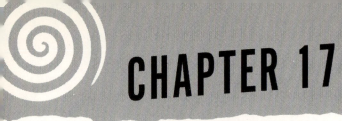

CHAPTER 17

MONDAY - TRIAL DAY 1
7.16pm

Ethan Hall lay back on his prison hospital bed and allowed himself a brief moment of reflection.

He had spent the rest of the afternoon focussing more on Duncan the security guard than on Mike Coopland and his overlong opening speech. Two hours. Two hours of a carefully rehearsed, self-satisfying, amateurish monologue. If Mike Coopland was the best they could send against him, God help the rest of them.

And God help Duncan.

Ethan chuckled. Seeding his influence had been as easy and enjoyable as it ever had. Now Duncan was going to become active on his behalf. One more part of his beautiful, simple plan.

There were two kinds of simple.

Ethan had known that since childhood; since, as a five year old, he had watched a spider build a web and a Bluebottle buzz straight into it and die. The spider had, with effortless ease, created a thing of great beauty and complexity, at once a home and a snare. In doing so, it had demonstrated the simplicity of the expert, of the Master. The fly had died because it was too simple – too stupid – to recognize and avoid the trap.

Two types of simple.

One simple choice: be the spider or the fly, be the Master or the prey.

Ethan closed his eyes and journeyed deep into recesses of his subconscious even he had not been able to access until recently. His time in the prison hospital had proven to be everything he had expected, a time of exploration and preparation and growth. The training camp. The very deliberate lull before the very destructive storm.

As Ethan travelled a route few had ever known existed, his voice spoke. He heard it from a distance. He heard it stretching, spidery-thin. He heard it saying, 'And you have to look and you have to listen, even if you don't know that's what you are doing and what you have done. And so things get in and they stir what you have inside, those memories and beliefs and fears that cling, those parts of you that are so silvery-fine you don't feel their grip, you don't realise they have restructured you so completely you have become a fixed target, easy to penetrate, easy to direct.'

'And the less noticeable it is, the more sticky the influence. The less remembered it is, the more accepted and powerful the belief. And every arena has walls that are used to shape and define it. They keep the influence in, keep it ricocheting around, returning and repeating and sinking in ever deeper, time after time after time.'

'You let others create the arenas you live in. You let others do this because you are weak and soft, because you have no idea how to take responsibility for your own lives, because you are the herd, good for only copying and blaming others; imprisoned without even realising it.'

'You think I'm the one in prison and I'm not. Nothing can contain my influence. I'm not the prisoner. I'm the one building prisons, inside you and all around. And once they're complete I'm going to throw away the keys. I'm going to leave you all in solitary confinement. Regimented and lost.'

 FAITH

Ethan Hall opened his eyes and stretched his spine. He felt the warm buzz in the back of his skull that he always felt whenever he memorised something. The words he had just spoken were contained and secure in his subconscious, like so many others of late.

Deprived of his notebook and pen, both hidden in a place where no one would find them, he had been forced to remember rather than write. No matter. His memory was impeccable. He trusted it completely, just as he trusted the power of his subconscious to create the most complex and devastating web.

Marcus Kline and those closest to him were flying towards it because he was drawing them in. The courtroom was the arena of his choosing. He would destroy them there; leave them clinging and lifeless. It was inevitable. His enemies were already committed, incapable of changing direction, trapped without even knowing it. He, however, had never felt such freedom.

CHAPTER 18

MONDAY - TRIAL DAY 1
11.05pm

Gavin Hickson was feeling good.

Freedom, he told himself for the sixth time that night, was the best of all drugs. Not that he would ever tell his clients. Not that he ever thought of them as clients. True, it was what he called them to their face or when he was talking about his business. But secretly, inside, Gavin knew what they were. They were addicts. Worthless, desperate-for-a-fix druggies who would do whatever it took to buy his product.

Even though it was sub-standard.

And why, for Christ's sake, should he bother about the quality if they didn't?

They gave up their right to fair treatment the day they chose to be addicts.

Besides, if they kept coming back to him it meant they were happy with what he provided. It was an equitable arrangement. They became increasingly lost in their wasteland and he got richer.

Gavin drained his tenth pint of Carling and burped. The back room of The Hare and Horses was buzzing.

A private party to celebrate his release.

He had done three years, just because some middle-class teenage girl had got drunk and taken some of his stuff. And then had a fucking heart attack and died.

Three years.

It made Gavin yearn for the revolution. The coming of the New Order. An even bigger chance than Brexit to stick it to the smug bastards who thought they were untouchable.

'Hey Gav! Wanna Bells?' Steve Daines was leaning against the bar. He was the most pissed person in the room. And that was saying something.

'Course I fuckin' do!' Gavin laughed. 'I'm free mate! 'Aven't ya noticed?' A cheer went up. Gavin punched the air in triumph.

Truthfully, he was knackered. It had been a long and tiring day. Freedom, he'd discovered, was exhausting when you'd forgotten what it felt like.

"Ere ya go, mate!' Steve almost dropped the whisky on the table. 'Get that down yo'r neck!'

'Cheers, pal.' Gavin forced another laugh and swallowed the large measure in one go. Even in his drunken state he felt it burn his throat. Definitely time to sneak home and leave the rest to it. Definitely should have eaten something today.

'I need a leak.'

Gavin made his way unsteadily to the Gents. From there he staggered to the back door and out into the cold winter night.

The Hare and Horses was a ten-minute walk from his terraced house. Tonight it took longer. Buildings were spinning around him. The pavements angled down, making him veer into the road. He threw up twice. Once in an alley. Once on a dustbin. When he finally arrived home he couldn't find his keys anywhere.

'Shit!'

He thumped the door. Hurt his hand. Realised dimly it must be bad if he could feel it despite the alcohol. The door swung open.

'Fuck me!'

He'd forgotten to lock it. Three years inside and you're out of practice when it comes to locking your own doors.

Gavin stumbled into the warmth. The keys weren't in the lock, so he pushed the single bolt and, after several attempts, managed to slide the chain into place. Find the keys tomorrow. When his eyes were working. And his balance was back.

Gavin made his way into the galley kitchen off the lounge. He needed toast. With plenty of butter. Maybe even jam. He opened the cupboard.

'Fuck!'

He hadn't been shopping. The cupboard was bare.

'Fuck!'

He shaped to punch the wall, but some deep-rooted survival instinct stopped him. Instead he went back into the lounge. Remembered then that he couldn't watch a porn channel because his Sky contract had expired. Three years inside and it was like starting again. From scratch. All because of some stupid middle-class cunt.

The blow hit him across the back of his head so hard he barely had time to register it before he lost consciousness.

When he opened his eyes his head hurt like hell. He was sitting in the middle of his lounge, tied to one of his cheap wooden dining chairs. He was gagged.

The man standing in front of him was wearing all black. Leather jacket, sweatshirt, jeans, gloves, trainers and a balaclava that covered all of his face but for his eyes. Gavin couldn't see clearly enough to tell what colour they were.

'You're scum.' The voice was deep, coated in controlled rage. 'You're scum. You don't deserve to have your freedom when you destroy the lives of others.'

Gavin tried instinctively to reply. The best he could make was a muffled sound. The intruder didn't blink.

'So I'm going to give you a taste of your own medicine. An eye-

 FAITH

watering taste.'

The intruder had placed a small shoulder bag on Gavin's grubby, brown settee. He reached into it, unhurried, as if what was happening was too good to rush.

He took out a syringe. Held it very deliberately in front of Gavin's face. The drug dealer gasped.

'That's right. It's heroin mixed with a little water. You prefer alcohol, I understand. Still. Beggars and all that.'

Gavin tried again to speak, to scream, to begin some sort – any sort – of dialogue.

The intruder took no notice. He pressed his left hand against Gavin's chest. Then he pointed the syringe towards his left eye.

'Eye-watering is only going to be the first part of it.'

He moved the syringe forward, slowly.

Gavin screamed, but no sound came out. Instead he choked behind the grey tape that gagged him. He squeezed his eyes tight shut.

'Here we go. One at a time.' The intruder gently and carefully inserted the syringe into the very centre of Gavin's left eye. He eased it all the way through before releasing some fluid. He withdrew it with equal care.

The pain made Gavin's body jump and flex as far as his bonds would allow. He retched, his almost empty stomach firing fluid into his mouth. He coughed, spluttered, struggled for breath.

The intruder nodded calmly. 'It's a shame you are drunk. It would feel much worse if you were sober.'

He pointed the syringe at Gavin's right eye and punctured it even more slowly than he had the left.

The chair moved and squeaked and threatened to come apart as Gavin reacted to the shock.

The intruder returned the syringe to the bag and took out a

large, single-edged knife. 'I'll give you a few minutes,' he said, 'and then I'm going to cut your throat.'

He sat back on the settee, resting the knife on his thighs, as he took a mobile phone out of his jacket pocket. He used it to take photos of the damage done to Gavin's eyes and to show what happened next. He took his time throughout.

When it was over he wiped the knife clean on Gavin's jeans before returning it to the bag. Then he uploaded the images onto social media. Doing that made him smile.

Pass it on, he thought as he left the house.

PART TWO
FEELINGS

CHAPTER 19

TUESDAY - TRIAL DAY 2
6am

Marcus Kline had stayed awake all night. He hadn't even tried to sleep. Which was flying in the face of his own rules. Rest and recovery were the most essential part of preparation, learning and growth. You couldn't perform well if you were not properly rested. Neuroscience was clear about this fact. The human brain, for all its brilliance, needed time out.

So, the night before the most important day of his life he had deliberately stayed awake.

What the hell was that all about?

Hopefully it was nothing to do with hell.

Even though he was once again making decisions he had no right to make.

Marcus tried to shake the memory free, but he couldn't. He tried to tell himself he had done the right thing, but he couldn't do that either. No matter what perspective he approached it from, he returned to the same conclusion. He should have told Peter Jones immediately about his meeting with Calvin Brent and what they had agreed. Only he hadn't. And he wasn't going to now.

Marcus looked at the ink black sky. The night, he thought, holding for as long as it can.

January.

The month of new beginnings.

The coldest month of the year in the northern hemisphere.

Many years ago he had written an article for a Sunday newspaper about the relationship between time and change. It had been a story about January. It was on his computer screen now. He had read it at least half a dozen times throughout the night. He couldn't help but look at it again.

Forwards and Back and Round and Round We Go

January, the first month in the Julian and Gregorian calendars, is a time of change. It is the first of seven months to contain thirty-one days. It begins with what we call New Years Day. It marks a time of opportunity and loss.

On New Years Day we look forward to what we might achieve in the coming year. We make resolutions. Sometimes we mean them. We look back at the previous year, gone overnight. We feel a mixture of emotions. We think – briefly, because it's an unpleasant thought – of our own mortality. Another year passed. Another step closer.

January is named after the Roman god Janus, the god of beginnings and endings, of transitions and time. Janus is usually depicted with two faces. One looks to the future. One to the past.

Modern scholars debate the fundamental nature of Janus. If the function of a god is to preside over all beginning and endings, the implications and the questions raised are significant. Why, for example, would a god let bad things, like war, ever begin? Why would they let the lives of good people, like Martin Luther King, end too soon?

Beyond that, a god of beginnings and endings and all associated change has to be inseparable from time. And not just the functional concept of time created by humankind to enable them to organise and manage their existence, but time as the very essence of universe-shift.

 FAITH

In the darkness of January we recognise, however subliminally, the inevitability of change. We sense the continual circling of the universe, the continual contracting and expanding of Life itself.

We drown January, at least the very start of it, in alcohol and enforced merriment in order to avoid the primal awareness brought by its inevitable chill: we are neither static nor permanent. We simply go forwards and back and round and round.

Unless we learn how to centre ourselves.

To be centred means to be fully present in the instant; to be experiencing the now of reality freed from the blinkers and restrictions of personal agendas and purely selfish need.

If we learn how to centre ourselves we can change the world.

Even in January.

Marcus stared at the words on the screen and remembered what it felt like to be centred. He remembered the sense of immediacy and freedom it created, the power that came with it. It was the state he entered into whenever working with clients, or needing inspiration to write. It was the state he had lost since Ethan Hall had defeated him.

And today we will meet again, he thought, in January of all months.

'What are you doing?'

Marcus spun round. Anne-Marie was standing in the doorway.

'I'm preparing for today.'

'Are those your notes?' She gestured towards the laptop.

'Sort of.' Marcus flipped the lid. 'How did you sleep?'

'No differently from last night.'

He nodded. If anything she looked even more tired than she had. 'Did you know the ancient Romans observed several feasts and festivals during January?'

'What?'

'It's true. One of them was called Carmentalia. In honour of the goddess Carmenta. She had her own temple. There were two feast days for her, celebrated primarily by women. Two days because they believed she had the ability to look into the future as well as the past. She was like the god Janus in that respect.'

'You're telling me this, why?'

'She was also the goddess of childbirth and prophecy. She was said to have invented the Latin alphabet and to be associated with technological innovation.'

'At the time of the Romans?'

'I guess innovation is relative.'

'And the point is?'

'It's in my mind, that's all. Technology. Social media. The damage it causes.' He paused. 'There's been another *Pass it on* killing. In Nottingham. Our twenty four hour news cycle has been full of it overnight.'

'You haven't slept?'

Marcus shrugged. 'Social media is killing us as a communicative species.'

'You're not really blaming some Roman god, are you?'

'No.' He managed a smile. 'The news story wasn't so much about the killing as it was the support it was getting. Can you imagine, you take pictures of your crime, show them to the world, add the hashtag *Pass it on* and thousands of people are suddenly keen to oblige. Not only that, they're making it clear they are on your side!'

'Who was killed?'

'Does it matter?'

It was Anne-Marie's turn to shrug. 'Once upon a time I would have said, no. I would have said that no matter who the victim is, there's no justification for murder. Now I'm not so sure.'

'Sometimes we have to fight hard to hold on to the beliefs that matter.' Marcus glanced out of the window. It was still dark. 'Guess what story followed on from that? Guess what is being associated, whether deliberately or not, to the *Pass it on* killings?'

'Oh God, don't say it's the trial.'

'Absolutely. Both are happening in Nottingham and at the same time, so it's a cheap and easy link to make.'

Anne-Marie took a step into the room. 'You don't think they are connected, do you?'

'I don't know. Logically, there's no reason to think so. Emotionally, it's just too easy to blame Ethan Hall for everything at the moment.' Marcus couldn't stop himself from running his right hand through his hair, remembering the feel of Ethan's scalpel on his skin.

'How much power does he have?'

There was something in her voice that brought his attention right back to the present.

'My best guess is that it's more than we can imagine and less than he believes.'

'How much power do you have?'

He laughed, a harsh, abrupt sound. 'Probably more than I currently believe and less than you imagine. Why?'

'I need to feel safe.'

'Of course.'

They were both silent for a moment. Then Anne-Marie said, 'Things start small and seem disconnected. That's how it seems, especially at the beginning. I'm coming to realise, though, that it's not completely true.'

'Oh?'

'We're all part of nature. Every natural thing begins small and then, over time, it grows. But, as a part of nature, everything is connected. That's the truth I'm coming to realise. Sometimes the growth and the connections are destructive, obscene even. But if we turn our backs and pretend that it's nothing to do with us we become complicit in every awful event that follows.'

He listened to her, unmoving. He watched her eyes flitter as she spoke.

'In 1929 the Nazi Party was tiny, measured as just a few hundredths of one percent of the world's population. Did you know that?'

He shook his head.

'Within a decade it was big and strong enough to threaten the world and cause previously unimaginable harm.'

'Before it was defeated.'

'But the cost...' She looked him in the face for the first time since entering the room. '...The cost was so great.'

'Yes.' He nodded slowly. 'There's always a cost.' He thought again of Janus and Carmenta and the dark coldness of January. 'There's always a cost,' he repeated. 'No matter which way you look.'

CHAPTER 20

TUESDAY - TRIAL DAY 2
6.57am

Peter Jones arrived in his office with two minutes to spare before the meeting was scheduled to start. Kevin McNeill was already there.

'Christ! You're early!'

'Aren't I always Boss?'

'No. I'm the one who's early, you're the one who's always got a very good reason for being five minutes late.'

'Not today, though.'

'Hmm. The learning point then is for me to organise meetings first thing in the morning, so you haven't had chance to let something else get in the way.'

'There's nothing more important than your meetings Boss.'

'Fuck off.'

'If you're sure you want me to, but we don't seem to have accomplished anything yet.'

'Smart arse.' Peter sat down behind his desk. 'I need to share something with you.'

'Fire away.' Kevin sat too.

'I've been alerted to a situation that has left me concerned about the possible wellbeing of an individual. It's a situation I can't get involved in. The best I can do is report it to the most appropriate authority.'

'And that's me?'

'Yes.'

'How come?'

'Because the individual concerned is my ex-partner.'

'Nic?' Kevin straightened in his chair.

'Yes.'

'What's the situation and how were you alerted?'

'It seems he's living in Bristol, alone as far as we can tell. The concern is for his mental stability. He phoned Marcus Kline yesterday. Right out of the blue. Marcus says he was rambling, incoherent at times. He was talking about his dead brother, Andrew.'

'Saying what?'

'That he was seeing him, that his brother kept appearing and encouraging him to follow. Then he'd disappear and Nic would spend the rest of the day roaming the streets looking for him.'

'Dear God. Was there any indication of...of mental problems before he left?'

'Other than the fact that he'd chosen to live with me?'

Kevin smiled because he was required to. It was called dark humour because they were the only times you used it.

'No,' Peter went on. 'He wasn't as happy as he'd once been, but you can work out the reasons for that as well anyone. Whilst he was obviously aware that things weren't going well between us, I don't think he had come to the conscious conclusion that we were beyond hope.'

'And you had?'

'Unfortunately I'd recognised certain signs.'

'But you hadn't shared that with him?'

'Not deliberately.'

'OK. So what do you want me to do?'

'As your Boss, absolutely nothing at all. That would be inappropriate on so many levels. As a concerned citizen, however,

I'm reporting a genuine concern. I think this individual might be at serious risk. I thought you ought to know.'

'You're absolutely right and I appreciate you sharing the information. It is definitely something I will look into as a matter of urgency.' Kevin made a point of taking out his notebook and writing a few words. 'Just so that you understand the process going forwards, I will contact Mr Marcus Kline and ask for his permission to trace this particular call on his phone. Assuming he is cooperative, we will be able to identify the number and then trace the location from which the call was made. At that point I'll make a call to my colleagues in Bristol. They, I'm sure, will send a uniformed officer to the address to check on the individual's state of health. This should all happen with great speed.'

'Good. Before it does, there's one other element to this that you need to be aware of.'

'Which is?'

'Marcus believes, and I'm very much inclined to agree with him, that the reason for this change in Nic's mental state might well be Ethan Hall.'

'What?'

'It makes sense if you think about it. During the time that still remains unaccounted for he could easily have caught up with Nic, even visited our house for God's sake, and cast one of his evil word-spells; convinced him that Andrew was still alive and that they could be together.'

'Christ!' Kevin wrote another note. 'I'll make sure the visiting officer asks the necessary questions. We definitely need to know if that happened.'

'Yeah. Thanks.'

Kevin closed his notebook, stood up and made his way to the

door. He stopped and looked back over his shoulder. 'Did you see the news, Boss?'

'Yes.' Peter nodded. His face stern. The pretence over. 'Two murders in less than twenty four hours, both posted on social media. This second one had DD carved into his forehead.'

'It stands for drug dealer.'

'I'd never have guessed.'

'Sorry Boss.' Kevin scowled as he remembered the images he had seen. 'It feels like there's some vigilante thing going on.'

'It certainly doesn't feel good.'

'Have you heard anything, on the qt?'

'No. But I do want to know all about it, just for my own piece of mind. You know how I feel about coincidences and this happening here, now, just seems like a step too far down the coincidence path.'

'Roger that. It isn't just the killings though, is it? What about the fuckers who do actually pass it on, spewing out their biased, vitriolic, violent bullshit opinions? I tell you, sometimes Boss I wonder just what sort of society we're protecting.'

'The silent majority are still the majority.'

'Well they should speak up more often and put those sick fuckers in their place.'

'Only then you start a conversation, and by doing so you not only acknowledge a disgusting point of view you imply it's worthy of debate.'

'I wasn't suggesting they get invited on Question Time, rather they were all told to fuck off and live together on an island away from the rest of us.'

'That's your solution whenever people hold views that are different to yours, is it?' Peter leaned back in his chair. 'Oh, and by the way, we live on an island.'

 FAITH

'Don't imply that I'm some sort of intolerant racist; you know I'm not. These trolls just make me so mad, that's all. I hate the way they conveniently forget that no matter who the actual victims are, whether they're criminals or not, there are always innocent family members and friends affected too.'

'And then there's the rule of law,' Peter said. 'It says that it's a crime to kill someone because you don't like them or because you think they've done something terrible or, even, if they have done something terrible. In the end, we are on the side of the rule of law. And so are the silent majority. That, DS McNeill, is why we come to work every day. I hope you haven't forgotten that.'

'I haven't Boss.' Kevin felt himself straighten instinctively. 'Anyway, I'll get off. There are some phone calls I need to make, a person I need to find in Bristol.'

'I have every confidence in you.'

'Thank you Boss.' Kevin closed the office door behind him.

Peter Jones listened to his footsteps in the corridor and thought of opportunities lost.

CHAPTER 21

TUESDAY - TRIAL DAY 2
7.09am

Calvin Brent wasn't feeling at his best. In fact, he was feeling decidedly uncomfortable; a mixture of concern and anger that had him pacing his office, talking to himself as he waited for the phone to ring.

He was uncomfortable because he didn't like unnecessary change. If a system or routine had been proven to work he let it run, focussing his energy and resources instead on problems or possibilities.

Today there was a change to a well-established routine.

An enforced change.

One he could do nothing about. One he had to go along with even though he didn't want to. Which was why he was angry.

'There has to be something wrong,' he repeated to himself. 'He wouldn't be calling at this time unless it's something really urgent. So what the hell is it that just can't wait? What could possibly be so bad that he's changed the routine? He was the one who taught me that consistency wins. Now he's breaking the rule! Shit!'

Calvin stopped pacing and looked at the mobile phone on his desk. Almost immediately it started ringing. As he went to pick it up he realised that his hand was shaking.

'Hello.'

'Morning, son.'

'Dad.'

Calvin knew better than to ask. His father would say what he had to in his own good time. Any attempt to rush him would backfire badly.

True, Calvin was the face of the business. The man who ran it on a daily basis, who kept tight control, managed the numbers, put down any opposition. But his father was still the ultimate power. That was the unspoken truth. Everyone knew when push came to shove, the Brent family business was still the old man's business.

Karl Brent's sixty-fifth birthday was fast approaching. He had been in prison for a decade. According to his records he had been a model prisoner. Despite that, according to his records, he had no chance of release until he was at least seventy-three. What his records didn't show was that he had taken his authority with him into prison. He ran the place.

He wasn't stupid. He didn't rub the Governor's face in it. He didn't make outrageous demands. As long as he was left alone to do as he pleased, in the style of his choosing, everyone got along just fine. Which was good news for all concerned. The prison guards felt safe. The other prisoners understood the hierarchy. The Governor appreciated the subtlety of the arrangement. Karl's ability to make unrestricted and unmonitored phone calls was the very least of it.

'How are you, lad?'

'I'm, er, doing good. Business is on the up. Profits are rising. I'm winning at cards. So, yeah, life is good.'

'Hmm.'

Karl had realised long ago that his son's passion for poker exceeded all else. If he'd had another son, one with a single, business focus, he would have put him in charge when the guilty verdict came in. Only he hadn't. Calvin was his only child. And he sure as hell wasn't going to give the business to an outsider, no matter how capable or loyal. And, to be fair, the boy had done well overall. Even if Karl had been required to solve a couple of problems at long-distance.

'We need to talk.'

'Yeah. Of course.'

Karl smiled at the tension in his son's voice. He could feel the question straining inside him. He decided to stretch it out a little longer.

'There are three things. Although, as you will come to appreciate, two are connected. Let's deal with the lesser one of those first.'

'Right.'

'Gavin Hickson.'

'Ah. Yeah. I heard all about it.'

'I should fucking hope you did. It was all over the news. I should fucking hope you know more about it than the BBC.'

Calvin felt the cold, hard edge of his father's irritation. It went from that to explosive action without the slightest warning. He couldn't help but remember the power in the back of his hand. Followed by the instruction to never cry.

'He was out boozing most the day. Organised a party for himself in the evening in the Double H. Left without telling anyone. Too pissed to know what he was doing or saying.'

'And then?'

'Nobody seems to know.'

'Nobody *seems* to know? Or nobody knows? Which is it?'

'Nobody knows. Anything. I've had people asking around. It was late when he left the pub. Dark. Cold. Streets were quiet. No one saw him on his way home. No one heard anything from inside his house.'

'And no one was seen leaving his house?'

'No.'

 FAITH

'You understand the importance of this, right? I don't give a fuck about Hickson. He's ten-a-penny. What I do give a fuck about is the message it sends! No one comes into our territory and makes a killing without getting permission first! So I want to know who did it.'

'It's a *Pass it on* killing, like the one the day before.'

'I've seen that and I don't give a fuck! People will be watching to see what we do. I want you to make sure you give them something that they can pass on. Got it?'

'Yeah. I'll make sure we find out who did it and take appropriate action.'

'What exactly will that appropriate action be?'

'It will be, er, to call you and give you all the information.'

'That is absolutely fucking right. Now, let's move on to the connected but much bigger topic.'

'OK.' Calvin swallowed. However difficult the conversation had been so far, he figured it was about to get a whole lot worse. He still couldn't bring himself to ask the question. He heard his father drawing on a cigarette. Bastard! Quite literally dragging it out.

'So,' Karl said finally, 'I've got another, very specific job for you. An opportunity has presented itself and we need to take advantage. It's an opportunity that I never thought we'd get and I suspect it's time-sensitive, so you're going to have to move quickly.'

'OK.'

'I want you to kill Peter Jones. I want him dead. And I want you to make it look like a *Pass it on* killing.'

Calvin moved the phone away from his ear and stared at in disbelief.

'D'you hear me?'

'Yeah. Yeah.' Calvin pressed the phone back in place. 'It just wasn't what I was expecting, that's all.'

'Were you not?'

'No. I mean I know you've always wanted to pay Jones back. I mean it's no more than the fucker deserves - '

' – But?'

'It's just a surprise, that's all. I think it's a brilliant idea. I'm just sorry I hadn't thought of it first.'

'Sorry you hadn't been smarter than me, you mean?'

'No! Nothing like that. Everyone knows you're the best there is when it comes to planning and making things happen. I'd just like to have worked it out myself, as a present for you.'

'Well, you can still give me the present,' Karl took another drag on his cigarette. 'Like I said, this is the perfect opportunity. Those *Pass it on* killings aren't going to stop until everyone involved is caught. But they're clearly in a hurry. Two in twenty four hours is going some. Reminds me of the time I dealt with the Robinsons. Difference being I didn't want to plaster it all over the Internet.'

'The Internet didn't exist when you sorted them out.'

'Well, it does now and we're going to use it. I want you to set someone on Jones. Make it clear that it's got to happen within days not weeks. Tell them to use a burner phone to post pictures of his dead body. Tell them to use the *Pass it on* hashtag.'

'What do you want done to him?'

'I don't care. As long as it's made public and there's nothing to connect it to us. Jones thinks that because he got me he'll get you too eventually. And he's good at getting people to share information with him, people who should know better. So we have to make our move. I owe him for what he's done to me and we both owe him for what he might do to you. Right?'

'Definitely. Makes sense to me.' Calvin nodded vigorously, his mind racing.

Owe him for what he might do.

It was an attitude for which Karl Brent was known throughout the city and beyond. Calvin wondered just how many men and women had been beaten or killed because of what they might do. What was the line, the mantra, he had heard so often so many years ago?

Oh yes.

We pay it forwards before they get chance to pay us back.

That was it. And when he had asked why that was so, the answer had been chilling and abrupt.

'It makes people think twice. The first time they think about what they'd like to do. The second time they think about staying alive.'

There was no doubting the success of his father's approach. People very quickly learnt to let Karl Brent know they were on his side. In fact, they were usually desperate to prove they could be trusted. That was why it had taken Peter Jones years before he had collected enough evidence to go to court. Even then it could have gone either way. It would have gone their way if they had been able to get to the jurors. Only Jones was too smart to let that happen. And Coopland, the prosecuting QC, had been too good at his job. The result had been a sickening twenty five years.

'Why don't we do Coopland too?' Calvin blurted the question.

'What?'

'He'd fit the *Pass it on* killings. There must be as many people hate barristers as there are people who hate the police. And that's what it's all about, isn't it? Paying back people who deserve it. So why not Coopland?'

'Because there's one thing Coopland and Jones have got in common that even a half-decent copper would recognise. That's me! You stupid fuck! How long do you think it would take before they joined those particular dots and started putting pressure on?'

Karl paused for a moment to let the point sink home. Then he continued, 'No, we can do Jones and get away with it. Besides, Coopland limited himself to what he did in the courtroom. Jones used to visit our home. Used to pop round for a chat, trying to wind me up, looking like he owned the place! So it's him and him only. Are we clear?'

'I'll get right on it.'

'Good.' Karl used the remains of his cigarette to light another. 'One other thing, when the job's done make sure the person who did it get's the most secure reward possible.'

'Understood.' The tension in Calvin's body began to ease for the first time that morning. At least now the surprises were over. He understood precisely what he had just been told to do. The truth was, he didn't need to be told. He had already decided the man he was going to task with killing Jones. And who would get the job of killing him once it was done.

'Excellent. Let's move on to the third topic. Ethan Hall. Let me remind you, I want that guilty verdict! I want the freak locked in here with me so I can teach him what happens to people who take the piss. I don't want the Peter Jones situation getting in the way of this. You need to manage both equally well. There won't be a second chance.'

'I understand that.'

'So, tell me, how is it progressing?'

'Good. I spoke to Kline last night. Matt's going to be well prepared.'

'Is that all?'

'What else?'

'For Christ's sake! I told you, you to do everything possible to make sure I get Hall! You let him use you! He made you look like a fucking idiot and got away with it! So it's clear to me that he's too

 FAITH

much for you to handle. That means I have to deal with him. And I don't care how many clever tricks he's got, or what mind games he can play, once he's in here he's mine. I'm going to watch that piece of shit die!'

'I'll do everything I can - '

' – You'll do more than you can fucking imagine! You'll not do everything you can, you'll do everything that's needed! Pay some jurors. Pay the judge! If they won't take money, give them some pain then ask again. Make them think twice! Use your brain. Get creative and fix that fucking trial!'

'You can count on it.' Calvin heard the nervousness in his own voice as the tension returned.

'I am counting on it. That's the point. That's what you need to remember. Son.'

The call ended.

'I'm not a fucking child!' Calvin looked at the phone in his palm. 'This time I'll show you once and for all!'

He set to work.

He had lives to end, a trial to win and a point to prove.

CHAPTER 22

TUESDAY - TRIAL DAY 2
7.31am

Nicholas Evans looked out of the window of his hotel room and saw his brother, Andrew, standing on the pavement below. If it hadn't been him, if he hadn't known for sure just who was waving up at him, Nic would have said that it was a mirage, a shimmering haze of a person, rather than the real thing.

Only he was sure. He was certain. Brothers have a special bond. Everyone knew that. It was a bond that couldn't be explained or understood in any logical, rational way. It was invisible. Unbreakable. Stronger than life.

Nic waved back.

Today, for the first time, Andrew gestured towards the famous Clifton suspension bridge just a few hundred yards away.

'We haven't gone that way before.' Nic mouthed the words, knowing that Andrew wouldn't be able hear him even if he shouted. 'I'll be right there.'

He ran down the three flights of stairs, his heart racing with excitement rather than the exercise. The lobby was crowded with a group of foreign tourists arguing over a map. Nic pushed through them and burst out onto the street.

Andrew had gone. Just as he always did. Just before he could get close.

No matter. This time he had at least shown him where to go.

Nic sprinted until he reached the Toll Booth. He slowed to a fast walk as he moved out onto the bridge. Andrew was still nowhere to be seen. To Nic's left cars were crossing in a continual, measured manner. To his right and over two hundred feet below the river Avon continued its own steady pace.

Nic looked down at the water. There was no chance Andrew had jumped. The fencing that ran along the side of the bridge, a mixture of metal and wire curving inwards at the top, was almost shoulder height and difficult to get over. Anyway, why would Andrew jump? He wouldn't want to be in the water, surely? It didn't look too clean. And, besides, why would he jump when he could choose to fly?

Nic came to a halt and looked up at the sky. It was grey and overcast. Impossible to tell if Andrew was in the clouds. Or beyond them. He'd certainly had enough time to get there. In Nic's own experience, flying was fast and easy and beautiful. So, much as he wanted to spend time with his brother, he couldn't blame him if he had simply flown away.

'Just because I fly at night doesn't mean it's wrong for you to do it now!' Nic shouted this time, hoping the wind would carry his voice. 'I understand if you had to go! And thank you for bringing me here!'

He laughed because it was true.

All of it.

He was grateful for being here. And he had been flying. Every night since he came to Bristol. He knew, of course, that some people would have called his flight-time *dreams*. But they were the same people who wouldn't have been able to see Andrew.

Nic glanced at the commuters passing by, trapped in their cars. He wanted to tell them, 'how you travel is a reflection of what is going on in your life'.

Then he looked up at the sky again.

Flying was reserved only for those going through a transitional stage, those who were high on life, those who were elevated above the mundane, every day ways of living. Flying didn't just offer personal freedom; it was the result of having set yourself free in the first place.

'If you want to reach new heights,' Nic shouted at the cars, 'you have to know how to fly!'

The drivers ignored him. The pedestrians quickened their pace. Nic put both hands on the metal fence and considered the view. He was already higher than the trees that lined the river. Higher than any rooftop he could see. Higher even than some birds. It still wasn't the same as flying. Despite his elevation he was still grounded. He didn't have the feeling of the air rushing around him, of unlimited space. He didn't have any sense of his own essential power.

'It's just a high-level prison for tourists and travellers,' he said as if Andrew could hear him. 'It's just another way of keeping you down, of keeping you in.'

'Excuse me, sir.'

Nic spun round. A gentle-faced, overweight man in a yellow high-vis jacket was standing on the pavement to his left.

'Yes?'

'Good morning, I'm a Bridge Attendant. I volunteer here on the bridge to help ensure people have a great experience.'

'Yes?'

'I've noticed that you've been standing here for a few minutes. You seem unsure about where to go or what to do next. I was wondering if I could help?'

'No. My brother wanted to show me this. He's teaching me.'

'Your brother?'

'Yes.'

 FAITH

'I'm sorry, I didn't notice him.'

'He moved on. Quickly. He's special.' Nic wanted to add, 'And you're not', but he knew it was best to be polite.

'Oh. Are you studying something to do with the bridge – engineering, perhaps?'

Nic laughed. He wanted to say, 'Don't be so fucking stupid!' Instead he replied, 'No. I'm a flier. I know how to let go and take off.' He found that very funny. Especially when the other man didn't.

'There is no flying allowed from the bridge, sir.' Now the man was looking serious.

'I can see that. The bridge is just for people going from one place to the next. From A to B and back again. This isn't really about a crossing over. This is really about repeat, repeat, repeat. To and fro. To and fro. To and fro. You keep coming back, don't you?'

'Well, yes.' The man stepped back a pace. 'I think it would be best if we turned around now and walked off the bridge together.'

Nic wanted to say, 'I think it would be best if I carried you over the edge so you could fly.' But something inside told him that was wrong, so he said, 'Of course. Thank you for coming to speak to me.'

'You're welcome, sir.' The man stepped to one side and gestured with his right arm so that Nic could take the lead.

He did. They walked in silence, back passed the Toll Booth. 'Thank you for visiting, sir. Have a good day,' the man said.

'Fly high!' Nic shouted without looking back. 'Fly high, then swoop down towards the water!'

He walked back to his hotel at a brisk pace, giggling all the way.

CHAPTER 23

TUESDAY - TRIAL DAY 2
8am

Mike Coopland stared at the crumpled photo he had kept in his wallet for decades. He took it out and looked at it several times a week. It was always easy to find a reason. Sometimes someone said something that sparked a memory. Sometimes he said something that sparked a memory. Sometimes he dislodged the photo accidently when taking out money or a credit card. Sometimes he just pretended that was what he'd done.

It was a photo of him as a young boy standing next to his father. They were on the beach at Great Yarmouth. It had been taken during one of their traditional summer holidays.

Back in the day.

His Dad was military upright, proud and lean. Young Mike was doing his best to copy the pose. Mum was behind the camera. In hindsight, that could have been a metaphor for her life.

Behind the camera.

Putting the rest of her family first. Perhaps that had been easier for women to do back in the day, before the psychology and technology of change? Perhaps everything had been easier then?

Mike used the question as a barrier, trying to answer it rather than think about how much he missed his parents. Before he had time to depress himself further, Peter Jones walked into the cafe. Mike put the photo away and put on his confident, smiley face.

'Good morning, old man. How are you today?'

'Good, thank you.' Peter Jones sat down. He had been Mike's *old man* for a long time. It was, he knew, more than a sign of affection. It was an acknowledgement of need. 'Did you get any sleep?'

'Enough.'

'You do know that, given your size, you need more than most of us?'

'Fuck off.'

'Says the Prosecuting Counsel.'

'After due consideration of the facts.'

'In which case, I expect your closing speech to be nothing short of profane.'

Mike couldn't keep the grin off his face. 'I can't promise that, but if the case has been shot to bits I might well pick up the electric guitar and sing.'

Peter laughed. Mike had once famously played his own unique version of *Stompin' At The Savoy* by Charlie Christian to persuade a jury to return a guilty verdict.

'The principle being, if you're back's against the wall and you think you're going to lose, go out playing jazz?'

'There's no better way.'

Peter ordered a coffee. 'That probably explains why I don't like that kind of music.'

'That certainly explains why I feel sorry for you.'

'Sometimes opposites attract.'

'Unless one's prosecuting and one's defending.'

'They're still drawn together.'

'Caught. You might say?'

Peter raised his open palms. 'As ever, I give in when we do the play on words.'

'As ever, I expect you to.' Mike took a swallow of his Latte.

FAITH

'So I can forget Ethan Hall and focus my energy on the dangers of Brexit?'

This time Mike laughed. 'I voted the way I voted and I don't regret it.'

'Yet.'

'At all.'

'Given the current information.'

'Given the fact that, in response to the argument presented, the nation acted as the jury and delivered their verdict.'

'And the jury's verdict is always right?'

'It's always the one we act on.'

Peter's coffee arrived. He sipped at it.

'I think it's all going to hell,' Mike said suddenly.

Peter shook his head. 'Not you as well, please. I had McNeill ranting earlier, wanting to paint a picture of doom.'

'He's got a point. In fact, he's got more than a point. People can't disagree and get on together anymore. It all feels more tribal, more aggressive. And all the time we are becoming more and more accepting of the violence in the world.'

'As ever, the violence is being caused by a minority. They just happen to be getting more media coverage than they used to.' Peter took another sip. 'Look, people in our professions can't let what we do destroy us. We've chosen to deal with the worst of everything, with those aspects of life and death that most people want to ignore or fictionalise. We, more than most, have to make ourselves remember the goodness that exists. We have to ensure we live in that.'

'You're an atheist and it sounds like you're preaching a sermon!'

'I'm an atheist who believes in Life. And I want my friend to get the most out of his.'

Mike finished his coffee and signalled for another. 'You really don't think that the world is going down the toilet?'

 FAITH

'No. The world is just different from when we both started, that's all. And just because some things change it doesn't mean everything has. It certainly doesn't mean the most essential things have. Anyway, I didn't ask to meet you to talk about your imaginary Armageddon.'

'Fair enough. What's the problem?'

'More of an update than a problem. I heard a whisper late last night that Marcus Kline had a meeting that neither of us could have predicted.'

'Oh?'

'With one Calvin Brent.'

'You are fucking joking!'

'Not at all. They had a stroll together in the Arboretum. Not hand in hand exactly, but certainly shoulder to shoulder.'

'What do you think that was about?'

'My source told me that Brent called the meeting, if you get my drift?'

'You mean Kline didn't have any choice?'

'Exactly. So the question then becomes what did Brent want? My best guess is that it's related to Ethan Hall and the trial.'

Mike considered. 'The fact that the two of them met has no bearing on the trial – unless Kline has been threatened or paid to change his testimony.'

'Brent wanting to weaken the case against Hall, you mean?'

'If there is a working relationship between Brent and Hall that you haven't uncovered, it would make sense. And it's not as if Brent would be shy about trying to corrupt a case.'

'True. I'm sure, though, that if Marcus had been pressured he would have contacted me.'

'Fear can make people behave in ways that are out of character.'

'I realise that.'

'Plus he's got an over-sized ego, so he might have decided to manage the situation himself.'

'Six months ago, I would have agreed with you. Now his confidence has been shaken to such a degree, I think that course of action is far less likely.' Peter's mobile phone rang. He checked the number and chose to ignore it. 'The other option,' he said, 'is that Brent wanted Marcus to help in some other way. You have got one of Brent's heavies lined up as witness.'

'The one Hall took hostage, yes.' Mike sniffed. 'Maybe Kline was asked to coach him?'

'Which would mean that Brent wants Hall locked up.'

'Why would he want that?'

Peter shrugged. 'I've no idea. But those couple of days when Ethan Hall was free and appears to have done nothing are still troubling me. Who knows what might have happened then?'

'A Brent-Hall partnership would be a frightening combination.'

'It would. It just strikes me as a highly unlikely one. You mentioned Marcus's ego, well those two could match him for sure and I can't see how they could ever agree to work together.'

'So basically we have only options and ideas and one guaranteed fact – that Kline and Brent met. That's assuming your source is reliable, of course.'

'There's no question of doubt about that.'

'So?'

'So I'm going to leave here and use my incredible detecting skills to find out exactly what happened, then I'll let you know.'

'Whilst you're doing that I am going to drink some more coffee with the minuscule but highly effective Brian Kaffee, in final preparation for Mr Kline's appearance as our first witness.'

'Brian isn't so small,' Peter said, standing up.

'The vast majority of you are small,' Mike flexed his chest. 'And remember, if I may misquote Dickens slightly, if there were no bad people, there would be no good barristers. Now, you go run about your business and leave me to do the serious work.'

Peter left to the sound of Mike's deep-chested laughter.

CHAPTER 24

TUESDAY - TRIAL DAY 2
8.44am

Marcus Kline was in town early. Walking the streets. Keeping his head down, his hands in his coat pockets. Most people ignored him. Only a couple had glanced twice. Neither had said anything.

He was walking up Byard Lane when Peter Jones called.

'Yes?'

'Where are you?'

'Does it matter?'

'Not so much.'

Marcus recognised the tone of voice and came to a halt. It was the DCI talking. 'What do you want?'

'I want to know why you met with Calvin Brent last night. I want to know why you haven't already informed me. I want to know that you're doing nothing that will damage Mike's case.'

'How do you know about that?'

'Wrong question. In fact, in this conversation you don't get to ask any questions. You get to provide the answers.'

'Well, the answer is you've got nothing to worry about.'

'Not good enough.'

'Listen, I'm in the witness box in less than a couple of hours. I don't need your dominant detective bullshit right now.'

'Right now you don't get to make any decisions, just as you don't get to ask any questions. And the reason for that, as you so rightly pointed out, is because you are about to appear as a significant witness in a very significant trial. So stop fucking about and tell me what happened.'

Marcus sighed. 'I haven't done anything wrong.'

'How can you possibly be sure of that? Unless Brent was schooling you in trial law?'

'Actually he was after my professional advice.'

'At last, the start of an answer. Keep going.'

'Brent's bothered about how his guy will cope with Ethan Hall. He wants him to be a reliable witness and, after what Hall did to him when he held him hostage, he's worried that he won't be.'

'Brent wants his guy to contribute to the prosecution's case?'

'That's what he said.'

'So what did he want from you?

'He wanted me to meet with his man, teach him some tricks so that Hall couldn't influence him easily, give him some techniques that would help him stay focussed. He made it very clear that, as far as he was concerned, I didn't have a choice in the matter.'

'He threatened you?'

'Not in any way that would make it worth reporting, but the threat was real nonetheless.'

'Please tell me that you managed to talk your way out of it.'

'I think so.'

'Influence is your area of expertise, how come you only think so?'

'Because violence and killing is his area of expertise and he wasn't happy when I told him that I had no intentions of working directly with his guy!'

'Working *directly*?'

'I suggested some things that he might do to prepare himself and then again when Ethan Hall is talking to him. I had to do something, didn't I? That seemed like the best way out.'

A woman walking by looked at Marcus as if she knew him. He turned to face a building, putting his back to the street.

'Truthfully, I'm not sure how much use my tips will be even if they're applied exactly as I said. Ethan had this guy hostage for several hours, so it's reasonable to think he'll have created some neural pathways that are close to unbreakable.'

'It sounds to me that there's no harm done,' Peter's mind raced through everything he had heard. 'And we get an extra insight we didn't have.'

'We do?'

'Yes. If you're right, Calvin Brent wants Ethan found guilty. That means they're not team-mates.'

'It doesn't mean they weren't.'

'I know.'

'So what are you going to do now?'

'Police work.'

'Thanks for sharing.'

Peter smiled. 'You did well with Brent. It was a tricky situation. Remember, if he or any of his men come near you again I want to know immediately. OK?'

'Understood.'

'And say nothing to any journalists that approach you – and they will once you're done in the witness box. Seriously Marcus, I don't want a repeat of the Dave Johnson fiasco, when I open my paper to discover that you've given an interview to a sleeze-ball journo just to promote your own agenda.'

'Yeah, I am still sorry about that. I let the pressure get to me. Johnson just happened to be in the right place at the right time.'

'Or the wrong place at the wrong time.'

'That, too.' Marcus sighed. 'Until this is over, I'm a journalist-free zone. I give you my word.'

 FAITH

'Good. By calling Johnson as a witness Mike has effectively quarantined him, so at least he's out of the picture. Now go and do whatever it takes to get yourself in the best possible state for the day ahead.'

'Will do.'

Peter ended the call. Then he looked out of the car window at the five bedroom detached house he was parked outside. A figure he couldn't see clearly was looking back at him from what he knew to be the kitchen.

Peter got out, locked the car behind him, and walked brusquely to the front door. He knocked four times, loud and rapid, as if he was angry and in a hurry. He waited only a few seconds and knocked again. Louder this time. He heard footsteps inside, heavy on a wooden floor, and stepped back half a pace as the door swung open.

'What the fuck do you want?' Calvin Brent asked.

CHAPTER 25

TUESDAY - TRIAL DAY 2
8.52am

'Happened to be in the neighbourhood, thought I'd pop in for a coffee,' Peter Jones said. 'Your dad always used to welcome me in.'

'It's funny, I was just talking about you.' Brent opened the door further and gestured inside.

'Only good things I hope.' Peter moved passed him and headed straight into the expansive dining kitchen filled with modern appliances and black, marble work surfaces. The man who had been watching the car was sitting on a stool by the island in the centre of the room. He had a glass of water in front of him.

'I don't know you, do I?' Peter said.

The man shrugged. Just. As if even that was more of an answer than the question deserved.

'He's a new employee,' Brent said, entering the room. 'A driver.'

'Of course he is.' Peter pointed at the glass. 'Half empty or half full?'

The man picked it up and drained it in one swallow. 'Empty and gone.' He said, pushing the glass away from him.

It was Peter's turn to shrug. He looked at Brent and jerked his thumb in the man's direction. 'Wow, do you think that was an attempt at symbolism? Seems you've got yourself a new *driver* who likes to mix philosophy with whatever other skills he's got.'

'I've got no idea what you're fucking talking about.'

'That's because I didn't make a poker reference. So let me try it this way: who's the joker?'

'I've already told you.'

'No you haven't. You've told me what you've employed him to do, not who he is.' Peter turned back to the man. 'What's your name?'

The man glanced at Brent. Peter saw the gangster nod briefly. 'Stu,' the man said.

'No surname?'

'Jolly.'

'You have got to be kidding me!'

'Please yourself.'

'Jolly by name but not by nature, eh?'

'Is that what you came here for?' Brent asked before his man could reply again. 'To see if there was anyone you could insult?'

'No, that was the last thing on my mind. When I want to insult someone I visit your dad inside and remind him of a few home truths.'

Brent flushed. Jolly's hands tightened into fists. Peter pretended not to notice.

'No, I came here because I'm interested in the meeting you had last night.'

'I had several meetings last night. I'm a busy man.'

'Whilst they might all be of interest to me, there's only one that I know about. That's the one with Marcus Kline. A little early evening walk in the Arboretum. A little quiet conversation. Obviously not quiet enough or I wouldn't have heard about it. Still, I did. And I'm here. And I want to know what you wanted from him.'

'Who says I wanted anything?'

'Don't be shy. You always want something. That's the nature of the beast. Sharks always keep moving. People like you always keep taking. So what were you after?'

'What have you heard?'

'Oh, please! Next you'll be asking me who my source is.' Peter clapped his hands together. 'Calvin, let's hurry this along shall we? I've got things to do at court after this – you know, the court where one of your other *drivers* is appearing as a witness sometime soon – and God alone knows what you've got planned for the rest of the day. So, stop wasting my time and yours and spill the beans. Talking of which, you never did offer me a coffee. Don't worry about that now, though. I think we're going to wrap this up in a couple of minutes, aren't we?'

Brent's mouth tightened for a second. Then he forced himself to relax. 'I'm a business leader, as you know Detective Chief Inspector. I thought it was about time I got to know Mr Kline. See if he would be able to help me with my corporate communications.'

'Your corporate communications?'

'That's right.'

Peter leaned forward. 'Well, here's the thing Mr Brent. I think for now and the foreseeable future it will be best if you keep Mr Kline out of your planning at every level.'

'Oh I see. You're not just a detective you're a management consultant as well, are you?' Brent smirked. Jolly laughed, once, hard like a cough.

'No, I am just a detective. A fucking good one, too. So when I detect something that I don't like, I act on it. And I keep acting on it until I get the result that I want. Whenever you find yourself in danger of forgetting that Calvin, just ask your dad.'

'Are we done here?' Brent failed to keep the anger from flashing in his eyes.

'Keep. Away. From. Kline.' Peter punctuated each word, pointing with his right forefinger at Brent's chest. 'Got the message?'

'You've been heard.'

'Good. In that case I'll wish you both a very good day.' Peter nodded at Jolly. 'Drive safely.' He looked back at Brent. 'Don't worry, I'll see myself out.'

Before either man could reply, Peter turned and left. He closed the front door very deliberately behind him and walked towards his car in a casual, unhurried manner. His heart was racing.

As he got inside he whispered to himself, 'Jones you are fucking madman!' Then he drove away without looking back.

Brent watched in silence until the car was out of view. 'What were the odds of that happening?'

'If you'd given me the signal, I'd have done him right here.' Jolly stood up and stretched.

'And done what with the body?' It was Brent's turn to point a finger. 'You got this job because you've done this type of thing before and because you owe me and my dad a favour. You pay off the debt by killing Jones quickly and making sure it can never be traced back to us. Doing him in my fucking kitchen hardly addresses the second part of the deal, does it?'

'I know how to improvise.'

'I don't want you to have to improvise! That's the fucking point! I want you to kill him and disappear the body in the quietest of ways. Then I want you to fuck off for six months. And I want you to keep your mouth shut about it for the rest of your life. That's what I want you to do. That's what my dad expects you to do.'

'Yeah. I got it.' Jolly poured himself another glass of water. 'I'd never seen Jones up close before. It's like everyone says. He's a real cunt.'

'He always has been.'

'It's going to be a fucking delight doing him. Now that he knows my face I'll just have to make sure he doesn't see me coming.'

'That's not going to be a problem, is it?'

'Nah. He's so far up his own arse, he'll not know what hits him.'

'Remember to carve a word into his face, take some pictures, and make it look like one of those *Pass it on* killings.'

'You can count on it.' Stuart Jolly beamed. 'That part will be even more fun than the kill.'

CHAPTER 26

TUESDAY - TRIAL DAY 2
9.17am

Marcus stood in quiet reflection for several minutes after his conversation with Peter Jones. Then he set off again on his repetitive walk.

He strode up High Pavement, ignoring his own office. It had been closed for a while. He had told his clients normal service would be resumed after the trial. He said it as if it was a matter of fact. He believed it was. He hoped they did, too.

Putting his office behind him he turned left along Stoney Street, passing New College before turning left onto Warser Gate and then after a few hundred metres turning left again onto Fletcher Gate.

He had repeated the route a couple of times. Doing laps. Always ending at the place he began. Going nowhere. Neither forward nor back. The trial, though, was getting closer with every step.

Marcus glanced automatically through the windows of The Cross Keys pub as he passed.

'Dear God!' He stopped abruptly, staring at the young woman busying herself inside the empty pub. 'Cassandra...'

She was dark-haired. In her early twenties. Italian heritage. He knew her. He wished he didn't. He stepped inside.

'Hi.'

Cassandra looked up from the table she was cleaning. She took a step backwards.

'Marcus.'

'You remember me.'

'Of course.'

'I didn't expect to see you here.' As he said it he knew she was hearing the unspoken ending.

Ever again.

He knew he was a mile away from his professional best.

The trial.

Calvin Brent.

Now her.

He felt lost. He was lost. Yet he couldn't ignore her. Not Cassandra.

'I needed to come back,' she said. 'It's always felt like home, and you can't allow yourself to be driven from your home.'

'You're absolutely right.' He said it because it was true and because he couldn't stop himself.

It made him feel like a fraud.

It made him think of the house in The Park that he and Anne-Marie had left because of Ethan Hall's invasion. He couldn't help but be reminded of how he hated their rented place. He couldn't help but think again, as he had secretly for months now, that when put under real pressure his inevitable response was to run away. Even if he disguised it as an attack. He couldn't help but come to the conclusion that he was a coward.

Cassandra looked at him and waited for what he had to say next. He remembered that, in her eyes, he was the expert. The guru. The one with the answers. Not so long ago he would have taken that for granted. Now he was reduced to walking laps around city streets.

'When did you return?' It was the best he could do.

'A few days ago. They always said there would be a job for me here if I ever came back, so...' She half-smiled. '...Do you want a coffee?'

'Please.'

'Take a seat.'

They both glanced at *that* table. They both pretended they hadn't. Marcus chose a table on the other side of the room. Cassandra disappeared behind the bar. Marcus tried to let his mind wander. It wasn't easy. Too much pressure. Not enough space.

The last time he had been here he had sat at the same table. And a woman had talked to him about Ethan Hall. Talked as if she knew him. As if she had a personal reason for hating him.

'Jesus...' He heard himself say it out loud. Every thought led back to Ethan Hall. Swiftly. No matter what the starting point. Absolutely no degrees of separation. 'Fuck!'

'One Americano.' Cassandra placed it on the table in front of him. 'Are you OK?'

'Me?' Marcus felt his heart jump. 'Not particularly.'

'Can I sit?' She gestured to the seat opposite.

'Sure.'

'I've read all about the trial.'

He nodded. 'Have you, er, talked to anyone about what happened?'

'Only my dad.' That half-smile again. 'He wasn't sure what to say, but he was good at holding me when I needed it.'

'Dads can be good at that.'

'Yeah. He's the best.'

He took a drink of his coffee. 'When this is all over, if you need to, you know that my office is only just up the road.'

'Thanks. I'll see how I feel. Is that alright?'

'Whatever works. I'm here if you need me.'

She ran her right hand through her hair. A nervous tic that he recognised despite his own awkwardness. He saw her tension increase. He knew the time had come. He softened his gaze. Tried to ease himself into his working state.

'I went to his grave yesterday,' she said. 'I did that clichéd thing of talking to the gravestone.'

'What did you say?'

'I told him that, even though we hardly knew each other, it had felt right. I told him that you couldn't measure something good by how long it lasts. That I missed him more than our time together suggested I should.' She wiped a tear away. 'I really went there because I still like to say his name.'

Simon.

Marcus could see him clearly in his mind's eye. He could hear his voice and his laughter, feel its vibration.

Simon.

His protégé. Ethan Hall's third victim. The closest thing to a son that Marcus had ever known.

The Cross Keys had been the place where Simon Westbury breakfasted most mornings, eating the same food, sitting at the same table. It was here he had met Cassandra.

'I talk to him, too,' Marcus said.

'Really?'

'Yes.'

'What do you say?'

He hesitated; felt his working state slipping away. 'Apologies mainly.'

'What on earth do you have to apologise for?'

'His death. Ethan Hall targeted him because of me.'

'But you can't blame yourself for what a madman did!'

'As human beings we have an almost infinite capability to blame, haven't you noticed? Sometimes we direct it at others, sometimes at ourselves.'

'Not you, surely? You're the famous influencer. You must have some tricks or something for managing your mind?'

'I'm just as human as everyone else. And, as I've learnt, I'm far better at helping others than I am myself.'

She reached out and touched his hand. 'Ethan Hall is going to be locked away forever, isn't he?'

'If he's found guilty it will certainly be for a very long time.'

'If? Do you mean there's a chance he might get off?' She pulled her hand away.

'I'm not a legal expert, but my understanding is that it's not clear-cut. The prosecution has a great deal of circumstantial evidence linking Ethan to...to Simon's death and to two others. But they are lacking as much direct, hard evidence as they'd like.'

'What about his attack on you?'

'He didn't kill me, so it's not the same thing.'

Cassandra's eyes watered again. 'He has to be found guilty. For all of this to have any ending at all, he has to be sentenced. The world has to see his guilt. It can't be any other way.' She shook her head, struggling for words. 'You have to make sure.'

'Everyone's doing all they can. We have a great barrister.'

'I came back because I needed to be here when it ended. It never crossed my mind, I mean...I never thought there was a chance he...' Her voice trailed off, her eyes staring into space.

He watched her and waited. It was all he could do. He felt like his mind had frozen.

Eventually she looked back at him. 'What should I do?' She asked.

'Have faith,' he said and regretted it instantly.

CHAPTER 27

TUESDAY - TRIAL DAY 2
9.22am

Mike Coopland ended the call and switched his phone off. All OK on the Marcus Kline-Calvin Brent front. Which was just as well. There was already enough scope for uncertainty and doubt without sticking any more nails into the prosecution's coffin.

Brian Kaffee looked up from the notes he had been reading for the last two minutes. 'You're smiling because?'

'Either because DCI Jones is good at his job, or because earlier this morning Ethan Hall felt such remorse for his crimes that he lay on his prison bed and suffocated himself with his own pillow.'

Kaffee chuckled. 'It's obviously the first, even though I'd prefer it to be the latter.'

'How come you're so sure? After all January is the month with the highest suicide rate.'

'No, it's not. That's a common misconception.'

'Really?'

'Yeah. It's easy to imagine that the dark, winter months encourage more suicides than any other time of the year, but it simply isn't true.'

'So when is it?'

'Springtime.'

'Oh, come on!' Mike punched Kaffee on his upper arm. 'Not even I could convince a jury that the sight of new buds appearing in the garden and lambs bleating in the fields drives people to top themselves!'

'Actually even you could convince a jury of that. Because the data is clear. Crystal, in fact. And ouch, by the way, that hurt.'

'I knew you were a miserable git, but I didn't appreciate you were an expert on suicides.'

'Just one of those things I read somewhere. It's all about the psychological effects of change, it seems. We don't all cope with it in a measured way. Spring comes, the weather warms up, we all come out of the emotional shell we've been hibernating in during winter, and shit happens.'

'The emotional shell?'

'That's right. There's research that suggests we close ourselves off, almost shut down emotionally, during the darkest, coldest months. Not you obviously, because you don't have any emotions to shut down. However, the rest of us, the more balanced and evolved members of society, we go through this experience on a yearly basis.'

'Fuck me.'

'Not even to save your life.'

'Couldn't blame you for that.' Mike frowned. 'I wonder if that's what Ethan Hall's been doing for the past months?'

'What?'

'Hibernating. Closing himself down. Getting ready.'

'To come out of his shell?'

'Yeah.'

'That's a very uncomfortable thought. Instead, I'd like to think he's been shivering in the cold at the prospect of what's going to happen to him.'

'I'd like to think that I once looked like Schwarzeneggar, but I didn't.'

'Forget the biceps, he could never have carried the wig the way you do.'

'Thanks.'

'Praise where it's due.'

'Hmm.' Mike's frown returned. 'We need to have a great day today. Then we have to hope that Hall is still half-asleep and screws up his cross-examination tomorrow. Then we have to get Anne-Marie Wells in and out in tidy fashion. Keep it simple and to the point. Get her to share a few more bits of the story and it's thank you very much.'

'It should be straight-forward.'

'Yeah. She should be the easy one.' Mike returned his hand, gently this time, onto Kaffee's arm. 'We just need to have a great day today,' he said again.

✿ ✿ ✿

Anne-Marie Wells couldn't get the sentence out of her mind. Everything reminded her of it.

I would willingly shorten my life to avoid all of this.

That's what she had said. That's what she meant. In fact, it was the most truthful thing she had said for months. Even though the words had escaped like rats jumping from a sinking ship. Gone before you even realised what was happening. Needing to be out no matter what the consequence. A sign of just how desperate the situation was.

Once Anne-Marie believed that losing the battle against terminal cancer was the definition of hopelessness. Now she knew better. Real hopelessness could only be experienced in times like this. When you were scared to fall asleep. And hated being awake. When you didn't want to talk for fear of what you said. And yet silence was a crushing weight.

 FAITH

She guessed these were the seeds of suicide. She could feel them growing inside her, more obvious even than the cancer, spreading, entwining, blocking out light. Not even her work offered respite. If anything, the current project was somehow adding to the pressure she was feeling, to the sense of being trapped in an increasingly limited space.

Anne-Marie was pacing around the house, from one room to the next, unable to settle, trying to find some place where she could breathe easily, repeating the same route time after time. The house didn't change despite her persistence. The routine wrapped around her.

I would willingly shorten my life.

Every room reinforced the truth of it. Every creak in the floorboards. Every wrong colour on the walls. Every memory reminded her that she didn't belong here.

And then, for the first time, unbidden, her mind asked itself the question, Shorten your life by how much?

Anne-Marie stopped pacing. Closed her eyes. Held her breath.

The answer came easily.

FAITH

CHAPTER 28

TUESDAY - TRIAL DAY 2
10.35am

Mike Coopland QC looked at Marcus Kline, sitting ramrod straight yet relaxed in the witness box, and offered him the briefest of nods. It had already been established that Marcus was appearing first as an expert witness and then as a witness of fact. The difference had been made clear to the jury.

They looked attentive, sitting in two rows of six, each person with their jury bundle – a black file containing relevant photos, documents and agreed facts - open in front of them. From their manner, Mike guessed that all of the jurors knew who Marcus Kline was and were keen to hear what the famous man had to say.

Time to begin.

Mike rested both hands on his lectern. 'Please tell the court your name.'

'Marcus Kline.'

'What is your profession, Mr Kline?'

'I am a Communications Consultant. I provide training and guidance on a personal and organisational level to a wide range of businesses and leaders across the globe. I help them manage and improve both their micro- and macro-communications. By which I mean the ways they interact with and influence their target audiences, be that an audience of one or an audience of one hundred million.'

'I see. What are your qualifications?'

'I have a PhD from Magdalen College, Oxford, in the Psychology of Interpersonal Communication. My thesis was titled *The Power of Words* and formed the basis for my first book. I am also a qualified Master Trainer in Neuro-Linguistic Programming, I have expertise in the use of Dr Paul Ekman's Facial Action Coding System and I am regarded as an authority on theoretical linguistics and generative grammar, which are both topics I lecture on at various universities. I also hold a Masters degree in Marketing Communications and an honorary Doctorate from The University of Nottingham. Finally, I am a qualified hypnotherapist and play a leading role in the National Council for Hypnotherapy.'

'How would you summarise your expertise?'

'I understand how to influence people both consciously and subconsciously.'

'How do you do this?'

'There are as many ways to influence as there are people on the planet. However, despite this, there are several underlying principles. Firstly, you have to understand your client or audience. You have to understand their preferred communications patterns, their emotional state in regard to the situation you are addressing and, importantly, their desired outcomes. Obviously this is much easier to do when you are seeking to influence only one person than when your seeking to influence many.'

'What is the next principle?'

'Once you have that understanding – and you have tested it thoroughly to ensure you are right – you match their communication patterns in ways that acknowledge their emotional state and show an understanding of their desired outcomes. You test continually to identify the degree to which you are creating rapport with your audience. You need to make them like and trust you; they need to feel understood and secure.'

'And when you have achieved this?'

'You take the lead. That means you do whatever is necessary, within legal and ethical boundaries, to move the client to their desired outcome. Again, this part of the interaction involves conscious and subconscious processes.'

'What are "conscious and subconscious processes"?'

'Conscious communication processes are those happening in the foreground of our mind, those we are aware of. The most obvious examples are the words we say, our thoughts and our feelings. Subconscious communication processes are those things that are happening in the background of our mind that we are not aware of. For example, neither yourself nor the ladies and gentlemen of the jury have been consciously thinking about the colour of your front door at home. Until now.'

Marcus glanced at the jurors and then looked back at Mike.

'Now you have all remembered what colour it is. Some of you actually visualised the door briefly in your mind's eye. In fact, you did that yourself, Mr Coopland. I know because of the way your eyes moved and because of other subtle changes to your physiology. My point is that knowledge of your front door existed in your mind not as a conscious presence – until I brought it forwards – but subconsciously. It was there, but you were not aware of it. This is true for all of our memories and so many other aspects of ourselves that we take for granted.'

'As a professional, indeed, in all aspects of my life, I operate on the belief that the subconscious is by far the most powerful part of our mind. It holds not only our memories, but also many resources we can bring to bear to create change.'

'Do you explain this to clients?'

'Always. People come to me when they want to improve their personal or professional performance and don't know how, or when they feel themselves being damaged by trauma or tragedy and can't stop it. In all cases they come to me when they cannot consciously create their desired outcome themselves.'

'I explain to them that any feelings of failure, helplessness or, in the worst cases, extreme hopelessness, are the result of the conscious mind being unable to solve the problem. Even though it is the smaller, weaker part of our mind, it is the part we are aware of, so we are easily influenced by it.'

'For example, we create beliefs based on feedback from our conscious. If the feedback is negative, so are the beliefs. Thus we find ourselves creating a vicious circle. By which I mean, when we are consciously unable to achieve our desired outcomes, we emphasise the feedback that highlights our inability, we inevitably then create negative beliefs about ourselves and they serve to limit our abilities even more. Round and round we go, screwing ourselves deeper and deeper, tighter and tighter, into a bad place.'

'In your professional experience, is this true for all people?'

'Yes. Unless they are very well trained in intrapersonal communication. And even then in some situations they would still need the help of a fellow professional.'

'What is intrapersonal communication?'

'It's the way we communicate with ourself. It includes our memories, our thoughts, our beliefs, our emotions, the ways we imagine, the ways we think about, or plan for, future events. It's what keeps us awake at night when we'd rather be asleep. It's how we make ourselves excited when there's something to look forward to. It's central to our sense of personal identity.'

'Is intrapersonal communication a conscious process?'

'On some levels it is. On some levels it isn't. For example, when I came forward and sat in the witness box the individual members of the jury were all aware of not only their initial thoughts about me, but also how I made them feel. If you asked them why they felt the way they did, they would each give you some answers that would be logical and, to varying degrees, true.'

'They wouldn't be the complete truth however, because we feel emotions before we think rationally. Our brain is designed for this to happen. Added to that, the jurors' feelings would have also been created by a variety of subconscious cues – aspects of my communication patterns that either match or mismatch theirs - that they were recognising beyond their conscious awareness.'

'It's a common experience, if you think about it. We have all met someone for the first time and taken an immediate like or dislike to them. We call it a gut reaction. Once upon a time it would have been called women's intuition.'

Marcus gave the jurors a second to let that settle in. He noticed Mike glance at one particular woman. She had already drawn Marcus's attention, making occasional notes without ever taking her eyes off him.

'Gut instinct would, indeed, be as good a term as any. That type of intuition – which often proves right, doesn't it? – is not only the prerogative of women. Men too, if they are sensitive enough to recognise it, experience this interaction between brain and stomach. It's a communication that occurs via the vagus nerve; a nerve rooted in the cerebellum and brainstem that runs down into your stomach, connecting with your heart and most other major organs along the way. This communication leaves us with an emotional certainty way before we have had chance to apply a rational analysis.'

'Simply put then, some aspects of our intrapersonal communication are consciously done. Others happen sub-consciously and we then become conscious of how they are

 FAITH

affecting us.' Marcus shrugged. 'In all forms of communication the subconscious runs the show.'

'How do you influence it deliberately?'

'Firstly by acknowledging its presence and making it my ultimate target. Secondly, by basing everything I do on the principles I outlined a few moments ago. Thirdly, by applying any combination of relevant techniques.'

'Is hypnosis one such technique?'

'Absolutely. In one form or another it's of central importance.'

'I see. What exactly is hypnosis?'

'It's a way of communicating that is intended to put someone – or, in some circumstances, yourself – into what is known as an hypnotic trance. Now that word trance is very much misunderstood by many people. It actually refers to a focusing of attention on a thought, idea, feeling, concept or thing, in a way that excludes focusing on anything else.'

'Once you understand that, you then realise we all go in and out of trances every day of our lives. When, for example, was the last time you drove to work and when you arrived found that you couldn't remember the journey?'

Two jurors laughed. Most smiled.

'Technically you had been in a trance whilst driving. We might commonly call it daydreaming. When was the last time you were so engrossed listening to music, or reading a book, or working out in the gym, that you lost track of time? Once again, you were, as I like to think of it, entranced by what you were doing.'

More smiles.

'It's also important to say that, to some degree all communication invites the receiver into a trance. You see, whenever we make a statement, the person hearing our statement cannot help but respond to our words and to the thoughts they stimulate. They will connect some meaning to what we say, and, at least for a moment, as they focus on that meaning, they will enter a trance state. Everyone in this courtroom is doing that right now as you all think about and make sense of what I have just said.'

Marcus heard his words and his body tightened automatically. For the first time since taking the witness box he had reminded himself that he was sharing a room with Ethan Hall.

CHAPTER 29

TUESDAY - TRIAL DAY 2
11.13am

The truth was the synesthete was in an hypnotic trance of his own making. He was deep within his own subconscious. Not that anyone would have known if they had looked into the dock. Even the two people closest to him, Duncan and the other security guard, were oblivious. They, like everyone else in the court, were focussed entirely on the witness.

It was exactly what Ethan had expected. He had long known how to find ways to grow in even the most challenging of environments. It was, he acknowledged, just one more advantage he possessed.

That was his final thought.

As he distanced himself from the conscious world, Ethan felt the mix of emotions pulsing inside Duncan. He took a moment to reinforce the work he had already done and then let himself move on. Flowing, comfortable and effortless, towards the greater connection.

In the darkness he sensed Marcus's sudden tension. It didn't touch him. It didn't affect him in any way. The rules of the herd did not apply. Not for him. Not here. In this state he was so far beyond them they had nothing in common. Here he was invulnerable. Faultless. Absolutely different.

So, as Marcus fought to regroup, he ignored the opportunity to press home an early advantage. Instead he simply noticed it as a traveller passing by en route to somewhere infinitely greater. When the time arrived he would open his eyes. He would look with a clarity none of them could imagine. He would hear with an acuity no human ever had. Then he would speak. Irresistibly.

❀ ❀ ❀

Mike Coopland didn't see the ripple of tension run through Marcus's body. He didn't see his witness change his breathing pattern as a way of regaining control. Rather he gave the jurors time to recognise the truth of Marcus's last answer, to appreciate his expertise, and then he asked the next obvious question.

'Can anyone be hypnotised?'

'It depends whom you ask. There are some professionals - it is inevitably those with limited experience - who argue that certain individuals are not susceptible to hypnosis. However in my experience over the past several decades, and in the opinion of all the world's most accomplished hypnotists, anyone can be hypnotised if the conditions are right.'

'What are those conditions?'

'The environment and the context of the interaction, the subject's motivation and, most important of all, the relationship between the subject and the hypnotist.'

'Environment matters because it creates an inevitable influence. We are always affected by the environments we are in, whether we are consciously aware of it or not. Context is usually connected to motivation. Strange as it might sound, clients don't always want to create the change they say they do. Some clients just want to use someone like me to prove to themselves they are beyond help. In such situations there are obviously more issues to address than if the client is highly motivated to change from the very beginning.'

'That leads me back to the nature of the relationship between therapist and client. You recall that I talked earlier about the need to create rapport, to be liked and trusted. That's essential here. You see there are basically two approaches to influencing others. The first is the ethical approach. It's based on understanding and trust, on a sense of rapport and safety. The second is non-ethical. Abusive. It's based on manipulation. It serves to satisfy the needs of the hypnotist rather than the client. I need to stress that none of the professionals I know would ever consider that second approach.'

'Yet it could be done?'

'Yes. An incredibly skilled hypnotist could dominate an unwilling subject.'

'To what effect?'

'Again it depends on the subject and the hypnotist. Ultimately, there are no limits. We know that people are using hypnosis to positive effect in the most amazing of ways. For example, it's commonly used during surgeries as a method of pain management when the patient is allergic to all forms of anaesthesia. So it follows that if the hypnotist had a more damaging, hurtful intent it could also be used to achieve great harm.'

'This would require incredible hypnotic skill?'

'Yes. Of the highest order.'

'Are you skilled enough?'

'Probably. But it's something I can't even begin to contemplate. I've developed my abilities to help people, not hurt them. I seek to create positive change, to improve the world. To me, misusing hypnosis in such a way would be akin to learning how to drive and then using your car as a terrorist weapon. There could be no justification for such behaviour.'

'I understand.' Mike ran his right hand down the side of the lectern. He wanted the jury to understand, too. He gave the note-takers chance to finish whatever they were writing.

'Are you the world's greatest hypnotist?'

Marcus hesitated. He forced himself to look only at his questioner. 'No. I'm not. I used to think I was, but I was wrong. I'm not the best there is.'

'How many are better than you?'

'One.'

'Who is that?'

'Ethan Hall. The defendant. The man in the dock.'

'How can you be sure?'

'Because, whilst I might not be the best hypnotist in the world, I am still a leading authority. I'm more than capable of recognising the level of skill someone possesses.'

'Can you categorise Mr Hall's skill?'

'It's outstanding. Beyond anything I have ever experienced.'

'Enough to dominate an unwilling subject?'

'Easily. In my professional opinion, his skill levels are such that the normal rules don't apply. He has an ability that is so high it is potentially unimaginable for most people.'

'Can you explain that to us?'

'He operates at a far greater speed than any other hypnotist I've ever met or heard of. He recognises communication patterns and belief systems and emotional states in fractions of a second. He uses words and gestures and his breathing to influence in the most powerful of ways. He does this effortlessly.'

'We have known for a long time that words affect brains. In more recent times neuroscience has been providing us with scientific proof of just how that happens, how our brains actually change in response to communication. Ethan Hall can affect another person's brain – he can dominate it - in any way that he chooses.

And he can do it more quickly than a snake can bite.'

'How far could such domination go?'

'Complete physical and psychological control. Think of it this way, words affect the human brain and the brain controls the mind and body. So when you influence the brain, you therefore influence the mind and body.'

'As I stated earlier, patients who have been hypnotised can undergo surgery without the need for anaesthetics and remain pain-free and calm throughout. Their mind and body have been so influenced, so controlled, by the hypnotist they are impervious to even the most invasive operation.'

'It follows, then, that if an incredibly skilled hypnotist wanted to control the mind and body of another person for their own reasons, to make them do whatever they wanted or to use them however they chose, including in matters of life and death, they would be able to do so.'

'And Ethan Hall is that skilled?'

'For a man of Ethan Hall's ability, that would be child's play.'

CHAPTER 30

TUESDAY - TRIAL DAY 2
1.27pm

Detective Sergeant Kevin McNeill wasn't looking forward to delivering his news. Despite that he hurried into the small room his Boss was using as a temporary office. Peter Jones was expecting him.

'What have you got for me?'

'Marcus Kline gave permission for us to trace the phone call. Colleagues in Bristol identified the address as a hotel near the Clifton suspension bridge. A PC visited an hour or so ago. Reception told him which room Mr Nicholas Evans was staying in. The PC said thanks and went to see him.'

'How was he?'

'Indignant. Angry, actually. Well, furious. Well, he became furious as the conversation went on.'

'What made him so angry?'

'You, according to the PC. It seems he started out being polite but obviously suspicious. He was very quick to ask for the name of the individual who had registered their concern about him. He became angry when he heard that Marcus Kline had told you about his phone call. He became furious when he discovered you had acted on it.'

'Technically I haven't.'

'Technically he didn't give a shit. The PC reported that Nic identified you as a bullying, egocentric, power freak. He was shouting by this point. He claimed that he'd left you because... well...' Kevin hesitated.

'Go on.'

'He claimed he'd left you because he'd finally come to realise the huge degree of psychological abuse you were submitting him to. He said he had been a domestic victim, trapped in a relationship that was killing him.' Kevin coughed. 'Look, I'm sorry Boss. I could just - '

'- Just get on with it. We've both heard a lot worse. And I certainly wasn't expecting you to report back with the news that he suddenly wanted a dinner date.'

'Fair enough. Nic said you were clearly using your authority to get him back, to pressure him into returning. He said it was typical of your abusive nature. He said he would sooner jump off the bridge than live any more of his life with you.'

'Beyond the outrage was there any sign of mental disturbance? Did the PC get any sense that Nic was hallucinatory?'

'No. Nothing at all. He actually asked him about his brother.'

'And?'

'Nic said that his family situation was no matter for either you or the police. He told the Constable that he felt his visit was so inappropriate he was going to report it. The term Police State was used a couple of times it seems.'

Peter sighed. 'So, overall, the PC did not see or hear enough to make him concerned about Nic's psychological welfare?'

'That would be correct. The PC said it was impossible to identify anything beyond the anger. And he said that, whilst he didn't agree with, or appreciate, Nic's argument and attitude, it was at least coherent. If you really were a psychological abuser and if Nic really was escaping from you, it makes sense that he'd be rattled to his core by a copper coming to see him.'

'Only none of that is true.'

'I know. Which means that Nic is functioning well enough to lie.'

'Which doesn't mean that he's mentally stable.'

'I know that, too. He might have been rambling when he spoke to Marcus Kline, but the PC's assessment doesn't leave us with anything immediately actionable on the danger-to-himself front.'

'And on the Ethan Hall front?'

'Nothing there, either. Nic was adamant he had never seen or heard from Ethan Hall. He said the suggestion was just another example of your manipulative ways.'

'So we've done all we can for now.'

'Officially.'

Peter shook his head. 'I'm not going after him. For a whole host of reasons. No, unless something bad happens and we find out about it, we'll just have to let things lie.'

'Yes Boss.'

'Good. By the way I had a chat with DCI Anderson about the *Pass it on* killings. Just in case you were wondering, the DD carved into the dead man's forehead stood for drug dealer.'

Kevin grinned. The situation with Nic had to be tearing at Jones's insides and still he came up with the joke, the pointed reminder. Typical. Always the Boss. Always putting work first. Always keeping his relationships with the team on point.

'Did the DCI say anything else Boss?'

'The perpetrators are using burner phones to upload the images onto social media, and then, of course, they're destroying them. No useful fingerprints were discovered at either crime scene. Although, because of some details SOCO have found, they do think it's highly likely they're after two killers.'

'Fuck!'

'I know. And the images have created ever-increasing social media responses. With every hour that passes there are more and more people supporting the murders and explicitly inciting others to do the same. Plus there are those with a few more working brain cells who are careful to state that, whilst they deplore acts of criminal violence, they do fully understand the motivation. They, of course, are the people who incite the mob and then feign innocence and pretend they didn't mean to, or that they were taken out of context, or were being satirical. Anyway, those fuckers are out in force, too.'

'And the silent majority?'

Jones nodded his approval. 'Well remembered Detective Sergeant.'

'Thank you, sir.'

'They are becoming a bit more vocal. But that's just leading to on-line verbal fights. And, it seems, the odd late night punch-up when the pub debate turns into a brawl.'

'The DCI must be under a lot of pressure.'

'He is. The powers that be are not simply looking down, they're leaning heavily already.'

'Poor sod.'

'Anderson's tough. And smart. He'll cope.'

'Did he say if there was anything at all that might connect...' Kevin gestured vaguely with his left hand.

'To Ethan Hall? No, there's nothing.'

'To be honest Boss a big part of me is relieved.'

'Well, I say nothing...' It was Peter's turn to let his voice trail off.

'Oh shit! You mean there is something?'

'Just the one thing. But it is significant.'

'What is it?'

Peter stood up and tapped his right hand onto his stomach.

Kevin groaned. 'Boss I keep telling you, your gut can be wrong! It's got to screw up every now and again; it can't be a perfect predictor can it? Please, at least tell me that it's only half your gut.'

'Which half of my gut would you like it to be DS McNeill?' Peter sat down again.

Kevin stepped back. 'With all due respect Boss, there's no way I'm answering that.'

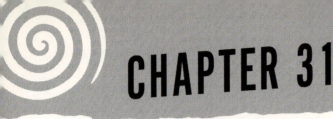

CHAPTER 31

TUESDAY - TRIAL DAY 2
2.01pm

Mike Coopland couldn't help but think to himself, We're halfway there.

The morning had gone well. Very well. Marcus Kline had been the perfect expert witness. His answers had been clear and concise, phrased so the jury could follow along easily yet delivered with the calm authority of a world leader in his field. He had even managed to incite some negative emotion towards Ethan Hall by emphasising his dangerous capabilities whilst, subtly, contrasting them with his own desire to help people.

By the time Marcus had finished, the content and purpose of Mike's opening speech had been supported and developed fully. Many of the jurors were studiously resisting any temptation to glance in Ethan's direction. Some were clearly uncomfortable at being so close to a manipulative, master hypnotist. The threat had been well established.

A very good morning indeed.

Now it was time for Marcus Kline, witness of fact. Now a different Marcus Kline was needed.

Mike placed his hands on the lectern and began.

'Mr Kline, do you ever help the police?'

'Yes. Occasionally I am asked to study a crime scene, to read the scenario as I would a human being, to see if there are any communication patterns or insights I can glean.'

'Have you been successful?'

'Yes, I've been told that I provide valuable support. And I have been asked to help on numerous occasions, so the police clearly think I'm doing something right.'

'When was the last time?'

'It began with the murder of a man named Derrick Smith. He was found dead, tied to a chair in his own home. He had been scalped and the top part of his head, the cranium, had been removed and placed on the carpet next to him.'

'And you know this, how?'

'I was shown the police film of the crime scene.'

'By whom?'

'Detective Chief Inspector Peter Jones.'

'He wanted what from you, precisely?'

'He didn't give me any specific instructions. Neither did he share any additional information. I can be most useful if I'm allowed to look at these things with a clear and open mind, in much the same way that I would look at a client. That gives me the best chance of seeing something I might otherwise miss.'

'And did you see something?'

'Yes. But before I say what, I need to clarify what I mean by "seeing". It isn't always a conscious, visual activity. Sometimes I'm responding to subconscious cues that I'm picking up. When that happens it's more an example of the gut instinct that I mentioned this morning. – If I'm allowed to refer back to that?'

Mike nodded.

'Good. Thank you. Anyway, with the Derrick Smith film it was definitely more of an intuitive response. I had the very clear impression that the killer wasn't concerned with torturing Mr Smith, even though he did, in fact, torture him. Rather I sensed that he was searching for something.'

'Searching where?'

'In Smith's head. In or around his brain to be exact.'

'Searching for what?'

'I couldn't tell at that time. It only became clear to me much later on in the investigation.'

'I see. We will return to that in a moment.' Mike looked down at his notes. He didn't need to read them. It was his favourite ploy whenever a witness started getting ahead of the story and he had to manufacture a break, no matter how brief, before getting them back on track. 'Treat questions as if you are climbing a staircase,' his mentor had taught him. 'Take them one step at a time and in the right order. That way you'll cover everything and arrive at the end in one piece.'

'Did you learn anymore before then?' Mike asked.

'Yes. I had a direct message from the killer almost immediately after I had seen the film.'

'What was the message?'

'He visited my home and cut a branch off the willow tree in our front garden. He painted the branch purple and left it on the grass, pointing at the house. I know that seems like a very unusual answer,' Marcus glanced at the jury, 'but I recognised it instantly as a form of symbolic language. It was meant for me to understand and no one else. It was meant for me because of my expertise.'

'You see both the tree and the colour are rich with symbolic meaning. They have been throughout the ages. For example, for Victorians the willow tree represented mourning and sadness. In eighteenth and nineteenth century art it symbolised immortality and rebirth. Purple has long been associated with nobility and prestige. It symbolises mystery, magic and power. It's the colour of kings and leaders, people of power.'

'Putting these together I knew, therefore, that the killer was identifying me as his target. Although I didn't know why he had chosen me, I was convinced that I was his ultimate victim.'

'Did you tell DCI Jones?'

'Yes. He wasn't convinced. Not at first anyway.'

'What happened to change his mind?'

'The next two murders. They were both connected to me. The next victim was Paul Clusker. He was one of my clients. The third victim was Simon Westbury. He was my...my employee.'

'You employed him to do what?'

'To assist with our clients. Simon wanted to become the world's next great communicator. I was teaching and training him.'

'How would you describe your relationship?'

'He was like a son to me.' Marcus fought back tears.

Mike softened his voice, 'And how was he killed?'

'In the same way as the other two. He was tied in a chair, scalped and then had his cranium removed.'

'I appreciate this is difficult, Mr Kline. We can all see how you feel. However, if I may continue?'

'Yes.'

'Thank you. Tell us, what happened next?'

'DCI Jones insisted we have a panic button installed in the house. He warned both myself and my wife to exercise extreme caution until the killer was arrested.'

'How did you respond?'

'Truthfully, not well. Simon's death had put me...well...I was in a bad place emotionally. A part of me, an angry part, wanted to find the killer and confront him myself. It was stupid I know, but grief and anger are closely linked and I wasn't managing them well.'

'Did you search for the killer?'

'I didn't need to. He came to me. He confronted me in the

garden. At night. Suddenly there he was, within touching distance.'

'Did you recognise him?'

'Yes. It was Ethan Hall.'

'Are you positive?'

'Absolutely.'

Every juror wrote that down.

'How did you feel?'

'So full of emotion I was lost to myself. But that angry part still thought I could defeat him.'

'Did you try to restrain him?'

'No. It became a war of words. That's what he was there for, in the first instance. To win a war of words.'

'And did he?'

'Yes. He hypnotised me as easily as he would anyone else. I could only do what he said. There was no option.'

'So you never struggled physically?'

'No. He had complete control over me. Even though he told me that he was going to do the same to me as he had the others, it was still impossible to fight back.'

'He admitted to killing the others?'

'Yes. He wanted to tell me about them. Especially Simon.'

'Did he tell you anything else?'

'He told me what he was searching for.'

'Which was?'

'To find the subconscious mind, to see it in action. Ethan Hall is a synesthete. It's a neurological condition. It means that he sees emotions as colours in the air around a person. He believes he can see their thoughts in the same way. Consequently he was convinced he would eventually be able to see the subconscious.'

'Do you find that plausible?'

'No. For all his incredible skill, I think Ethan Hall is completely

 166

misguided on this matter.'

'Why did he target you?'

'He said it was because of my reputation and skill. On one level he wanted to prove himself better than me and on another he thought my subconscious would be somehow more obvious, more worthy of study.'

'What did he do to you?'

'He tied me to a chair in my dining room. He took a hammer and drill and a scalpel out of his bag and placed them on the table next to me.' Marcus felt himself tense as the images came to mind. 'This sounds a really stupid thing to say, but those objects were the most real things in the world right then.'

'Did he use those objects?'

'He began to. He started with the scalpel. He put it there,' Marcus touched his right temple with his forefinger. He realised he was shaking. 'I could feel it and I could see it in the mirror, out of the corner of my eye. He was so calm. The way a person is who has done something well many times before, when they know exactly what they are doing.'

'Why didn't he kill you?'

'Because...'

'Mr Kline?'

'Because...' The memories were swirling. The sudden noise. The confusion. The shouting. And then...

'Mr Kline?'

Marcus shook his head. 'He didn't kill me,' he said finally, 'because a policeman shot him.'

Mike Coopland QC looked at the jury. Twelve men and women who, according to the signals they were giving, had just climbed the staircase with him.

CHAPTER 32

TUESDAY - TRIAL DAY 2
6.20pm

Dave Johnson was impressed. From what his courtroom spy had told him Marcus Kline had done a bloody good job. Dave was willing to believe that the tears and emotion towards the end were false, that Kline had most probably rehearsed until he could make it look natural, but it was still obviously good enough to convince those who didn't have his journalist's training and experience.

He swirled the remaining Guinness around in the bottom of his pint glass and considered how he would include today's happenings in his planned book on Marcus Kline and Ethan Hall - working title *The Twisted Relationship*.

It was still all too easy to remember the phone conversation he had shared with the killer right back at the start of it all. At the time it had been terrifying. Later, after a few days and enough booze, he had recognised it for the opportunity it was. The chance to follow the story from beginning to end. To be the journalist at the centre of it all.

And so far the story was going along just fine. He had written several features about it for some national newspapers. He had even managed one scoop! But it was the book that was going to bring it all together. To make his name. To make him more than drinking money.

Dave looked across the bar to the far side of The Piano and Pitcher. Mike Coopland and his Junior, a small man called Kaffee, were both on their fourth drink. They were looking happy. And with good reason. He guessed they got pissed, or close to it, every night of every trial.

Celebration or consolation.

There was always a reason to drink if you needed to find one. Until you reached the point where you didn't need to find one. Then, in his experience, one of two things happened.

You either got honest with yourself, which meant you stopped drinking or you carried on and became a miserable drunk.

Or you just accepted your lot. Took it in good grace. Acknowledged that everybody was fucked one way or another, so it didn't matter if you fucked them a little bit more along the way. At which point you became a lonely drunk who was, at least, still trying to make something of himself.

And every drunk was lonely.

Every drunk knew that.

Even those who always got drunk with other drunks.

Especially those.

Dave watched Kaffee go to the bar. He saw a change come over Coopland. Left alone, the big man instantly became more thoughtful. And whatever he was thinking about was making him frown, making him uncomfortable, distracting him from the busy, bustling environment.

So easily lost in your own troubled world, Dave thought. One day you're going to become the miserable drunk.

'Christ, I needed that!' Harry Smith sat down, ending Dave's observation of the QC. 'I was bursting.'

'Beer has that effect.'

'So you're definitely going to name me in the book, and say how I helped?'

'Definitely. I will include you in the acknowledgements and

publicly thank you for being my eyes and ears in the court.'

'And I'll get a free, signed copy?'

'Along with all the beer you want until the trial ends.'

'Excellent.' Harry took a drink. 'It must piss you off, not being able to be there yourself.'

'It's the price I have to pay for being a prosecution witness. It's standard court procedure. Witnesses can't watch the trial until after they've given their evidence, and even then it's at the Judge's discretion.'

'How do you feel, you know, about being a witness in such a big trial?'

'What, are you the fucking journalist now?'

'Just interested. I think I'd be shitting myself.'

Dave smiled. A smile of calm, confidence. He held it just long enough to emphasise his superiority. 'It's inevitable for someone like me. Journalists who are doing their job well always find themselves at the heart of the action. We're the storytellers see? We gather the facts, find the best angle – you can think of it as a hook that grabs the readers and pulls them in – and get the story out there. To be honest with you, I've always been amazed that the police haven't thought to learn from the best journalists. We could teach them a thing or two about tracking events, getting the right information.'

'What other big stories have you done?'

Dave emptied his glass. 'Plenty of other big ones,' he lied, 'but nothing as big as this. See, most people think it's pretty easy to get in the papers. They think if you are doing something good, or if you've done something bad, we're bound to want to write about it. Well that's just bollocks. We're looking for things that are newsworthy and, unless there's something that we just can't afford to miss, like this Marcus Kline Ethan Hall thing, there is no guarantee we'll be interested.'

Dave leaned across the table, put his hand conspiratorially on Harry's left forearm. 'Between you and me, what people never realise is that most of the time journalists decide what's newsworthy and what isn't. We don't simply report the news. We make it. We choose what to tell you about and how to tell you about it. We're the people who decide how everyone thinks. It's not politicians. It's not the Church. And it's certainly not the arty-farty types! It's us, the journalists. We shape the fucking world.'

'Let me give you an example. Some years ago, I contacted this guy and said I wanted to do a story about him and his business. He was a dog breeder, see? Staffordshire bull terriers. Ugly fuckers. Anyway, it was at the time when we were all reporting about these types of dogs attacking people – kids especially. It's always good for a story if kids are being hurt.'

'So I told him that I wanted to write about his point of view and his experiences. He was thrilled at the chance to set the record straight. That's what he said. Silly fuck. I spent an afternoon with him. Got loads of quotes. Took some pictures of his dogs with their mouths wide open. They looked like fucking sharks I tell you. I thanked him very much for his time, nice and polite. Turned it into a great story with the headline *Breeding Killers*.'

'Bloke went berserk. Said I'd only quoted bits of what he said, that the photos and the captions I'd put with them were misleading. Claimed I was destroying his life's work. I told him he could have said No. Asked him which part of the term *news story* he didn't understand.' Dave let go of Harry's forearm. 'See? I created a story that fitted perfectly into the bigger story everyone was telling. That's how I made it newsworthy.'

Harry sat back. 'But you could have told it from his perspective, couldn't you? Given, you know, the alternative point of view. Given your readers something different to think about.'

'That's the sort of naive thinking I lost a long time ago. Readers don't want to work that hard. They want it simple. Straight forward. Easy to understand. They don't want to have to do mental gymnastics just to make sense of the news. They don't want to be treated like they're at school, learning stuff. No, they want to have things explained to them in an entertaining way that lets them talk about it with confidence in the pub. So the story about Dogman was always going to be simple and fit in with what we professionals would call the larger narrative.'

'Jesus...' Harry looked pointedly at his empty glass.

Dave slid a ten pound note across the table just as his mobile phone began ringing. 'Get two more,' he said.

'Right.' Harry took the empty glasses with him.

Dave checked the caller ID. There was no name. The number was withheld. Nothing unusual there. Not for a journalist. And it can't be Ethan Hall, he told himself. As he always did these days whenever the caller's identity was unknown.

Truth be told, if he had been offered an exclusive Ethan Hall interview he would have refused it. He didn't need it. Not for his book. He'd already got plenty for that, with more to come. So why the fuck would he want to be in a room with that madman?

Dave shivered at the thought. Some news stories are not worth the risk, he reminded himself as he accepted the call.

'This is Dave Johnson. Who's this?'

'Someone with information for you.'

'Information about what?'

'The Ethan Hall trial.'

Dave's stomach tightened. 'Who are you?'

'Are you interested?'

'Depends what you've got, how reliable you are. I'm a busy man.

 172

I don't waste my time. So before we do anything else you've got to convince me.'

'Listen, I know your involvement in the case. I know Coopland is calling you as a witness. I know you've got plans to profit from all of this. I can give you details and insights into the main man that you can't get from anywhere else.'

'The main man?'

'Ethan Hall.'

Dave licked his lips, swallowed, took a deep breath. 'What sort of details and insights?'

'Behind the scenes. Up close and personal.'

'How current?'

'Up to the minute.'

'I see. Is what you've got based on first-hand experience, or have you got a source?'

'It's first-hand.'

'So you have access to Ethan Hall?'

'I'm not going to answer any more questions on the phone. Right? If you want to know more we've got to meet.'

'I need to be sure of your credibility.'

'Your choice. Hang up or tell me you want to meet tonight. Either way, you've got two seconds to make your decision.'

'Alright! Alright. I'll meet you.'

'Good choice.' The caller was silent for a moment. Then he said, 'Midnight. On Mapperley Plains. There's a car park behind the Co-op. Park there. Come alone.'

The phone went dead.

Dave realised his hand was sweating.

'Who was it?' Harry placed the two beers on the table and sat down.

'It was, er, an informant.' Dave returned the mobile to his jacket pocket and took a large swig of his Guinness.

'Someone who gets information for you on a regular basis?'

'No. No, it was, er, someone who wanted to keep their identity a secret.'

'Fuck me, that's like proper spy stuff. I didn't realise it could get that serious.'

Dave forced the superior smile back on to his face. 'Yeah. It's all part of the job. Thing is, when you're as experienced as me, it's easy to work out who you're talking to even if they want to remain anonymous.'

'How do you do that?'

'Stay calm. Ask the right questions. Listen to what they say.'

'So who was it?'

'It's not that I know his name or anything like that. What I have been able to work out, though, is what he does for a living.'

'And?'

'He's something to do with the prison.'

'How do you know?'

'Because of what he offered me, and what he said he knew.'

'Go on.'

Dave took another swig. 'I've got to be careful what I say, mate. I can't just sit in the middle of a crowded pub and start blurting out confidential stuff. I'm a professional, remember? And I can't afford to take unnecessary risks.'

'Yeah, but I'm on your team, aren't I? I've proven to you that I'm reliable. Come on, you can trust me.'

Dave pretended to consider. He loved the fact that, for a moment at least, he had managed to make Harry forget about his beer. 'The most I can tell you,' he said finally, lowering his voice, 'is that later tonight I'm going to get some more amazing stuff for the book. Stuff that no other journalist would ever have a chance of getting.'

'Wow! You are a fucking star!'

'Thank you, my friend.' Dave raised his glass.

Harry followed suit.

Dave's smile came naturally this time. It felt good being in control.

CHAPTER 33

TUESDAY - TRIAL DAY 2
11.43pm

The three-bedroomed detached house was in darkness apart from one downstairs light. He guessed it was the lounge. He couldn't know for sure because the curtains were closed, but it was the most obvious choice. The front door was to the right of the building. Inside a hall would lead straight into the kitchen at the back of the property. The dining room would be to the left of that. If not, it would have one of those popular large kitchen-dining affairs. Something like Calvin Brent's, but not as big or as expensive. Peter Jones couldn't afford a kitchen like that on his policeman's salary.

'And you're not a man for back-handers, are you?' Stu Jolly asked the question quietly as if Jones was next to him, sitting in the front passenger seat of his dark blue Ford Mondeo.

Stu had a habit of talking out loud to those he was targeting whenever he was studying or planning or just thinking about them. He knew that about himself. He knew why he did it, too. It made the targets feel closer. It made him feel a sense of inevitability about what was going to happen.

'So what are you doing in there?' He asked. 'You're not watching the TV, if you were I'd see the lights flashing. You're not moving around either, because I'd see your shadow through those curtains. So what are you doing? Sitting there, reading a book, listening to music, drinking a whisky? Whatever it is, you'd better enjoy it. You won't get many more chances.'

Stu wouldn't have picked this job by choice. True, there was great kudos in doing a copper but it brought a lot of pressure, too. A lot of risk. The bottom line, though, was that saying no to Calvin Brent was far bigger risk. In fact, that didn't so much bring risk with it as an absolute guarantee.

'I'd have been dead by the end of the week,' he said. 'Dead and disappeared. So, DCI Jones, sooner you than me.'

The other problem he faced was the time limit. It had to be done quickly. 'But not rushed,' as Brent had told him repeatedly. 'Being fast doesn't mean rushing. Being fast just means getting the timing right, it means fitting in at the first available opportunity.'

Brent was right, of course. He usually was. That's why he was the top of the tree. Well, almost the top. And fitting in was something Stu knew how to do in all sorts of ways. It was easier than most people would have thought because targets, just like everyone else on the planet, all had one thing in common. Routines. Habits. Call them what you will. People were creatures who created and valued repetition.

'Even you DCI Jones.'

Stu let his mind wander back to the beginning of his criminal career. He had begun as a burglar. Robbing homes that looked like they were worth a visit. Breaking and entering they called it back then. Not that he ever broke anything. Entering and taking was his speciality. He was good at it, too. His success, as he taught others, was based on his ten-step rule.

Step one: Choose homes in wealthy areas or, and this was the one exception, a home that you know for a fact has something of value inside.

Step two: Only choose homes with a six foot fence around them, or something else that blocks the view from the street.

Step three: Avoid homes with dogs.

Step four: Study the daily routines of the homeowners and of their neighbours.

Step five: Study a house plan or, if unable to access one, just study the house and work out which room is where.

Step six: Know your entry point.

Step seven: Once inside always ensure you leave two escape routes open.

Step eight: Always wear gloves.

Step nine: Only take the best stuff.

Step ten: Don't disrespect the property; never trash the place just for fun.

In the trade it was referred to jokingly as Jolly's ten-step programme – guaranteed to earn you enough money to turn you into an alcoholic. He liked that. He liked the fact too that, with a few changes, it worked equally well for other endeavours.

'Like the one I'm here for now. You see, DCI Jones, routines don't just get you burgled, they can also get you killed. All someone needs to do is find the routine that leaves you most vulnerable. A routine that isolates you for a period of time. One that means your body is unlikely to be found in a hurry. And we all have routines like that, DCI Jones. Even you.'

Stu checked his watch. If his information was right, and he had no reason to doubt it, Jones should be appearing any moment now.

And he did.

Dressed in a thick country coat to protect from the cold, with a cap pulled down over his brow, Jones locked the front door behind him and walked out of his garden and onto the pavement. He glanced right then left, before putting both hands into his coat pockets and setting off on his regular late night walk.

He headed away from the busy road, the A610, away from the centre of the village and towards the fields and quiet lanes.

Perfect.

Stu watched him disappear into the darkness. He made no attempt to follow. Not tonight.

'I'll see you soon, DCI Jones.'

He turned the ignition and the Ford's engine coughed and came to life.

Step nine, he thought to himself, is one of those that applies no matter what the job. Sometimes, though, taking the best stuff meant leaving nothing behind.

CHAPTER 34

TUESDAY - TRIAL DAY 2
11.56pm

The car park was empty and dark. Dave Johnson parked his ageing Fiat in the middle of it. He undid his seat belt and twisted right then left, checking for signs of life.

Nothing.

He couldn't help but wonder if he was being played. He figured there were plenty of people who knew of his relationship to the trial. Out of that number there were bound to be a few morons who would think it funny to waste his time. It was, he concluded with a mixture of anger and pride, the price you paid for becoming a kind of celebrity.

A sudden noise brought him out of his reverie. He looked through the windscreen, his eyes straining, his heart hammering. A city fox was tearing open a discarded shopping bag less than five metres from the car. It stopped abruptly and turned its head in his direction, as if sensing his sudden interest.

'You scavenging little bastard!' Dave glared back.

The fox turned and trotted away into the shadows.

'That's it! Fuck off and die!'

Gloved knuckles rapped the Fiat's front passenger window. Dave jumped. A large male figure was outside. He rapped a second time. Dave opened the door. His hand was shaking. The man got in without hesitation.

'You made the right decision,' he said.

'Wh – What?'

'Showing up. It wouldn't have been the same without you.'

'What have you got for me?' Dave tried to sound authoritative. He straightened in his seat.

'Something special. Something you really need.'

'Oh, I see.' The penny dropped. The man wanted paying. He was starting a negotiation. Dave felt the power move back in his direction. 'Listen, you have to tell me what you've got before I can tell you what it's worth. You've probably never done this before, so let me make clear that's the way these things work.'

Dave took his Dictaphone from out of his jacket pocket.

The man put a large hand over the top of Dave's. 'Before you start recording, I'm going to whisper what I've got for you.'

He didn't wait for a response. Instead he leaned across the car, putting his right arm around Dave's shoulders. It was unexpectedly heavy. Dave felt his sudden confidence wilt beneath it. The man moved his face close. Dave could almost feel his lips against his skin. The man began whispering in his ear.

Dave tensed, squirmed, tried to fight himself free. The big arm tightened and pressed, holding him in place. Dave tried to turn his head, to push it against the other's face. The man wouldn't let him, keeping his own forehead tight against Dave's temple.

The whispering continued.

Dave tried to drive his left elbow up. The man felt the movement and prevented it with ease, using his left forearm to pin Dave's arm in place on his own thigh.

The whispering continued.

Dave screamed, trying to drown out the words. Spittle flew out of his mouth. Sweat was running down his face. The car windscreen began to fog.

The whispering continued.

'For God's sake, you've got it wrong!' Dave shouted as loud as he could, but he was struggling to breathe properly, his chest heaving as the fear mounted. He made one more attempt, but the words almost stuck in his throat. 'I tell the truth! That's my job! To let people know!' He began sobbing. And coughing. And spluttering.

He didn't notice that the man's left arm had moved. He didn't notice because he was desperate to clear his airways, because the whispering continued.

'Please...' Dave tried to force the words out. 'Please...Aargh!' He retched. 'Please...Just...'

The man's left hand now held a knife. He thrust it upwards violently. Dave thought he was having a heart attack. The pain pinned him to the back of the seat, his spine stretching and arching. Dave wondered why there was a fire inside his chest, why the flames reached higher when he gasped. Then he felt himself shudder and heard himself groan and his body lost control.

The whispering stopped.

The man withdrew the knife slowly. He used it to carve a simple four-letter word into Dave's left cheek. It was a messy business.

When he was done, the man dropped the knife onto the grubby mat in front of the driver's seat and took out a mobile phone. He took three pictures, one of them a close-up of the scored cheek. Satisfied with his work he opened the passenger door and eased himself out into the dark night.

A city fox was standing in front of the car watching him. He guessed it was the one from earlier. He guessed it could smell blood.

CHAPTER 35

WEDNESDAY - TRIAL DAY 3
10.33am

Duncan had taken the handcuffs off.

Mr Justice Mulvenny had ruled that, for practical reasons and to avoid any unnecessary prejudice, the handcuffs couldn't remain on during cross-examination.

To avoid any unnecessary prejudice.

That was just bullshit. The trial was the witch-hunt he had always known it would be. Only two days in and the jury's prejudice was fixed firmly in place. Ethan couldn't see one who wasn't already convinced.

It had been easy enough for Coopland to do. You didn't have to prove anything beyond a reasonable doubt if you could scare people enough. Fear was all it took. All it had ever taken. Especially when your target was an outsider. Especially when they were also very different.

As Ethan Hall rose to his feet he made a point of looking at his bare wrists and rubbing them gently with his palms. He flexed his fingers cautiously. Just for fun. On either side of him Duncan and his colleague watched closely.

Handcuffs removed, but still in the dock. That had been the Judge's decision. Even though the accused was defending himself, he was still the accused. So he asked his questions from behind a Perspex screen. Visible but caged.

To ensure all possible prejudice.

Ethan inhaled softly and deeply, easing his diaphragm forwards. He held the breath for a silent four-count before exhaling equally gently through his nose. One breath. That was all he needed. Ready now to do what only he could.

'Mr Hall, are you ready to begin your cross-examination?'

'I am, my Lord.'

'Very well.'

For the first time since the trial began Ethan Hall looked across the court directly at Marcus Kline.

Neither looked into the other's eyes. Neither was thinking. Only Ethan was salivating.

'Mr Kline, to confirm, we have met before?'

'Yes.'

'How well do you remember it?'

'In great detail.'

'You remember where we met?'

'Yes.'

'You remember what we did?'

'Yes.'

'You remember what we talked about?'

'Yes.'

'So you remember my voice?'

'Yes.' Marcus swallowed.

Ethan watched it happen in slow motion. One swallow, caused by a pressure in the back of Marcus's throat; a pressure his words were creating. Already.

'Mr Kline, you believe everyone can be hypnotised?'

'Yes. As I said, if the conditions are right.'

'Everyone, without exception?'

'I believe so.'

'Do you believe I could be?'

'What?' Marcus jerked backwards. For reasons he didn't understand the question felt as if it had penetrated his chest. He held back a gasp.

'Could I be hypnotised?'

'Erm, well, it has to be possible, yes.' The feeling in Marcus's chest moved and spread, cocooning his heart. Automatically his mind filled with a single thought.

His words are inside me!

'How would you go about it?'

Marcus shifted awkwardly in his seat. In his, Mike Coopland tensed.

'Mr Kline?'

'I, er...' Marcus wanted to inhale deeply but daren't, afraid – crazily - that his heart might burst. He forced his mouth to work, not caring what came out. 'I would need to have a clearly established and agreed purpose, as I explained yesterday. Then I would shift my state slightly and by changing my language patterns and delivery style I would lead you into a trance.'

'Is that all?'

'More or less.'

'Which precisely - more or less?'

'Well,' Marcus coughed into his hand, he felt something jump inside his chest and then an extra pressure, 'my answer was, of course, just an overview of the process. There's an awful lot of technique and skill and subtlety involved.'

'Too much for jurors to understand?'

'No. No. It would just take a long time to explain it fully, that's all.'

'I see.' Ethan nodded. 'You were Mr Coopland's expert witness?'

'Yes.'

'Did you answer his questions fully?'

 FAITH

'Yes. Of course.'

'So why not answer mine fully?'

'I'm, I'm sorry?'

'You are an expert, aren't you?'

'Yes.'

'So why provide only an overview?'

Marcus gestured vaguely with open palms. The words that had invaded his chest were calling for all of his attention. He could feel them being strengthened every time Ethan Hall forced him to say *Yes* in reply to his questions. Marcus fought silently, frantically, to ignore them.

Mike Coopland, sitting with his arms folded across his chest, realised he was gripping himself tightly. Ethan Hall was questioning Marcus as a trained and experienced barrister would! And it was clear that Marcus was on the back foot, the confidence of the previous day evaporating fast. How the hell had Ethan Hall learnt how to perform like this? Beyond that, what would happen if Ethan started hypnotising Marcus, too? Dear God, what if he already was?

'Do you have an answer?' Ethan mimicked Marcus's gesture.

'Y-Yes. I didn't appreciate you were asking for a detailed, authoritative response.'

'You are an authority, aren't you?'

'Y-Yes.'

'A world leading authority?'

'Y-Yes.' Now it felt as if the words inside him were burrowing into his heart. Something in the back of his brain began to fear for his survival.

'So you could answer as such?'

'Y-Yes.' Marcus felt a bead of sweat trickle down the left side of his face.

Ethan Hall raised both arms and gently massaged his left wrist with his right hand. Mike Coopland looked across at the jury. They were watching Ethan. They looked comfortable. And interested. As far as Mike could remember not one of them had made any notes since Ethan had asked his first question.

'You said you remembered our meeting?' Ethan pressed his thumb against the pulsing vein in his wrist as he spoke. Marcus Kline felt his heart jump.

'Y-Yes.'

'Where did it take place?' Ethan lowered his hands, letting them hang by his sides.

Marcus felt an instant release. Not complete, but enough to let him breathe in more deeply without fear. The question and the answer it enabled helped too. 'In the front garden of what used to be my home.'

'Can you describe the garden – authoritatively?'

The word – that increasingly dreaded and painful word – jumped into the forefront of Marcus's consciousness. He could bypass it this time though by offering a detailed description. Only for some reason, the images were not appearing in his mind. The images of the garden he had loved were simply not there. They had disappeared from his memory. Marcus felt his mouth dry.

'It was, er, dark at the time, when you were there. So, er, it couldn't be seen clearly.'

'You lived there for how long?'

'Erm, many years. I'm not sure how long.'

'So you saw it in daylight?'

Marcus nodded.

'Answer verbally, please.'

'Y-Yes.' *That* word. The burrowing began again. Words eating his heart. His memory turned into the darkest winter night.

'Then please describe your garden.'

'I...I can't. I, er, seem to have forgotten the, erm, details.'

Mike Coopland glanced over his shoulder at Brian Kaffee, sitting behind him. He looked as shell-shocked as Mike felt.

Ethan continued without a pause.

'You have forgotten your front garden?'

'Y-Yes.'

'Have you also forgotten our conversation?'

Marcus realised that he had as soon as he heard the question. He knew it before he even tried to remember. And he couldn't bring himself to explore the darkness of the night. Even though...

'Yes or no, Mr Kline?'

...Even though he was allowing himself to be driven back into the same agonising trap.

'Y-Yes.'

'Have you also forgotten what happened?'

'Y-Yes.'

Marcus couldn't stop himself from saying it. It was true. But the truth wasn't the most important thing. Not here. Not now. The most important thing was escaping from *that* word, from the way it activated the other words Ethan Hall had somehow placed inside him. The most important thing, according to the back of Marcus's brain was not winning, but survival.

Mike Coopland saw his key witness on the verge of complete surrender and realised he had only one option. He needed an adjournment. He had to give Marcus Kline chance to regroup and begin again later.

Mike rose to his feet and addressed Stephen Mulvenny with all the confidence he could muster.

CHAPTER 36

WEDNESDAY - TRIAL DAY 3
11.18am

The jury had been dismissed; the arguments had been made. The Judge had refused Mike's application. Ethan Hall had seemed impervious to it all. When the jury returned he continued as if there had been no interruption.

'Mr Kline, how are you feeling?' Ethan's voice floated across the courtroom.

'What?' Marcus paled. It was the second question to pin him back in his seat. He felt the words rush through the burrows already made and begin to create their own.

'How are you feeling? Now?'

'I'm, er, fine.'

Ethan smiled. It looked as if he was pleased.

'You believe I am a killer?'

'Y-Yes.'

'You use hypnosis to help people?'

'I do.' Marcus forced himself away from *that* word.

'Might I not also?'

'What?'

'Use hypnosis to help people?'

'You use hypnosis to destroy and kill.'

'You believe I do?'

'I know you do!'

'Is believing the same as knowing?'

'No.'

'How are they different?'

This time the question freed his mind. 'Beliefs are thoughts that have hardened into a type of certainty that isn't based on fact and is based more on desire, on what we hope to be the case. Knowing is data-based.'

'You said you believe I kill?'

'Y-Yes.'

'And you don't believe I help?'

'No.'

'And you have no supporting data?'

'No.'

'For either belief?'

'No.'

'And you can't remember our meeting?'

'No.' Marcus felt the pressure, the threat, easing out of his body; he realised there was safety in the word *No.* His brain urged his mind to cling to it. Survival at all costs.

'Have you ever hypnotised me?'

'No.'

'But you can't remember our meeting?'

'No.'

'So how can you be sure?'

The question darkened the winter night in his memory. 'I, er...I'm sure because I...because you can't be hypnotised.'

Mike Coopland fought the urge to put his head into his hands.

'Didn't you say everyone could be?'

'I, er...No...I, er, can't remember. Right. Now.' Marcus heard himself speak and didn't care. The words were no longer moving inside him. Now he had the chance to get them out and *No* was his only hope. He clung. Hard.

'Mr Kline, are you unbiased here?'

'No.'

'Are you committed to the truth?'

'No.'

'Can we then trust your answers?'

'No.'

Can we trust you at all?

'No.'

'Do you trust our court system?'

'No.'

'Finally, Mr Kline, do you trust this jury?

'No.'

Mike Coopland didn't need to look at the twelve men and women to his right to know their response. The staircase he had so carefully built had just been demolished.

CHAPTER 37

WEDNESDAY - TRIAL DAY 3
6.41pm

Peter Jones was far from happy.

It was a bad news day. In fact, it was close to being the worst ever. A third *Pass it on* killing and a Marcus Kline disaster in the witness box. After Ethan had finished his questioning Mike Coopland's re-examination had, in the barrister's own words, 'Managed only to slow the flow of blood from a fatal wound.'

The press was having a field day. Dave Johnson's dead body had been found with the word *Fake* carved into his face. The murder was being presented by the media as a literal attack on the freedom and integrity of the press. Johnson was being talked of as a dedicated, old school journalist who had been a tragic victim. Peter guessed it gave the story a greater poignancy to say *old school* rather than cynical and uncaring.

In contrast, Marcus's reputation was taking a beating. A classic case, Peter thought, of the English welcoming the chance to kick a celebrity figure when they were down.

Beyond that, Mike Coopland was as angry and confused as Peter had ever seen him. He would be in the bar now. If Peter knew him at all, he and Kaffee would be in the bar for quite a few hours yet.

'Talk to your friend for me, will you?' Mike had said, not even attempting to keep the frustration out of his voice. 'And then see if you can have a word with Anne-Marie. I don't want her stress levels increasing because of her husband's shambolic performance. We need a good show from her now more than ever.'

'Will do.'

Which was proving easier to say than to achieve. Marcus's phone was switched off and, ideally, Peter wanted to talk to him before he called his wife. Still, when push came to shove, pragmatism always won the day.

I'll give Marcus until 7pm, he told himself, and then I'll call Anne-Marie regardless.

Peter checked his watch as DS McNeill rapped his familiar knock on the office door and stepped inside.

'You wanted to see me Boss?'

'Yes. I had a phone call from our latest CHIS saying he needs to see me tonight. He says it's vital.'

'What – he called you instead of me?'

'That's precisely what he did.'

'But you made the rules clear to him, he talks to me as his handler and I talk to you as the supervisor. You don't break that chain of communication!'

'Well, he has.'

'Maybe he's not as reliable as we thought he might be? Maybe he's playing us?'

'It's possible, but I don't think so. He was bang on the money last time. That buys him the benefit of the doubt. Also I was struck by the fact that he said it was vital. Firstly because it's not the sort of word I'd associate with him. Secondly because he didn't say it was important or urgent. It was clear that to him vital is just about as desperate as it gets.'

'Have you got any idea what it's all about?'

'Nope.'

'Fair enough. So what are we going to do?'

 FAITH

'Follow the usual protocol. I pointed out to him that for this arrangement to work he has to follow the rules. Our rules. I told him you could deal with vital, that's what you were trained for. I told him that throughout the Force you were known as Vitality Man.'

'Fuck off!'

Peter grinned. 'Anyway, he settled down and agreed to meet with you.'

'Right. I'll get on it.'

'Good. Let me know straight away if what he has to say is, er, you know...'

'...Vital. Yeah, I will Boss.' McNeill left.

Peter checked his watch. 6.53. Wait another seven minutes, he thought. Then phone Anne-Marie.

✿✿✿

Anne-Marie Wells was watching her husband sitting silently in an armchair staring into space. He hadn't spoken since he came home. He hadn't moved. If she had taken a photo of him now she would have titled it *Hollow*.

Anne-Marie didn't know what to say or do for the best. She had long found it almost impossible to resist Marcus's emotional state. He influenced her more obviously and easily than anyone else on the planet.

Apart from one.

Her mind flooded automatically with images of Ethan Hall intermingled with imaginings of what would happen when she appeared in court. She forced herself to look through them, to return her attention to the immediate reality of her husband. She had heard the news. She knew what had happened. At least, she knew the media version. What she didn't know was how to help him.

The first thing, she decided, was to shake off the mood he was sharing with her. What was it he always said?

If you keep doing what you've always done you will always get what you always have.

That was it. That was the first part of his argument for the value of change.

If you keep doing what you've always done...

Time to change then, she told herself. Time to take the lead.

'Action cures fear,' she said suddenly. 'Isn't that what you tell your clients? Action cures fear. And you're taking no action. Inside or out as far as I can tell. You haven't done since you came home. At some point you've got to move and you need to make sure your first move is in the right direction. Wherever that might be. And time is passing. So let's make a start.'

He couldn't help but look at her.

'Good. Now it's clear that you know I'm here, let's talk. Let's start naming the monster. We both know that once you begin to engage in your own state change your brain will do what it's been trained to. You've had a bad day. But you are still Marcus Kline. And if you give your brilliant brain something more positive to work with, it will start firing along more positive neural pathways. Right?'

She forced a smile. She saw a glimmer of *something* in Marcus's eyes.

'When did you become so smart?' He mumbled.

'I learnt it from my husband,' she said. 'Now, just what is going on?'

His eyes looked away from her, roaming the room, watering.

'Just say anything that comes to mind,' she said gently. 'Trust yourself.'

'I lost...' He said. '...Again.'

'Explain what you mean by losing.'

'He beat me. He...did what he wanted to.'

'And?'

'I couldn't stop him. I let everyone down.'

'And?'

'His words.'

'What about them?'

'He...put them inside me.' His eyes fixed on the carpet. 'I could feel them physically. Inside. Eating my heart. It was real. I had to get them out. No matter what. I couldn't survive with his words inside me. Doing what they were doing. I know it sounds crazy, but it's true.'

Anne-Marie shivered. He didn't see. He was too lost in his own experience.

She spoke without meaning to. 'I never thought that...'

He looked up. 'Thought what?'

A part of her needed to say, 'that he could penetrate you, too'. Only the rest of her would not allow it. She had no doubt she would shatter like glass if that truth ever escaped her lips.

Then her mobile phone rang.

'You'd better answer it,' Marcus said.

She did.

It was Peter Jones. He wanted to know if Marcus was home. He wanted to know how he was. He wanted to remind her that all she had to do tomorrow was answer every question as honestly as possible.

CHAPTER 38

THURSDAY - TRIAL DAY 4
2.02pm

The courtroom was exactly the same as the one in her dream.

She had almost fainted when she entered it this morning. If anything, she was feeling even worse now.

Somehow she made it to the witness box, even though she had no idea what kept her upright and moving. When she sat, her legs were shaking. Her brow was moist with sweat, but she chose to ignore it. Her hands gripped first each other, then the chair, then each other again. With every in-breath she could feel the presence of Ethan Hall in the room.

Anne-Marie did her best to ignore it by focussing on the large, commanding figure of Mike Coopland. He had questioned her calmly and deliberately in the session before lunch. His questions, as expected, had been about the night Ethan Hall had invaded their home.

She realised he was using them to lead her, step by step, through her experience; using them to help her keep her thoughts on track; giving her the time and space to tell her story to the jury. On several occasions she found herself drawn to look at them as she spoke. Two of the women smiled gently and nodded with, what Anne-Marie took to be, encouragement whenever their eyes met. Three of the men also seemed to be explicitly sympathetic. Of the others, several avoided her deliberately by looking down or writing notes.

After each answer, Mike was there again. Standing between her and Ethan Hall. Giving her the opportunity to add more detail, or clarify a point, or move the story along.

She had quickly lost track of time, caught in the repetitive nature of the interaction.

Mike asked his brief, easy to understand questions. She replied with as much detail as she could remember and, often, levels of emotion she simply couldn't control. Once he had asked if she needed to take a break. She had shaken her head vigorously and urged him to continue.

He had.

As she spoke, the event she was reliving began to merge in her mind with the event she had kept secret. At times she had to cut her answer short and start again. Too often she was reminded of the fact that her husband was not present. He had promised her he would stay in the house and do nothing. She could only hope he was being true to his word.

In the end it came to a sudden and obvious stop. Mike had no more questions to ask. She had nothing more to tell.

The lunch break had passed in a blur.

Now she was here again. In the same room. In the same seat.

With Ethan Hall looking at her. Saying nothing. Giving her time to remember.

'The truth is inside you, swirling and swelling and soon to come out. Isn't it?'

'It...it can't. It mustn't.'

She heard the words and realised they were hers. Everyone heard them. Some jurors looked at each other questioningly. One man scowled.

Ethan Hall cocked his head to one side. 'Who are you talking to?'

'Erm...myself. Myself. I'm sorry. I was just, erm...'

'What can't or mustn't happen?'

'Nothing! Really. Honestly. I apologise. I'm ready to begin.'

She saw his eyes light up.

'You are sure you're ready?'

He left his mouth open. She could see the tip of his tongue. She wanted to scream.

'Yes.'

'Good.' He rubbed his hands together. He paused again.

'This is the place where intimacies are revealed...'

'No, please!'

This time some jurors gasped at her outburst. The Judge leaned forward and looked at her directly.

'Mrs Kline?'

'I apologise. Again. It's just, erm, difficult. I'm OK now. Thank you.'

'Very well.'

Anne-Marie turned back to face the room. She was vaguely aware of Mike Coopland watching her with a concerned look on his face. Somehow he seemed much further away than this morning.

Ethan Hall turned his gaze towards the ceiling and asked, 'Do you trust your husband?'

'I, er...Yes. Yes, of course I do. He is a great man. A trustworthy man.'

'And you believe that firmly?'

'Yes.'

'Despite his claim he was untrustworthy?'

'I don't think he meant that.'

'Proof then of his untrustworthiness?'

'No! What I mean is, I don't think he was thinking clearly when

 FAITH

he said those things.'

'What makes you think that?'

'I, er, I think it was because of you.'

'Doing what exactly?'

'Influencing him, manipulating him into saying something he didn't believe.'

'Were you in court then?'

'No.'

'So how can you know?'

'Because I know my husband! Because of what he told me!'

'Which was?'

'That you...You...Used your skills...To make your words...'

'To make my words do what?'

Anne-Marie glanced down. Her hands were clenched in her lap, veins pressing against white skin. Beneath her jacket her blouse was damp against her shoulder blades. She couldn't say it. She couldn't repeat what Marcus had said. It would take her far too close to her own secret. She couldn't risk the glass shattering.

'To make him claim things that weren't true.' She said finally.

'That is your untrustworthy husband's claim?'

'You know it's the truth!'

'Can you read my mind?'

'No!' Anne-Marie shook her head angrily.

'Do you have any evidence?'

'No!'

Ethan gestured airily with both hands, looking around the court as he did so. 'Have you ever been here before?'

'What?'

'Have you ever been here before?'

'No. No, of course not.'

'So you don't know this place?'

'This is the place where intimacies are revealed...'

'No!'

'Are you trustworthy, Mrs Kline?'

'Yes!'

'How would you define trustworthiness?'

'It's honesty, reliability. When a person is trustworthy it means that people believe what they say and expect them to keep their promises, to honour their commitments.'

'And people believe that of you?'

'Yes. I'm sure people who know me well would say that I am reliable and honest.'

'Trustworthy?'

'Yes.'

'And you've never been here before?'

'No.'

'And your evidence can be trusted?'

'Yes. Absolutely.'

'Excellent!' Ethan beamed. 'How many times have we met?'

'What?' Anne-Marie felt the room contract around her.

'How many times have we met?'

'I, er, I wouldn't call what happened at our home a meeting. I just saw you and what you were doing to my husband.'

'So your answer is?'

Anne-Marie looked at Mike Coopland. He was further away than ever. She was alone. Cast adrift. One question. One moment in time.

I would willingly shorten my life to avoid all of this.

How wrong she had been. She would sooner be dead.

'Mrs Kline, how many times?'

Ethan Hall was the only person she could see with clarity. Everything about him appeared gentle, soft, verging on sadness.

She managed to hate him for just a few more seconds and then all her strength was gone.

She spoke because she had to. 'Once. We have met once.'

'Where?'

'In the rented house where my husband and I are currently living.'

She heard the noise build and move around the courtroom. She watched Ethan wait, calmly, until it was silenced.

'When did we meet?'

'After you escaped from the hospital. Not long before you were arrested.'

The noise was louder this time. The silence even more noticeable.

'And what happened when we met?'

Anne-Marie's eyes roamed the room. There was no way out. Mike Coopland shot into focus. He looked smaller and weaker than she remembered him. She thought he looked terrified, but she couldn't be sure. She couldn't be sure of anything apart from the weight of the silence and the damage she was about to cause.

'What happened, Mrs Kline?'

Anne-Marie looked down at her hands. They were lifeless, palm down on her thighs. The same shiny pink nails as in her dream. She forced herself to look up, to face him, to face them all.

'You cured me of cancer,' she said.

And the silence broke.

PART THREE
FAITH

CHAPTER 39

THURSDAY - TRIAL DAY 4
7pm

There is a difference between sure and certain.

I said that at the very beginning.

Sure is more certain than reasonable doubt and less certain than certain.

The herd thinks these are all matters of fact. That's what they are taught. It's the greatest of all lies. Feelings come first. Feelings turn some thoughts into those things the herd calls Beliefs. When a member of the herd says they are 'Sure' they are caught somewhere between hoping and believing. When a member of the herd says they are 'Certain' those hopes and beliefs have grown and thickened like cataracts, blinding them.

For these people – for you - the only thing that is reasonable is, indeed, Doubt.

You know little.

Your beliefs are flawed.

You place your hope in those leaders who tell you the easy story and make you feel good.

You do everything you can to deny the Doubt that is gnawing inside you.

You fill yourselves with thoughts and hopes and beliefs. You bury yourselves beneath your possessions. You disappear for a while behind the drugs of your choice. Every one of you turned into so many contradictory and competing parts. Every one of you trying to deny the Reasonable Doubt that is your only birthright.

It's the universal cover-up.

Making you all so available to me.

The only challenge I face is to resist the boredom.

Long ago I stopped being excited at what I could make you do. By how easy it was. It's easier now, of course. You are more desperate. You share your desperation in so many ways. You repeat yourselves and pretend you are different and pretend you are important through so many different channels. You shout your anger and your outrage and your immature conclusions around the world.

Whilst I make you feel grateful for the impending chaos.

If I had chosen to be an obvious leader in the way of Marcus Kline many of you would have followed me to the ends of the earth. You would have been grateful for the way I removed your Doubt, believed what I taught you to believe, proved your faith by acting as I encouraged.

Only I don't need to hear you chanting my name.

There are better ways to make things spread.

Nature teaches us so.

There are weeds and vines that can grow up to four metres in just ten weeks, their roots underground spreading nearly twice as far in the same time.

From a seed to a monster silently, in darkness, so quickly.

Such a beautiful lesson!

Missed by you all. Lost behind your noise and your stench.

The man they sent against me uses his fake-confidence as perfume to cover his Doubt. He believes it protects him. He believes no one knows. Only I smell him better than the best hunting dog ever could. For all his pomp he is no different than the rest.

He is Doubt-full.

I, however, have no Doubt. That is why my feelings are different

to yours, why my mind is different.
  I am never only sure.
  Certainty is my companion.
  My only one.
  And I can see more clearly than you can possibly imagine.

CHAPTER 40

THURSDAY - TRIAL DAY 4
7.07pm

The Piano and Pitcher was even busier than usual. Mike Coopland didn't know why and he didn't care. His capacity to care had been syphoned into a single place.

'How far away does your family feel right now?' He asked Brian Kaffee. 'Emotionally, where are they?'

'Miles away.' Kaffee pulled at his already open shirt collar. 'When we are winning, or when we've won, they seem miles away until I get home and then I just want to hug them and tell them what's happened and spend an appropriate amount of time with them. When it's like this, they're so far over the horizon it's almost impossible to remember what they look like. How awful is that?'

'It's awful. And it's the same for me, too.' Mike picked up the bottle of Malbec and poured them both a large glass. It was their third bottle. Incredibly, Kaffee was matching him swallow for swallow. 'But when was it ever like this? Tell me, when have you ever had a couple of days in court like the last two?'

'I never have. I've never seen or felt anything like it. You?'

'No.' Mike had a drink.

Kaffee joined him. 'Do you think he hypnotised her into saying what she did?'

'No. I think it was the truth. I think she simply couldn't lie.'

'As trustworthy as she professed to be?'

'Sadly, yes.'

'So Ethan Hall played us?'

'He certainly did. When he asked Marcus if he might also use hypnosis to heal, he was preparing the way for what he knew Anne-Marie would say. When he made Marcus admit his supposed untrustworthiness, he was doing the same again. Contradictions and contrasts. Time-honoured ways of discrediting the witnesses who are harmful to your case, whilst at the same time crediting those who are supportive. It's all the more powerful when the witness who is suddenly supporting you was supposed to be on the other side.'

'So you believe he actually cured her of terminal cancer?'

'Honestly, I'm at a point where I'm prepared to believe anything. Intellectually I can't make sense of it at all. Experientially I have nothing to compare it to.'

'But?'

'But if I was on a jury and asked to make a decision, I'd say that he cured her.'

'How sure are you?'

'Sure enough. You know as well as I do, sometimes the evidence leads you to the conclusion that the improbable actually happened. When that happens you have to re-jig your own mindset and run with it.'

'When was the last time you ran anywhere?' Kaffee forced a smile.

'Fair point. I'm not so much running towards this conclusion, as being forced in its direction. I didn't believe Peter Jones when he first warned me about the danger Ethan Hall posed in the courtroom. I didn't accept the hypnosis thing, and I know you didn't either. Now I'm certain that he hypnotised Marcus into saying what he did. And if he can do that to Marcus Kline, then what the hell can he do with the rest of us?'

'But doesn't this all go together to prove that he is the threat, the killer, that we say he is?'

'That's irrelevant. We're back to the point that we've built our case on circumstantial evidence. The only direct witness we've got, apart from Marcus himself, is Anne-Marie who, admittedly, is credible to the jury and said she saw him with Marcus. She couldn't say, though, that she saw him attacking her husband. And she did say that, whilst on the run from the police, he went out of his way to save her life. As for the other two murders, we're even further away from those than when we started.' Mike reached angrily for his wine; some of it ran down his chin as he drank. 'I should never have pushed on the charges the way I did.'

'You pushed because you believe in justice! You know, justice - that quaint old notion I'm sure the British must have invented because it's too damned good for it to have originated anywhere else. That's why we're here. That's why we have times in our lives when even our families seem distant. We can't give up on it now.'

'I'm not giving up on it, I just can't see a way to undo the damage that's been done. I fear I've fucked us all.'

'You haven't. It isn't over yet. And if I may remind you of our favourite film, Tom Cruise as the delectable Lieutenant Kaffee went through just such a mid-trial slump before nailing Jack Nicholson.'

'But he still didn't get the verdict he was after.'

'Not quite. He did better than anyone thought he would, though.'

'And that was with Aaron Sorkin writing the script for him. I'm increasingly coming to think that our scriptwriter is Ethan Hall.'

'Then, with all due respect, that's the thinking you've got to change. This isn't a film. It's real life. And it's a form of real life you – we – are very good at. So you've got to get your mind into gear and start doing the things that only you can.'

'That's easy for you to say.'

'I know. And I haven't got a clue what those things are, but that's your job. Mine is to remind you that you can work it out and to get you back up on your feet.'

Mike raised his glass. 'Here's to friends like you.' He drank deeply.

Kaffee joined the toast. They were both thoughtful for a moment. Mike looked out, across the bar. Kaffee swirled the wine in his glass.

'So she's carried her Ethan Hall secret for over six months now,' he said. 'Poor girl. It must have been tearing apart, especially given who her husband is.'

'Yeah.' Mike took another drink of his wine. 'God alone knows what sort of conversation they're having right now.'

CHAPTER 41

THURSDAY - TRIAL DAY 4
7.37pm

They were sitting in silence, as they had only recently.

This time the silence was filled with more active, dangerous emotion. They were both creating it. They were both in danger of becoming its victim.

He was struggling to look at her because he hated himself so much, because of what his failure meant, because he was terrified that he might have already started hating her for not telling him.

She simply couldn't handle the fact that, beyond all of the other swirling emotions, she felt grateful. Grateful that Ethan Hall hadn't asked the next question. Grateful for the chance to hold on to the bigger secret, the one that was destroying her life as surely as the cancer once was.

Something in the back of her mind was telling her the challenge they both faced was saying the first thing. Offering the first explanation. Sharing the first insight. Just starting.

The same part of her mind was insisting that silence was the enemy. That soon it would grow beyond their control. That it would spread, reaching out into the places they valued most, capable of corrupting the very foundations of their relationship.

So Anne-Marie began by saying, 'I didn't ask him to.'

He replied more swiftly than she expected.

'It would have been a wise thing to do. Any port in a storm. Life at all costs.'

'He didn't give me any choice.'

'He rarely does. And then it's only to increase the pain.'

'I didn't even realise I was hypnotised until...until later. It was so different from...'

He looked at her.

She changed direction. 'Have you ever been hypnotised so deeply?'

'Only by him.'

'Of course.' She felt stupid. How could she have forgotten?

'He is irresistible,' he said. 'I fully understand that. When he failed to kill me he chose to punish and hurt me in different ways. Curing you when he knew I couldn't was, in one sense, the most powerfully twisted thing he could do. Obviously I wanted – want – you to be healthy and well more than anything else in life. But when it feels as if the Devil has made it happen everything gets conflicted.'

'Do you wish he hadn't done it?'

'God, no! That's the point. I was delighted when you were told you were in remission. You know that. And I would have done anything to make it happen.'

'Even asked Ethan Hall for help?'

Marcus shook his head. 'I could never have trusted him. There's nothing he could have said that would have convinced me it was safe to let him near you. He isn't a healer. And curing you doesn't make him one.'

'Really?'

'Healing is as much a state of mind as it is actions taken. He healed you to hurt me and to satisfy his own ego. You were secondary to his personal needs.'

'What about you? In the past?'

'What about me?'

'To what extent was all the good you did driven by your own personal and professional needs?'

That stopped the conversation. He sank back into his armchair and closed his eyes.

She forced herself to wait.

After what seemed like an age he said, 'You're right. I didn't realise it at the time. I think I was continually drip-feeding my ego and it grew accordingly. Bit by bit. Until it could barely fit into my office.'

'Or anywhere else.' She risked a smile.

He returned it. 'Or anywhere else.'

'Despite that, I don't think you are remotely like Ethan Hall.'

'That's good to know.' Another smile.

'Seriously! You're right to say that genuine healing and helping grows out of a certain mindset, and it's definitely a state of mind that horrible man doesn't possess. He saved my life and yet I agree with you wholeheartedly – he is awful and he isn't to be trusted.'

'So you don't feel grateful?'

'Grateful for what?' Her mind flashed back to the trial, to the moment when she was sure he was going to ask that next question.

'For your cure.'

'Yes. No. Maybe. I'm as conflicted as you. For different reasons perhaps, but...' She shrugged.

'At least now it's out in the open. No more secrets that you have to carry. And you could have told me, you know. I might not have responded well initially – I think we can both accept that without debate – but we would have worked it out. Just as we are doing now.'

'There is nothing you can't share with me,' he went on. 'The fact that I couldn't make the difference with your cancer doesn't mean that I'm not here for you. Always. I need you to be sure of that.'

'I am. And I'm always here for you, too. We're a team.'

She needed him to stop talking secrets.

'Mike was as nice as he could be,' she said. 'Nicer than I had any right to expect after my testimony. He told me the justice system depended on honesty; that whilst the courts dealt with crimes, telling the truth wasn't one of them. Peter, of course, was as lovely and supportive as ever.'

Marcus saw her skin colour slightly; the first shift away from the grey pallor she had carried since returning home. 'Yes, our good DCI saves all his harsh words for me.'

This time she laughed. 'Tough love.'

'I believe so.' He considered. 'Maybe all love is tough.'

'In different ways. All love is beautiful too.'

'In different ways.' He could feel his usual self tiptoeing forward. ' I fear there's now a real chance Ethan Hall will be found not guilty.'

'I know. We could well have combined to give out greatest enemy the freedom he craves.'

'And to let down Peter and Mike.'

'And all the others.'

'Yes.'

They both thought of Simon.

'If I had to do it again tomorrow,' she said, 'I'd answer the same questions in the same way.'

'And I couldn't prevent myself from doing the same either.'

'Sooner or later he will make a mistake.'

'I agree. The problem is, it needs to be sooner; we don't have later.'

'Maybe there's a third option.' She straightened.

'Which is?'

'Before. Maybe he made a mistake before he was arrested. Maybe there's something just waiting to be uncovered?'

'But Peter and his team have been through everything already.'

'True. But that doesn't mean they found everything. They didn't know he visited me, for example.'

'Because you hadn't told them.'

'For all sorts of good reasons.'

'So you think there could be other people out there who haven't come forward?'

'Why not?' In fact, the more I think about it the more likely it seems. That man couldn't isolate himself completely and wouldn't want to. He's the master manipulator, right? Isn't he always going to need a victim or a plaything?'

'Yes, he is.' Marcus stood up and began to pace the room. 'He needs to feed his ego just as I always did. As I still do, I guess. We can't be the only people he's targeted since he got out of hospital. We just think we are because - '

' – Because we're wrapped up in our own lives and no one else's!'

'Exactly.'

'So what shall we do?'

'I'll call Peter and tell him our thoughts.'

'I'm sure he'll be pleased to hear from you.'

'Yeah. I'll brace myself for some more tough love.'

They chuckled.

'Maybe it isn't over yet,' Marcus said. 'Maybe we still have a chance.'

CHAPTER 42

THURSDAY - TRIAL DAY 4
7.51pm

Peter Jones had assembled the team, seven Detective Constables minus DS McNeill who had not yet returned from meeting his CHIS, for an emergency briefing. He didn't use the word *emergency* when talking to them, even though he knew that's exactly what the situation was. Instead he talked of urgency and great importance.

'The bottom line,' he said, 'is that Mike's case is falling apart through no fault of his own. So we need to focus all of our attention for the next day or two on that time period when Ethan Hall was off the grid. We need to find something that we haven't managed to yet. And there will be something. I guarantee you.'

'Why are you so sure Boss?' One of the younger Detective Constables asked the question.

'Because it's in his nature to keep moving after prey. And because we now know he visited Anne-Marie and that he also visited Nicholas Evans - '

' – But Evans is denying it.'

'I don't agree. Not quite, anyway. He's saying they never met, but I think that's because he genuinely can't remember what happened. I don't think he's deliberately denying something he knows to be true. Ethan Hall messes with people's minds. He does that as well as causing them physical harm. Sadly, I'm sure that Nic's denial and outrage at our contacting him are both honest responses.'

'From a damaged mind?'

'From a confused mind, yes.'

'But he didn't leave Anne-Marie Wells confused or forgetful.'

'That wouldn't have suited his purposes. He needed her to remember that he cured her. That added to her pain, to the punishment. And beyond how it made Anne-Marie feel, I'm sure he was hoping that one way or another it might force her and Marcus apart.'

'How so?'

'Well, if she had kept the secret – and, let's face it, it was a huge one – then she was committed to carrying a terrible burden for the rest of her life. And given Marcus's skill set it was likely that sooner or later he'd realise she was hiding something. If he then asked her about it and she lied to him, he'd know. Then, no doubt, he'd start wondering what she was hiding. Relationships have floundered on smaller rocks than that.'

'On the other hand, if she had told him what happened, if she had admitted to it straight away, she was risking a very different kind of problem. I know Marcus well. He loves his wife as much as any man could. But that wouldn't prevent him from struggling with the fact that Ethan had saved her. In fact, I'm sure he'd recognise it for the attack on him it was meant to be.'

'Boss, I still think there's a major problem we face in uncovering something new.'

It was Janet Harris, the most experienced DC on the team. Peter trusted her as much as he did McNeill.

'If what you're saying about Nic is right, and I'm sure the odds are that it is, then it's very possible that anyone Hall targeted during those missing days had their memory wiped clean before he left them. Or, even worse, they might be dead and still undiscovered.'

'It's a very fair point. Marcus struggled to remember things when he was in the witness box with Ethan questioning him. And we are certain, but still lacking the hard evidence to prove, that Ethan's a killer. As I said, though, the bottom line is that we don't have a choice in the matter. We need to find something or someone more, or else in all probability Ethan goes free. So I need you to retrace, revisit, and re-evaluate every possibility. Everything, including sleep, is secondary right now. Clear?'

'Yes Boss!'

The team rose to their feet and began to leave the room.

'Janet?'

She turned back. 'Yes Boss?'

'You're right. I think the odds are against us. However, as you know, I've always been a lucky copper and I don't see why my luck should run out now. Do you?'

'Absolutely not Boss.' She grinned.

'Good. Let's make sure the team is filled with optimists rather than realists until this over. OK?'

'Understood.'

As Janet turned to go, DS McNeill arrived. She nodded as they passed, but he ignored her. She guessed the worried look on his face meant his mind was elsewhere. She made a point of closing the door behind her.

'What is it?' Peter also recognised the look.

'Bad, is what it is Boss.'

'That's what we deal with here. So get on with it.'

'The CHIS says there's been a hit put out on you.'

'Go on.'

'The word is that Karl Brent thinks this is a good time to get his revenge. So he's got Calvin to recruit someone.'

'Why is this such a good time?'

'The *Pass it on* killings. The aim is to make your murder look like one of those. It's based on the thinking that there are enough people out there who believe coppers are corrupt and deserve what they get.'

'They can't know how long the *Pass it on* killings will continue for, so logic says they're going make their move pretty damn quickly.'

'That's why the CHIS said it was vital, Boss.'

'Well done, Detective Sergeant.' A crooked smile. The briefest moment of silent introspection. Then, 'I don't suppose by any chance we know who, what, where and when?'

'We've got bits of information and he's going to see if he can find out more. He's shakey at the minute, though. For all sorts of obvious reasons.'

'Yeah. At the moment we're all on a tightrope trying to go at full speed.' Peter sighed. 'Right. Let's keep this away from the team. They've got enough on their plates as it is. We'll talk through in detail what you've got, then we'll engage with other appropriate colleagues.'

'Roger that.'

'And if it all goes wrong and they manage to shoot me, there's just one thing we can hope for.'

'What's that Boss?'

'That they don't hit anything vital.'

CHAPTER 43

FRIDAY - TRIAL DAY 5
2.54pm

Calvin Brent was furious. He glared at Matt, who was standing awkwardly on the other side of his desk.

'What do you mean, you couldn't remember a damn thing?'

'I jus' couldn't. As soon as I got in the witness box, I 'ad t'look at 'im. Y'know, Ethan. There was nothin' I could do abowt it. My eyes just went straight to 'im. Like a magnet. An' after that I couldn't answer anythin'. It still feels like my mind's bin rubbed clean. Like a blackboard.'

'But it wasn't just that, was it?' Calvin shouted the question and didn't wait for the answer. 'The only thing you said you could remember was that you'd been feeling suicidal and your friend – your fucking friend! – Ethan Hall had been trying to talk you out of sticking a knife in yourself! Where the fuck did that come from?'

'I don' know. But I believed it at the time. 'Onest, Boss! It were like the only memory I could see in my mind's eye.'

'I got Marcus Kline to prepare you for this! Which, given how fucking useless he was as a witness, should have warned me!' Calvin slammed the desk with his right palm. 'What the fuck am I going to say to my dad? Eh? How do I explain to him that Ethan Hall is winning the trial?'

'Ethan 'All's a freak, Boss. Looking at 'im is bad enough, but when 'e speaks t'ya somethin' changes in yo'r 'ead. 'Onestly. If 'e 'asn't done it to ya it's 'ard to imagine.'

'I don't want to have to imagine anything! What I pay you for – what I pay everybody for – is results! By which I mean, the results that I fucking want not the results that someone else does. How difficult is that to understand?'

'It isn't Boss.' Matt hung his head.

'So, tell me, how many chances have I given you, Matt?'

'I, er, I don't know.'

'The answer should be none. I should never have had to give you any second chances because you should never have fucked up! But you have! If you'd managed to stay in control of Hall in the first place, we'd never have been in this fucking mess! He'd have been dead by now and you would still have had my trust.'

Matt blanched. 'What makes ya think ya can't trust me Boss?'

'Your fucking failures! Right now I wouldn't even trust you to drive a car in a straight line.' Calvin hit the desk a second time. Matt took a step back. 'So here's want I want you to do,' Calvin lowered his voice. 'I want you to fuck off. I want you to stay out of the pubs. I want you to keep out of sight. I want you to do fuck-all until either I get in touch with you, or someone else does. Do you reckon you can manage to remember that?'

'Yes Boss.'

'You'd fucking better.' Calvin waved his hand in the direction of the door. Matt was gone within seconds. Calvin took a deep breath, opened the right-hand side desk drawer picked up a mobile phone and made a call.

' 'Ello?' The voice was thin, cautious.

'Darren. It's me.' Calvin waited. God help the little fuck if he didn't know who me was. Even though he was way too far down the food chain to ever expect a personal call.

'Mr Brent! Right! Yeah…That's a…a surprise.' The voice thinned even more, caution now giving way to fear.

Just as it should.

'Are you on your own?'

'Y-yes, sir. Yeah. I'm at 'ome.'

'Good.' Calvin took his time. Gave the fear chance to grow. Fear sharpened the mind. That's what his dad said. And he needed Darren's mind to be as sharp as he could get it. 'Two things you need to know, Darren. First thing is that I'm going to ask you some questions and I expect your answers to be honest and detailed. Understand that?'

'Yes, sir.'

'Good. Second thing is if you ever mention this conversation to anyone, I will get to hear of it. And then I will be very pissed off. Do you understand that?'

'Y-Yes, sir. Of course. I won't say nothin'.'

'Right. For reasons that are none of your concern, I want to know everything that you and Ethan Hall did when he stayed with you. I'm talking about both times. The time when he'd escaped from hospital and the time way before that when he was still a nobody. So take your mind back and focus really fucking hard.'

'This last time 'e wasn't with me fer long.'

'Don't tell me what I already know and don't answer questions I haven't fucking asked!'

'Sorry, Mr Brent.'

'Right. Let's start with that first time, years ago. Was it clear then that he was dangerous?'

'No. Erm, I mean, not what ya'd call dangerous. More like 'e was just weird. An' 'e thought 'e was better than the rest of us. An' 'e kept to 'imself.'

'Was he doing any of this hypnosis shit?'

' 'E wasn't famous for it, like 'e is now.'

'I didn't ask you that.' Calvin hardened his tone.

'Sorry. No. What I meant was 'e was doing stuff, but it was more like 'e was practisin'. Working' stuff owt. If ya know what I mean?'

'Did he ever do anything to you? Did you ever see him do anything to anyone else?'

' 'E didn't do owt t'me, because we were mates. An' I made sure I never got on the wrong side of 'im. I didn't actually see 'im do owt to anyone else either, but there was this story going round that 'e brought a local tart back to the flat and hypnotised 'er into layin' on the bed an' doin' 'erself. Story was that 'e never touched 'er, but 'e kept 'er there for two days. By the time 'e'd finished she was like she'd been nearly fucked t'death.'

'Were you in the flat at the time?'

'Nah. I was in Carlisle.'

'Do you remember who the woman was?'

'Sorry, Mr Brent. She was just a local tart, willing' to pull a few tricks fer some drug money.'

'Anything else from that time?'

'Nothin' that springs t' mind. One day Ethan just disappeared and I never 'eard from 'im or saw 'im again until he turned up 'ere after the 'ospital thing.'

'Had he changed from those earlier days?'

'Yeah. It was like 'e'd turned 'imself into whatever it was 'e'd bin workin' on. You know? If I 'ad'n't known we were mates I'd of bin worried abowt 'avin' 'im around.'

'But you, being the man you are, weren't worried?' Calvin made no attempt to hide his sarcasm.

'Well, not worried as such, but, ya know, careful. Like when 'e wanted t'meet you, I didn't try an' argue with 'im. Besides, I figured you'd want t'see 'im for yorself.'

'It's good to know you were making decisions on my behalf.'

'No! No, sir. Not makin' decisions for ya, just tryin' t'be 'elpful.'

'Well, be helpful now and tell me what you did to keep on Ethan Hall's good side.'

'I just did whatever 'e said. Tried to 'elp 'im as best I could.'

'And when he came to your house, he didn't bring anything with him? He only had the clothes he was standing up in?'

'Yeah. Tha's right. Well...Sort of.'

Calvin heard the fear increase some more. He said nothing. The silence, he knew, was as punishing as a punch to the stomach. After only several seconds, Darren's words came rushing out.

'See the thing is 'e 'ad a notebook with 'im. Said 'e'd collected it after 'e left the 'ospital. 'E'd 'idden it somewhere. Didn't say where. Anyway, when 'e was owt the 'ouse, I 'ad a look round the bedroom 'e was usin'. I found the notebook 'idden behind the chest a drawers.'

'And?'

'It was full of 'is writin'. All sorts of shit t'be 'onest. It was like 'e was writin' down all the thoughts in 'is mind. Abowt 'ow 'e was different from the rest of us an' what 'e was goin' t'do to us.'

'Do to who?'

'E wasn' really clear. 'E kept writin' abowt the 'erd. An' 'ow 'e 'ated the 'erd. It was like 'e 'ad this big plan 'e was makin' 'appen. In one bit 'e even says there's a war comin'.'

'A war?'

'Yeah. It was all madness an' stuff.'

'What did you do with the notebook?'

'I put it back a' course. Didn' say nothin' abowt it.'

He used the silence again.

'But I, er, took photos of every page wi' me phone. Thought it might act as a bit of insurance or somethin' if things ever got a bit tricky between us.'

'You've still got them?'

'Yeah. Yeah, Mr Brent I 'ave.'

Calvin clenched his fist in triumph. 'Send copies over to me on this number. Do it as soon as I hang up.'

'Will do, Mr Brent. Are they, d'ya think, valuable?'

'They might help me solve a problem that I've got. And they're not your photos any more Darren. They're mine. Understand?'

'Yeah. Yeah a' course. 'Appy to 'elp Mr Brent. Ya know tha'.'

'Good. Make sure you remember what I told you at the start of our conversation.'

'I won't say a word, Mr Brent.'

'Good man. Now send me the photos.' Calvin ended the call.

Ethan Hall's personal notebook! All it needed to contain was one thing that proved he was a killer and the plan was back on track. What a result that would be!

Calvin poured himself a large measure of Blue Label and raised the glass in a toast to his good fortune.

CHAPTER 44

FRIDAY - TRIAL DAY 5
10.21pm

Mike Coopland swayed unsteadily on his feet, stared at the blurred image of the witness, and asked, 'What the hell happens now?'

The witness gurgled. It sounded to Mike as if he had started to laugh but a sudden inhalation had choked it back.

'Answer the question.'

The witness took a deep breath and replied. 'You know as well as I do. You carry on to the bitter end. And it's going to be very fucking bitter, you can be sure of that. So, what happens now is that you stay drunk for most of the weekend and, through your drunken haze, you prepare for your final witnesses – the Pathologist then Peter Jones. By the close of play on Monday you'll be finished. In more ways than one.'

'The truth is,' the witness went on, 'that unless a miracle happens there won't be a case to answer. Certainly not on the murder charges. Not after what's happened. When this point is raised you will, of course, fight your corner not believing a word of it and Mulvenny will rule against you. Everything connected to Marcus Kline has become so confused Christ alone knows what will happen there.'

'Regardless, you will have quite royally fucked up the most significant case of your career. Everyone who thought you'd pushed too hard on the charges will tell you. All the people who will now doubt your ability will say nothing. Not to your face. But the word will be shared. The result is inevitable. Your reputation will be in tatters.'

Mike rocked back on his heels. Took another slurp of Malbec. Blinked and tried to bring the witness into focus. 'Was he unbeatable, or did I make too many mistakes?'

Mike heard his own question and counted the words automatically. Ten.

Ten!

Any barrister who had studied the Hampel Method of Advocacy knew that short questions were the ideal. He had taken it a stage further and limited himself to six words or less. It was what he taught when providing Advocacy training.

Six words maximum.

Use it to build up a rhythm. Create a pace and a flow. Make it easy for the jury to understand and follow. Sequence the questions so the witness can tell the story you want them to easily and clearly. Sometimes that's the story they want to tell you. Sometimes it's the story they are trying to avoid. Either way, six words maximum, never a leading question, always sequenced well.

Sandwich this between an opening speech that gets the jury on your side and a closing speech that reminds them they were right to trust you all along and, if you started with a fighting chance, nine times out of ten you get the result.

So why had he just asked a ten-word question?

'What does it matter?' He said out loud. 'Six words or less has failed. So fuck it, let's ask it again, "Was he unbeatable, or did I make too many mistakes?"'

His reflection in the large, lounge mirror answered immediately.

'He is unbeatable and you made only one mistake. That was in thinking you could beat him. No one could have. That won't stop all the others deciding what you did wrong and what they would have done differently, but he'd have stuffed them too. Just as easily as he has you.'

The answer didn't make him feel any better.

The reflection went on, 'And you're wrong when you say that six words or less failed. They failed you. They didn't fail Ethan Hall. He used them perfectly.'

'But how did he know to do that?'

'You taught him. Whatever other study he's done in the last six months to prepare himself for trial, you gave him the final and most important lesson. You showed him how to examine a witness. He just watched you, listened to how you construct and use questions, and then followed your lead. The Trojan Horse in this conflict was your own skill.'

'I don't want to go back into court on Monday.'

'That's a first.'

'Well, I don't.'

'Tough shit. It isn't over until the fat barrister sings. I've heard you say that countless times over the last decade.'

'This fat barrister plays guitar better than he sings.'

'That's the point, isn't it?'

Mike took another slurp. 'I can't think of any way I can turn this around. The Pathologist's evidence is ultimately of little significance – which is a first. Peter can only help me wrap up the prosecution's case and at the moment we might as well be wrapping up an empty box. Worse than that, I'm now genuinely worried about what Ethan Hall might do with him.'

'The only reason he left this afternoon's witnesses alone is because they were insignificant in the grand scheme of things. The Pathologist will be the same. But my final witness, my final offering to him, is the DCI who arrested him.'

'What do you think he's going to do to him? Eh? Whatever Ethan

Hall did to Nic, assuming Pete is right about that, is only going to be the first act. Jesus Christ! He could make Pete say anything, whilst he's under oath! And I don't know how to stop him.'

The reflection clearly didn't have a response. Instead it emptied the wine glass in one urgent swallow and blurred some more.

Mike Coopland staggered into the kitchen in search of another bottle.

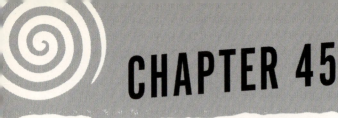

CHAPTER 45

FRIDAY - TRIAL DAY 5
11.41pm

DCI Peter Jones turned the unmarked police car left off a quiet Bulwell street into a dead-end road lined with graffiti-covered garages.

'He's here Boss.' Kevin McNeill pointed at the dark shape of a car parked, facing out, at the far end of the road. 'Ready for a quick exit, by the look of it.'

'Yeah. He's not getting one of those tonight.' Peter flashed his headlights. The signal was returned.

'You're not thinking of doing this interview in Morse Code, are you?' McNeill chuckled.

'Stick to your day job, Detective Sergeant.' Peter eased the car to a halt less than ten metres in front of the other. 'I'm in the front next to him, you're in the back seat.'

'Got it.'

'Right. Let's go and make a difference.'

They got out and walked slowly and deliberately towards the parked car.

'Stinks of piss out here,' McNeill said. 'Lets hope that now he's seen you, he's not shitting himself.'

'We do this in a sewer if we have to.'

'I'd say we're not far short of that already.'

Peter rapped his knuckles on the front passenger window. He heard the click as the doors unlocked. He got inside and settled into the seat with a smile on his face and a coldness in his eyes. He gave the man next to him chance to see both as McNeill climbed in behind them.

'DCI Jones!' The man's surprise was tangible. He glanced back at McNeill. 'I thought that, er, we wa'n't s'pposed t'meet.'

'Unless I decided it was necessary. And tonight I decided it was.' Peter slapped his right palm down hard on the bigger man's left thigh. He smiled again, waiting a second to ensure he had his complete attention before continuing. 'I have some questions for you. Which must mean you have some answers for me. Now, DS McNeill could have asked you himself, but tonight I really wanted to impress on you just how important it is that we get the answers. So I thought I'd come along and listen to what you've got to say in person.'

'But, but wha' if I don' know the answers?' Another glance back at McNeill.

'Aah, but you do. That's the thing. This isn't a school test. I'm not here to try and catch you out. No, I'm only going to ask you questions that I know you have the answers to. And don't look so worried, Matt. You've done a great job for us so far. Under difficult circumstances. Mind you, if I hadn't saved you from Ethan Hall you would have been dead and buried months ago – don't know who'd have paid for the funeral, but it wouldn't have been Calvin Brent that's for sure – and we would have all moved on. So, let me begin by reminding you that you do owe me a very significant favour.'

'Yeah. I appreciate tha' Mr Jones.'

'I know you do, Matt. And, for very obvious reasons, I appreciate the help you are giving us, especially with regards to the threat on my life. However, challenging times call for the bravest of responses. That's why we're all here. You see, Matt, in challenging times you have to stand up and be accountable. You have to make it clear which side of the fence you are on. Are you on my side? Or are you on the other side? That's the most important thing people want to know in challenging times. You understand that. Right?'

Matt stared hard through the windscreen, his eyes flickering from side to side.

Peter slapped his thigh again.

'Good! Now, whilst the statement you gave about how you came to be taken hostage by Ethan Hall was duly accepted and filed, and the witnesses who corroborated your statement were all word perfect, we both know it was bullshit. We both know it was a big, fat lie that we couldn't disprove. So here's the first question that I know you have the answer to. What the fuck were you really up to with Ethan Hall before we came to your rescue?'

Matt swallowed. 'Wha' I told ya before was the truth.'

'Just like what you said in the courtroom today was the truth?'

'I couldn' 'elp tha'! 'E did somethin' t' my 'ead! Tha's dead straight Mr Jones.'

'OK, Matt. For a whole host of reasons I can believe that. You see, whilst I can only guess about any possible relationship between your Boss and Ethan Hall, I am certain that you would be delighted to see Hall behind bars for a very long time. I mean, let's face it, if Ethan get's a not guilty verdict – and, between you and me, that's looking very likely right now – then I wouldn't bet against him coming back to finish what he started with you. Eh? After all, you have shown him which side of the fence you're on where he's concerned. Haven't you? And there's nothing about him that suggests he's the forgiving type.'

'Talking of which, and the only way you can check that what I'm about to say is true is by asking DS McNeill, I'm not the forgiving type either. Not in challenging times. So if you don't help me put

Ethan Hall away, I won't be able to help you when he comes looking for you. It really is that simple. You are in that classic situation Matt, you know, between a rock and a hard place. The good thing, let me remind you, is that you do know the answer to my question. So you do have a way out.'

'Tell us what you know, Matt,' McNeill whispered, leaning forward, bringing his face close to the big man's shoulder. 'That's in your own best interest. That's what I'd do if I were in your shoes.'

'It i'n't tha' straight forwards, tho, is it?'

'Ultimately it is.' McNeill stayed close. 'In fact, the truth is you've already made your choice. You did that a while ago when you offered to provide us with information. Think about it! You're on our side now! And it's the safest place to be as long as no one knows you are with us and Ethan Hall is in prison. C'mon, Matt! Do what's best for yourself.'

McNeill sat back. Peter Jones didn't move. The enforcer's breath steamed the windscreen.

'This stays between us, right? If I tell ya, it won't mean tha' I 'ave t' appear anywhere or be seen with ya?'

'We just need information we can act on,' Peter said calmly. 'Just like you've given us before.'

'Right. OK. Well, I, er,' Matt rubbed his chin, 'I drove 'im to this guy's 'ouse.'

'You drove Ethan?'

'Yeah.'

'To what guy's house?'

'A bloke called Robin Campbell.'

'Why did Ethan want to see him?'

' 'E, er, didn' tell me. I didn' ask. I just took 'im there.'

'In whose car?'

'My own.' Matt turned to face McNeill. 'Look, I'm tellin' ya where I took 'im and' wha' 'e did. Tha's enough right?'

The DS didn't blink. 'There's no point asking me when my Boss is here.'

'And I am,' Peter Jones turned his eyes ice-cold again. 'So I expect you to talk only to me. And I expect you to answer questions, not ask the fuckers.'

Matt looked back at the DCI.

'OK, for now let's work on the assumption that you took him there in your own car,' Peter softened his voice and his gaze. 'What did he say or do with this Robin Campbell?'

'I wasn' there w'en they were talkin', I jus' came in at the end.'

'What had happened by then?'

'Campbell was unconscious. 'E'd 'ad some sort of attack, shit 'imself an' puked up an' everythin'. It was a right fuckin' mess.'

'And you're sure that Ethan Hall did that to him, that he didn't just arrive and find him that way?'

'Yeah. There's no doubt. Not from the way Ethan was talkin' afterwards.'

'Do you know why he did it?'

'No. Not really.' Matt hesitated. ' 'E 'ad 'is own reasons, I guess.'

'I'm sure he did,' Peter said dryly. 'What was the situation when you left?'

'It was the same. 'E was unconscious on the floor.'

'And Ethan didn't go back?'

'No.'

'Why not?'

' 'E didn't get chance to, did 'e? You nicked 'im.'

Peter nodded. The gaps in the story were significant, but understandable. A CHIS was nearly always obliged to tread that fine line between being useful and protecting themselves.

We're all on a tightrope trying to go at full speed.

'Ok, Matt. One last, easy question to end on.'

'Alright, Mr Jones.' Relief was evident in the big man's voice.

'Tell me, where does Mr Robin Campbell live?'

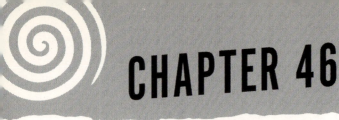

CHAPTER 46

FRIDAY - TRIAL DAY 5
Midnight

Marcus Kline had returned to the cold of the back garden.

He could feel the winter air beginning to numb his hands and face. He stamped his right foot then his left, rubbed both palms over his cheeks as if washing himself brusquely, felt the chill in the night touch him again as soon as he lowered his hands.

He had called Peter Jones earlier. He had told him that both he and Anne-Marie thought there might other victims as yet unidentified. He had talked of mistakes made before, rather than after. The response he had received was short and to the point.

'Good thinking.'

It had been clear he was talking to the DCI and not his friend.

Marcus blew a long out-breath into the darkness. It showed itself briefly, part cloud, part mist, before disappearing, absorbed into the vastness.

I was continually drip-feeding my ego.

Of all the things they had said to each other tonight, of all the things they had shared, that was the most significant; the root, the one at the very heart of the problems they had faced.

My ego.

How out of control had it become? How much worse would it have got if it hadn't been for Ethan Hall? How absolutely bloody crazy was that? Talk about learning from loss.

Marcus walked to the furthest edge of the garden. The grass

crunched beneath his feet. Something fluttered by, almost within reach. A dark cloud crossed the moon. It was hard to imagine that Spring was waiting it's turn.

He resisted the temptation to look back at the house. Instead he squatted down and touched the frozen earth.

All love is beautiful.

The second most important thing they had said was that they were a team. A team that might have broken apart completely if Ethan Hall had not dared them to confront themselves. Only they had met the challenge. Brought themselves back together.

From the brink.

Marcus let the earth numb his fingers even more. Winter, he considered, was Nature's ways of showing tough love. And there was beauty in winter just as there was in every season.

'Round and round we go,' he whispered. 'And this is the time for shedding, for the loss that precedes the new growth. We just have to learn how to deal with the exposure and the cold. We just have to survive for long enough, then we can move on. That's the way of it. We can't win every battle.'

He stood up, wiped his hands and blew out another long breath.

He imagined his ego was inside it.

CHAPTER 47

SATURDAY
10.23am

The good news was that Robin Campbell had not been reported dead. The bad news was that he no longer lived at the address given by Matt. But he had lived there. And with that as a starting point tracking him down hadn't proven to be a big deal.

If you wanted to be impossible to find, you needed a strong desire, a reliable network of contacts and some significant skill. Whilst Robin Campbell was clearly keen to hide, he had neither the network nor the ability to do so. It had taken McNeill three phone calls and the job was done.

He stood back now as DC Janet Harris knocked assertively on the door of a second floor apartment six roads back from the seafront at Skegness. It was opened a moment later by a slim, short man with thinning grey hair and a goatee beard.

'Yes?'

'Mr Campbell?' Janet asked the question.

'Yes.'

'I'm DC Harris,' Janet waved her ID card. 'This is my colleague, Detective Sergeant McNeill. Can we come in?'

'What's it about?'

'It's about an ongoing investigation that we believe you can help us with. So we would really appreciate your voluntary assistance.' Janet smiled and put her right hand on the door.

'Well, I suppose so. Although I only have a few minutes and I can't think there's anything I know that would be of benefit to the police.'

'We're paid to make those assessments, Mr Campbell. Thank you.' Janet stepped forward and he retreated before her.

Kevin closed the door behind them both and followed them into a large, square lounge. Janet sat without being asked in the centre of the dark blue, leather settee. Kevin chose one of the two matching armchairs. Campbell was the last to sit.

'Nice place,' Janet said, looking around the room. 'Been here long?'

'Some months now.' Campbell scratched at his right knee. 'So what, er, what is this investigation you think I might know something about?'

'It's a very serious matter.'

'Yes, but as I said - '

' – Mr Campbell, what was your involvement with Ethan Hall?' Kevin sat forward, clasping his hands, resting his forearms on his thighs. Janet relaxed back into the settee.

Campbell's eyes widened. 'I, erm, I don't know the man. Obviously I've read in the papers about his crimes and the trial, but that's all. I used to be an art dealer, I don't have anything to do with the criminal element.'

'Is that a fact?'

'Yes!' Campbell tried to sound indignant.

'Mr Campbell you implied that you are in a hurry and, frankly, so are we. So I'm going to do us both a favour and move this on quickly.' Kevin tapped his left foot on the carpeted floor. 'We know that Ethan Hall paid you a visit shortly before he was rearrested. We know that as a consequence of this meeting you were left unconscious. We know that he had plans to return before you regained consciousness. We believe his motive was not to reinstate your good health, but quite the opposite. We also believe he might walk free from court sometime soon, which means he'll be able to tie up any loose ends. We think you are one of those. Now, given all of that, why don't you fill in all the missing details? Starting with why Hall came after you in the first place.'

Campbell looked at Janet. She raised an eyebrow. Campbell looked back at Kevin.

'To be honest with you - '

' – That would be nice.'

'I, er, I don't actually know why Hall visited me. Really! I had never seen or heard of him before then.'

'Did you have any enemies at the time?'

'Erm, well, I had faced some financial difficulties. It's been a difficult few years for many of us in the art trade. I wasn't the only one who was finding it nearly impossible.'

'I'm sure you weren't. So what had you done, borrowed money?'

'Yes.'

'From whom?'

'The banks were refusing to help, so I went to a man called Calvin Brent.'

'Oh dear. Not the best choice of lender, Mr Campbell. How much did he give you?'

'Lots.' Campbell licked his lips. 'And with the interest he put on it, I was never going to catch up.'

'And Mr Brent was being demanding, was he?'

'Yes, but that's all I'm going to say with reference to him.'

'And then one day, right out of the blue, Ethan Hall knocked on your door?'

Campbell nodded. 'It was the strangest thing. As soon as I saw him it was like looking at someone you knew, but you couldn't quite remember where from. He said something, I genuinely can't remember what, and the next thing we were in my lounge and he was talking and all I could do was listen.'

'Can you remember anything he said?'

'He talked about my allergy. I'm seriously allergic to nuts. I have to be very careful.' Campbell's face and throat reddened slightly.

'And then?'

'He kept talking until I passed out. When I regained consciousness he had gone and I was in a terrible mess.' He blushed.

'You didn't report it?'

'No. I didn't want to make matters worse. I didn't want to get involved. So I moved. Quickly.'

'I see. I'm guessing Mr Brent hasn't discovered your new address yet?'

'No. So I'm not sure if that means I should stay here, or if it would be better to move on. Perhaps you can give me your professional opinion?'

'That's above our pay grade, Mr Campbell.' Kevin's face hardened. 'But I can tell you this, you are the victim of a serious crime perpetrated, if your account is true, by Ethan Hall. Given that, I need a formal written statement from you. You also need to ready yourself for the very real possibility that you will be summoned as a witness in the current trial of the said Ethan Hall.'

'You can't make me do that!' Campbell stood up and backed away into a corner of the room. 'You cannot make me do that! I am not going to get involved. I have the right to say No and I'm exercising it!'

'Mr Campbell, beyond what we can and cannot do, you need to consider one thing above all else,' Janet rose as she spoke. 'DS McNeill was one hundred percent correct when he told you that Ethan Hall is likely to go free and when he does we fully expect

 FAITH

him to complete all unfinished business. We can protect you from him and Calvin Brent, but we need your testimony to help us do that.'

'You're legally bound to protect me anyway!'

'If you contact any of our officers to report a crime we will, of course, do everything we can to help you. Likewise if we actually come across you being victimised, we will commit to your immediate protection. However, we cannot protect you from something we do not see or that you refuse to tell us about.'

'I could just keep out of sight.'

'Not forever, sir.' Janet raised her hands, palm up. 'Your choice is simple. Do the right thing and help us to help you, or spend every day for the rest of your life – however long or short that is – waiting for the inevitable.'

Campbell shook his head angrily. 'This whole system is so corrupt!'

'No sir, the system works really well when people support it.' Janet looked across at McNeill and he too rose to his feet. 'Now what are you going to do?'

CHAPTER 48

SATURDAY
1.14pm

Peter Jones didn't hesitate. When Calvin Brent opened his front door he stepped inside without waiting to be asked and strode into the kitchen.

'Calvin, you invite me round and you still don't put the coffee on.' Peter sat on a stool next to the island. Exactly where Stu Jolly had been sitting. Drinking water.

'Empty and gone,' the so-called driver had said.

Peter wondered briefly just what he was doing on behalf of Calvin Brent. Something bad, no doubt of that. Jolly was a different kind of villain to most, with a violent streak controlled and directed by a dismissive and distant demeanour. That much had been obvious from the moment Peter had set eyes on him.

'I asked you here for a business meeting, not a social,' Brent said, taking a position at the far end of the room.

Peter's mind shot back to the present. 'If you're looking for an investor, you're talking to the wrong man.'

'Funny.'

'We aim to please. Well, not everyone obviously. There are some we get a positive thrill out of upsetting.'

'That's a dangerous way to get your thrills.'

'Oh? Do tell.'

'I'm just saying. When people get upset they behave irrationally, do things they wouldn't normally do, make the world an unsafe place. If I were you, I'd be careful who I upset.'

'Some people who are upset behave more irrationally than others, do they?'

'You ought to know that in your line of work, DCI Jones. See, if you stick a harpoon in a small fish it just fights a little bit then it gives up and dies. Stick a harpoon in a much bigger fish - '

'- Like a white whale?'

'Exactly. Stick a harpoon in that and it destroys you and your fucking boat.'

'It might drag you down, but whilst it's doing that you can just keep stabbing away can't you? Anyway, I'm not one for fishing – not that sort of fishing. I'm more of a hunting man myself.'

'Is that a fact?'

'Yeah. I like to be part of a well-trained team, with some well-trained dogs, flushing the birds out of their hiding places and up into the air where they can be picked off one by one.'

'That must be exciting.' Brent feigned a yawn.

'It's lots of things. Most of them you wouldn't understand.'

'Why's that?'

'Because it requires a certain attitude to life that you weren't born with.'

'You're a fucking psychologist now, are you?'

'Unqualified, but I have my moments.'

'Do you know what they call a psychologist who doesn't have a qualification?'

'I'm guessing you're going to tell me.'

'A twat.'

'I think I'm definitely winning on the humour front.'

'You're not winning on any front.'

'Is that a fact?'

'Yeah.'

'And you'd know that, would you?'

'I know more than you can imagine.'

'I have a very vivid imagination.' Peter smiled. 'How's Jolly doing, by the way?'

'What?'

'Just asking.' Peter stood up and took a step towards the gangster. 'Enough of the pleasantries. Why did you call me?'

Brent fell silent for a moment.

Making one final calculation, Peter thought. Just double-checking one last time that you're making the right move.

'I might have something that would be of value to you.'

'You might have or you do have?'

'Thing is, if I do have this item and if I do give it to you, we need to do a deal.'

'We can talk about the possibility of a deal once I've decided if this mysterious item is as valuable as you think it is.'

'I need some guarantee first.'

'The only guarantee I can give you is that I'll listen to your proposal, but I'll only do that after I've checked the item.'

'You're making this really fucking difficult.'

'You called me. I can leave now if you want me to; go and make my own coffee.'

'You really are a fucking psychologist without a qualification! Do you know that?'

Peter grinned. 'I've been called worse. C'mon Calvin, I appreciate it goes against the grain to be helping me out, but my guess is you've already decided that it's to your advantage too. So let's get on with it. Throw your harpoon and let's see where it lands.'

'You are fucking unbelievable.'

'I'll take that as a compliment.'

Brent sighed. 'Ethan Hall has a note book.'

'Containing?'

'All sorts of shit. How much he hates the rest of us. What he thought he saw when he looked at the brains of those people he killed. Some vague stuff about how he'll destroy society and make us all start again.'

'You have this book?'

'I've seen the pages.'

'How?'

'I was shown them by an ex-friend of Hall's. He's the guy who gave him a room when he escaped from hospital.'

'He has the book?'

'No. But he has photos of every page.'

'On his phone?'

'Yeah.'

'I need to talk to him and I need his phone.'

'Now we're at the time when we need to negotiate.'

'I haven't seen anything yet. I don't know for sure these pages exist, or that they were written by Ethan Hall.'

'You'll have to trust me.'

'And find myself being dragged down by a whale?'

'For Christ's sake, remember what you said earlier! Why would I lie to you about this? I don't want you in my fucking house anymore than you want to be here.'

'But you want Ethan Hall in prison?'

Calvin shrugged. 'Any law-abiding citizen would want a man like that locked up.'

'Locked up in a place that's run on one level at least by their old man?'

'Listen, let's leave my old man out of this. I know the trial's fucked up and I'm offering to help. You don't need to bother yourself with why. What I've seen is genuine and I can get it for you, but I need your word on something before I do.'

'My word on what?'

'This guy's phone, you could probably find other stuff on it. If you went looking.'

'Stuff relating to illegal activity?'

'That's not for me to say.'

'Of course it isn't.' Peter fell silent, making it look as if the decision was a difficult one. 'OK. I'll tell you what I'll do, if these photos are what you say they are, you can take the Sim card out and keep it. Right now Ethan Hall is more important to me than any illegal activity this guy might have been involved in, or any contacts he might have. Do we have a deal?'

'I can trust you on this, right?'

'Fuck off! I'm the copper here, remember?'

'There are plenty of coppers who lie.'

'Not this one.' Peter put out his hand. 'I'm not interested in hunting you at the moment. Ethan Hall is my priority and, let's face it, you'll still be here afterwards.'

Brent nodded. 'Yeah. I'll still be here.'

He shook Peter's hand, briefly, strongly.

They both knew what the handshake meant.

CHAPTER 49

SUNDAY
9.42am

DC Janet Harris made no attempt to stifle a yawn as she walked out of the Lace Market car park. Yesterday had been long, tiring and successful. Robin Campbell had, begrudgingly, made the right decision. His statement was now on record. Mike Coopland had served a notice of additional evidence to the Judge and to Ethan Hall. Campbell would be appearing as a witness on Monday.

And now, incredibly, it seemed a second potential witness had come out of the woodwork. A woman had phoned right out of the blue, claiming to have been a victim of Ethan Hall. Peter Jones had spoken to her. Taken it seriously enough to send Janet to meet her.

'Nine forty-five in the Cross Keys,' he had said. 'If this is as real as I think it is, the tide could be turning. We could be sending Mike back out to battle with two new witnesses and Ethan Hall's notes. So get this one right, Janet.'

Get this one right.

As if she'd ever got one wrong.

She stopped on the kerbside as a bus passed, coughing out black smoke. She stayed a second longer than she needed to, looking for two others, making herself smile.

If ever there was a day for them to come in threes...

The pub was empty apart from a couple having breakfast. She ordered a large pot of tea with two cups and sat as far away from the couple as she could. She was halfway through her first drink before a skinny, pale-skinned woman with short mousey brown hair walked hesitantly into the bar. She was wearing dark blue Levi jeans, a black stained jumper and a well-worn brown leather jacket. Not enough to keep out the cold.

Janet smiled and pointed to the second cup. The woman approached and sat down.

'Milk and sugar?'

The woman nodded. Janet poured.

'You're Tina Smith?'

The woman nodded again.

'I'm DC Janet Harris.' She showed her ID card. 'You spoke to my Boss, DCI Jones.'

'Yeah.'

'He wants you to know how grateful he is that you've chosen to talk to us. Not many people do. Especially after...' Janet let her voice trail away. She offered a sympathetic and reassuring look. One of the best in her arsenal. Ideal for situations like this. 'Tina, why don't you just tell me what happened with Ethan Hall?'

'I need a drink first.' She picked up the cup using both hands. Needing the warmth. Working hard to keep her hands steady. She only sipped at the tea. 'I'm dyin',' she said. 'They reckon I might last six months. I might make it t' summer.'

'I'm sorry.'

'It's all the shit I've been takin' over the years. Done me in. Should 'ave known better, but...' She put the cup down; kept her hands on it. 'Tha's why I phoned. I saw on the news that 'e was likely t'get away with everythin'. Thought I can't let tha' 'appen, and there's nothin' 'e can do t'me. Not now. Ya stop bein' scared when you know yo'r dyin'.'

'Tina, can you just share with me what you told my Boss?'

'Yeah. It was years ago. He offered t'pay me t'do stuff for 'im.'

'He wanted sex?'

'Sort of. He wanted t'watch me doin' it t' myself.'

'And you agreed?'

'I needed the money. I 'ad a boyfriend at the time. 'E didn' mind as long as I didn' do certain things with the punters.'

'I understand.'

'So I went back to 'is place and got on the bed.'

'What did he do?'

' 'E got angry because 'e said I didn' do it right. An' then 'e started talkin' t' me. An' I couldn' get off the bed. I couldn' move, but I started cumin'. The more 'e talked the more I came. An' 'e didn' stop. 'E just kept makin' me do it. When it started 'urtin' 'e enjoyed it even more.'

'And you told him no? You made it clear you wanted him to stop?'

'I was beggin'. But 'e said it was my own fault. An' I couldn' get 'is words out of my 'ead. Even when I was screamin' and cryin', I could still 'ear everythin' he was sayin'.'

'How did it end?'

' 'E just stopped. I don' know why. I kept passin' out, so I can't remember it towards the end.'

'He just let you go?'

'One time I opened my eyes an' 'e wasn' there anymore. I managed t' get myself into the shower. Stayed there for ages. Getting' clean. Tryin' to think straight, get my strength back.'

'Did you tell your boyfriend?'

'No.'

'Did you tell anyone?'

'No. Even after Ethan Hall 'ad gone, I just wanted t' bury it.'

'I understand.'

'Everythin' they're sayin' about 'im is true.'

'We know that. We just need more people like you and more evidence to help us prove it. Shall I order us some more tea? And some breakfast, too?'

Tina nodded. She reached out across the table with a thin, boney hand. 'He still haunts my dreams,' she said. 'Every night.'

CHAPTER 50

SUNDAY
11.17am

Peter Jones hadn't visited them since the trial began. Now, as they sat together in the lounge, he wanted to share the news in person.

'We've made amazing progress in the last thirty six hours,' he said. 'New witnesses, new evidence. Mike's back in with a fighting chance.'

'How much of a chance?' It was Marcus who asked the question; Anne-Marie was silent, thoughtful and attentive.

'Difficult to quantify. But it's as you were both thinking, there were other people out there with stories to tell about how Ethan Hall had victimised them.'

'Every strength comes with at least one weakness attached,' Marcus said.

'What does that mean?'

'Ethan Hall's strength is his ability to influence others. Exercising that strength has become addictive for him. Like all true addicts, he finds more and more reasons to justify his addiction. That's the weakness that has become attached. Along with the fact that, because he is so uniquely skilled, he's forgotten that he's still a human being. Ultimately he's just like the rest of us. He might give the appearance that he's buried his emotional self so deep it's beyond reach, but I'm sure that's not the reality.'

'Why?'

'Because he is driven by his own selfish desires and by hate.

You can't get much more emotional than that. Whether he ever acknowledges it to himself or not, he's just as emotional as everyone else.'

'But he controls people with such ease. He can do things that seem unbelievable.' Peter glanced at Anne-Marie.

'True. But I realised something on Friday night, standing out in the garden, freezing. A difference between me and him that I hadn't consciously identified before.'

'What is it?' Anne-Marie asked before Peter could.

'When I'm working to influence others, that is precisely what I'm doing. Working. I might have a compulsion to help and, as I've been forced to admit an egotistical desire to be successful, – although I've begun addressing that - but essentially it's still work. That's how I view, think and feel about it.'

'Ethan Hall, on the other hand, is in fight mode all the time. He is continually attacking people, relationships, beliefs. You have to remember that a human being experiences on average around four hundred and fifty emotional responses every day, and usually it's a variety of emotions. Ethan is different. He is only operating from the fight or flight response. And, although in certain circumstances fight or flight is an appropriate and necessary response, it is not one we are supposed to maintain indefinitely.'

'So are you saying he's wearing himself out?' It was Peter again.

'Yes. Slowly but surely. The great artist Paul Cezanne said, "Genius is the ability to renew one's emotions in daily experience." Ethan isn't doing that. He might be a genius – albeit a twisted and dangerous one – but he is in emotional overdrive constantly, even if he doesn't know it.'

'So what price will he pay?'

'Eventually?' Marcus gestured expansively. 'His physical and psychological systems will break down, possibly irreversibly. It's impossible to know quite how or when. He could manifest with something like PTSD or even a complete emotional breakdown, or his body might just give out on him. Whatever happens, the weakness that's attached to his strength will get him in the end.'

'That couldn't happen soon enough.' Peter said. He thought of Nic and quickly redirected his attention to Anne-Marie. 'You are both going to stay out of the courtroom tomorrow?'

'Yes. I don't ever want to go back there,' she said. 'Even to watch.'

'I'll let you know what's happened.'

'I know you will.' She frowned. 'Can you tell us anything about the new witnesses and the new evidence?'

'You just need to know that in different ways they all cast serious doubt on Ethan's claim that he's misunderstood. In fact, they all support the case that, rather than being a healer, he is both a killer and a sexual abuser.'

'Abuser?' Anne-Marie straightened in her chair. 'I never said that.'

Both Marcus Kline and Peter Jones shifted instinctively into work mode. The DCI took control, raising his palm – a stop signal – in the direction of the communication consultant.

'Anne-Marie, why would you have said that?' There was both gentleness and demand in his question.

Comfort and control.

She found it impossible to defend against. Suddenly the weight on her chest was the only thing she could feel and she needed to rid herself of it. She realised for the first time that it was crushing her. She looked at her friend and prayed the DCI could see the truth she was hiding.

'Anne-Marie,' he said, 'when Ethan Hall visited you here and cured you of your cancer, did he do anything else?'

She nodded.

'I understand.' Peter kept his eyes on her as he said, 'Marcus, now more than ever I need you to trust me and do as I ask. Leave the room. Go out into the back garden. Look at the valley and the sky. Stay there until I join you.'

Marcus Kline stood slowly, pressed his left hand gently on Anne-Marie's right shoulder and left the room, closing the door behind him.

Peter waited until he heard the kitchen door open and close and he could see Marcus in the garden. Then he said, 'Once upon a time he wouldn't have done that.'

She smiled, even though the tears were already flowing. 'Once upon a time, he couldn't have.'

He returned her smile. At this moment he wasn't functioning as her friend. It was the best way he could show his love. For her and everyone else. 'For all sorts of reasons I'm not going to ask you many questions. Someone else needs to do that. And I have the perfect person on my team.'

'Thank you.'

'Just tell me this, did Ethan Hall abuse you?'

She nodded.

'Sexually?'

She nodded again.

'OK. This might seem like a really stupid question, but it is my last one about what happened. Did he touch you?'

'No!' Her hands came away from her face. She let the tears run down. 'How did you know?'

He shrugged apologetically. *Can't tell you.* And then she worked it out.

'My God, he did it to someone else before he did it to me!'

She remembered her conversation with Marcus.

Before.

That's what they had said. Ethan Hall had done things to people before. Theirs were not the only lives in the world.

'I'm a photographer,' she said. 'But I haven't been living it. Otherwise I would have known.'

'Known what?'

'It doesn't matter.' She shook her head. 'What happens now?'

'I'd like you to come to the station with me. I'll ask my very wonderful colleague to take your statement.'

'Then?'

He did that smile again. The one that showed his love. 'I think Mike will want to recall you as a witness.'

She nodded again, differently this time.

'Ethan Hall won't have changed,' Peter said, 'but you have. You've freed yourself from the burdens he wanted you to carry. The burdens he believed would destroy you slowly, over time. The best advice I can give you now is to focus on that, on how you've changed.'

It was true. Her chest was feeling lighter already. She inhaled and enjoyed it for the first time in months. Then she remembered.

'There is a quote,' she said, 'from someone I've long been inspired by. The quote is "Life is a movie; death is a photograph." It's helped me in the past. It can help me again now.'

'How?'

'It's how I can learn to trust myself again. I'll give you a statement. I'll be a witness again. I'll tell the world what Ethan Hall did to me.'

'And?'

'Whilst I'm doing it, I'll turn him and the courtroom into a series of photographs in my mind. I know how to create and manage those.'

'Better than most people on the planet,' he reminded her.

'Yes!' She had stopped crying. 'Better than most.'

They both looked out of the window.

'I need to go and talk to Marcus,' Peter said. 'Is that OK?'

'Tell him we are freeing ourselves.'

'I will.'

As Peter walked through the kitchen his phone beeped. He stopped to check it. It was a message from McNeill. There had been another *Pass it on* killing. The victim was a minor politician. An Italian. Living in Rome.

CHAPTER 51

SUNDAY
11.45pm

Stu Jolly spat the tasteless chewing gum onto the floor of the Ford Mondeo and replaced it immediately with a fresh stick. He always chewed gum when he went to work. Something to do with the increased adrenalin in his body, he guessed.

The first time he had stabbed a man had been in prison. Actually, that wasn't quite right. He hadn't stabbed him, he had slashed him twice across the face with a cute little tool made from a toothbrush and two Stanley knife blades. There was almost no chance of killing someone by accident with a weapon like that. What it did do, though, was leave a couple of cuts that couldn't be stitched. And it guaranteed that no other inmates tried to take your cigarettes.

No, the first time he had stabbed a man – pushed a blade into a body as deep as he could and twisted it repeatedly – had been sometime after that. It had been outside a pub. A drunken thing. The man had nearly died. The police had run into a wall of silence. Stu's reputation as a man with a knife had been established. Sometimes that earned him extra cash.

Over time he came to realise that two of his ten steps were as true for using a blade as they were for robbing a house.

Step six: Know your entry point.

Step seven: Once inside always ensure you leave two escape routes open.

He wasn't a man for a frenzied attack. He figured anyone could do that. He was always more deliberate, more targeted. He always knew his entry point. He knew what to do with the blade when it was inside, too. That was the real skill. Most people thought that sticking the knife in was the big deal, the part that mattered most. But it wasn't. It was what you did when your blade was inside that caused the real damage, followed by how and where you took it out. There were always at least two options for that, depending on what result you were after.

Tonight the result would be terminal. His weapon of choice was a heavy duty kitchen knife with an eight inch blade. He only ever used everyday knives. Stanleys or something like if he just wanted to make a mess. A kitchen knife if he had to go deeper. There was no point in spending money on a fancy hunting or fighting knife. They didn't do the job any better and they were certainly easier to trace.

Jolly stretched his legs and yawned, loud and long. Adrenalin, he told himself. And then the front door of the house he was watching opened, just as he knew it would, and the figure stepped outside, just as he always had. Jolly picked the knife off the passenger seat and watched Peter Jones lock the door and set off on his evening walk.

Routines. They can get you killed.

He let him get fifty metres away before he got out of the car. Jones was wearing the same thick country coat and cap, pulled down low over his forehead. His hands were stuffed into his pockets.

Jolly went in pursuit, walking brusquely, holding the knife in his right hand, the blade pointing upwards against his inner forearm. At the pace he was going he figured he would reach Jones within a couple of minutes. Enough time for them to be out of sight of all the houses.

 FAITH

He felt his heartbeat quicken. Adrenalin. Killing a copper. The biggest job of his career. Not one he would have volunteered for. Too late for that now. Just get it done, then get out of the country. Spend six months in Spain. Soak up the sun. Drink a few beers. Keep out of trouble.

Just get it done.

The distance between them had halved. Jolly resisted the temptation to walk faster.

Ten more paces and all the lights were behind them.

The road narrowed, hedges and ditches on either side. Jolly resisted the temptation to look back over his shoulder. The darkness was his friend.

Another ten paces and he was close enough to get his footsteps in sync with Jones. He changed his grip on the knife, turning the blade down so it was pointing towards the ground.

Jones's head was bent forwards, his shoulders rounded against the cold. His back was an open target. Jolly fought the urge to sprint the last eight paces.

No noise now.

Give him no warning.

You can't defend against a surprise attack.

Four more paces then left hand up and over Jones's left shoulder, palm clamping over his mouth, right hand driving the blade into and through his kidneys. A brief twisting, sawing action then pull the blade out, jerk the head back and slice left to right across the throat. Job done.

Three more paces.

Jolly tightened his grip on the knife, raised his left hand. Twenty seconds from now it would all be over. He pulled the knife back slightly, bending his elbow, readying himself to punch it forward as powerfully as he could.

Two more paces.

Ten seconds.

Torchlight exploded in his eyes. Figures – he couldn't see how many – appeared from nowhere.

'Armed police! Put down the knife! Put down the knife!'

Jolly spun round, trying to get out of the light, looking instinctively for an escape route. There wasn't one. He was surrounded.

'Put down the knife! Now!'

Jolly turned back to face Peter Jones. He was already beyond the circle of men. His hands were out of his pockets.

Jolly dropped the knife.

'Now, on your knees!'

He sank down. They made sure it hurt as they handcuffed him. As he was being walked away, Jolly heard Peter Jones say, 'At least now I can get out of this damned vest!' And the man who had given the commands laughed without humour or sympathy.

CHAPTER 52

MONDAY - TRIAL DAY 6
11.30am

Mike Coopland QC believed in second chances. For just about everybody. It wasn't a belief he shared widely. For reasons he had never been able to fathom he found it easier to make loud and frequent proclamations that would have convinced any audience his natural political home was somewhere to the right of Margaret Thatcher. However, if asked the right questions – six words or less – the truth would have soon become clear.

Second chances.

Integral to human learning. To a caring society. To winning a trial.

Mike had been handed a second chance by the brilliance of Peter Jones and his team. He began the day intending to make the most of it.

Mr Justice Stephen Mulvenny was waiting for him to speak.

'My Lord, you will have seen the notice of additional evidence. In these circumstances a matter of law arises that should be heard in the absence of the jury.'

'Of course.'

The jury was dismissed.

Mike continued. 'I understand your Lordship has a difficult balancing exercise in ensuring that Ethan Hall has a fair trial, yet the nature of this new evidence supports and reinforces the prosecution's concerns expressed when we began about the unique abilities of the defendant.'

'We intend to seek your Lordship's permission to recall Anne-Marie Kline. Given that both her testimony and that from one of our new witnesses is based on allegations of a sexual nature it is inappropriate for Ethan Hall to cross-examine either person directly. So we ask for a court-appointed advocate to do so on his behalf.'

Mike heard a noise from behind him in the dock. He didn't look. As he was defending himself, Ethan had received copies of the new witness statements. The morning start-time had been put back to give him chance to prepare. That was only right and proper. So was Mike's request for an advocate. He expected that to scramble the hypnotist's brain. A good old-fashioned right-hander. Bang on target.

Mulvenny moved things along as he was obliged to.

'Mr Hall, you heard the prosecution's application. What would you like to say about the recall of Anne-Marie Kline and, secondly, on the appointment of an advocate?'

The reply came swiftly. There was an edge of tension in the voice. 'My Lord, I am not charged with sexual misconduct. That is not what this trial is about. I therefore object in the strongest possible terms to the recall of Anne-Marie Kline and to the introduction of any such testimony. Given that, the use of an advocate becomes a moot point.'

Mike forced himself to remain impassive. Once again Ethan was performing like an accomplished barrister. The argument he had presented was the only viable one. He was absolutely right to remind the Judge of the nature of the trial and the charges he was facing.

As Mulvenny retired to consider his decision, Mike felt as if his second chance was balancing on a knife-edge.

The balancing act was over fifteen minutes later.

 FAITH

'I am going to allow the recall of Anne-Marie Kline,' Mulvenny said. 'With regard to the allegations of a sexual nature, the law is clear. Witnesses may not be cross-examined by the alleged perpetrator of the crime. Protection will therefore be afforded to them and an advocate will be appointed.'

Mike glanced over his shoulder at Kaffee. The smaller man offered the briefest of nods. Further back, Ethan Hall felt the heat of rage warming his face and the first stirrings of a feeling he couldn't identify in the pit of his stomach.

'No advocate can replace you,' the voice in his mind said. 'You didn't foresee this! It's the first thing you've missed! And they have your notes, too. Your private notes. They'll use them against you! They'll think they know you!'

The first of the new witnesses was Robin Campbell. He looked at the courtroom with a mixture of fear and resentfulness on his face. Mike doubted if that would change.

'Mr Campbell, what is your profession?'

'I'm an art dealer.'

'What does that entail?'

'I buy and sell different works of art, paintings mostly.'

'Established artists only, or newcomers too?'

'Both.'

'With equal success?'

'It varies.'

Mike allowed himself a half-smile. He wanted to say, 'If I'd needed a petulant, sulky child in the witness box I'd have invited my sixteen year old daughter.'

Instead he said, 'How has business been of late?'

'Bad.'

'How are your finances currently?'

'Bad.'

'How were they a year ago?'

'Bad.'

'Bad enough to need a loan?'

'Yes.'

'Did you acquire a loan?'

'Yes.'

'From whom?'

'A private lender.'

'Was it Mr Calvin Brent?'

'Yes.'

'How were the interest rates?'

'Steep.'

'Could you afford repayments?'

'Not to his satisfaction.'

'When did you encounter Ethan Hall?'

The sudden shift in focus made Campbell hesitate. Just as Mike hoped it would. It gave the jury time to reinforce in their minds the implied connection between Calvin Brent, a man with a fearsome reputation as an underworld Boss, and Ethan Hall.

'It was, er, nearly seven months ago.'

'You were making repayments by then?'

'Yes.'

'To Calvin Brent?'

'Yes.'

'But not to his satisfaction?'

'No.'

'Where did you encounter Ethan Hall?'

'He came to my home.'

'Did you invite him?'

'No.'

'Did you know him?'

'No.'

'Did you let him into your home?'

'Yes.'

'Why, if you didn't know him?'

'I couldn't stop myself.'

'You couldn't simply close the door?'

'No.'

'Why not?'

'I, er...' Campbell scratched at his goatee. 'It was like I'd lost control of my mind, of my normal thought processes. It was like he belonged in a memory I couldn't quite reach.'

'Even though you'd never met before?'

'Yes.'

'What happened next?'

'We went into my lounge. He started talking to me. All I could do was listen.'

'What did he talk about?'

'I have a life-threatening nut allergy. He talked about that.'

'He knew of your allergy?'

'Yes.'

'Had you told him?'

'No.'

'But somehow he knew?'

'Yes.'

'Even though you'd never met before?'

'Yes.'

'How did his words affect you?'

'They, erm, made me start having a serious allergic reaction.' Another scratch of the beard. 'A really bad one.'

'Had you eaten nuts?'

'No.'

'Touched any?'

'No.'

'Yet you had a severe reaction?'

'Yes.' Campbell's left hand touched his throat. 'He talked me into it. I don't know how! I can't understand it! I could have died!'

'How so, Mr Campbell?'

'I collapsed. I lost consciousness. He put me in a coma and left me on the floor. Just because I owed money!'

Mike allowed himself a second to look thoughtful; allowed the silence to frame Campbell's last words. So often, he reflected, the sulky witness said the most.

'Thank you, Mr Campbell.'

Mulvenny looked to the dock. 'Mr Hall?'

Ethan rose to his feet. The heat of rage was still upon him; the feeling in his stomach was an even bigger distraction. 'Are you sure I visited you?'

'Yes.'

'And we talked?'

'Yes.'

'Did we discuss your finances?'

'No.'

'Did I ever mention your finances?'

'No.'

'Did I ever threaten you?'

'No.'

'Did I ever mention Calvin Brent?'

'No.'

'I talked only about your allergy?'

'Yes.'

'About how dangerous it was?'

'Yes.' Another touch of the throat.

'About how I could heal you?'

'No. That's not what you said.'

'What did I actually say?'

'I can't remember the detail.' Robin swallowed.

'What if I asked you to?'

'I'd refuse.'

'Why?'

'Because I try to avoid thinking about it.'

'Why do you do that?'

Sitting with his back to the synesthete Mike Coopland heard the question and tensed with anticipation. Finally! He thought. A question you shouldn't have asked!

Robin swallowed again. 'It's too real. It's like a film playing in my mind and I get caught up in the film even though I don't want to. It's like I'm reliving the whole thing from the inside out.'

Another swallow. Another scratch. Another touch of the throat. Mike noticed an increasing redness on the man's cheeks and neck.

'And then I start feeling just like I did on the day. My body doesn't know how to stop it. Everything starts...' His eyes glazed as his breathing quickened. The redness on his skin began to darken. '...and it's unstoppable. No matter what I thay to mythelf, I can't juth make it...'

'When did you first approach Calvin Brent asking for a loan?' Ethan Hall's voice was louder than necessary.

Transfixed as he was by Robin Campbell, Mike counted automatically. Eleven words! Eleven loud, hurried words!

'...The film keepth running until ith - '

'Answer my question about Calvin Brent!'

Mike was sure Campbell's face was beginning to swell. Mulvenny had seen it too. He took control.

'Mr Hall, be silent! Mr Campbell, look at me!"

Robin ignored the instruction. 'The film hath to play till the end...'

'Clerk!' Mulvenny signalled to the sixty five year old man dressed in a black jacket and pinstripe trousers. 'See if the witness has an auto-injector on his person!'

The Clerk moved quickly and calmly. Mike knew him. A former Army Major. Used to acting under pressure.

'Here my Lord!' He pulled an EpiPen out of Campbell's jacket pocket. He didn't wait for the instruction. He removed the safety cap and pressed it firmly at right angles against Campbell's thigh. Mike heard the click as the auto-injector activated and a dose of adrenalin was released. Campbell slumped back against the chair.

Mike Coopland realised he had been holding his breath.

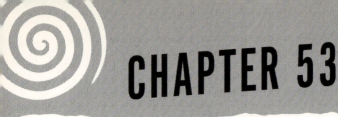

CHAPTER 53

MONDAY - TRIAL DAY 6
2.04pm

As Tina Smith took her seat in the witness box Mr Justice Stephen Mulvenny looked first at Ethan Hall, then at the assembled journalists and members of the public and finally at the jury. It was a final, silent reminder. After the drama of the morning, normal service was about to be resumed.

Or else.

He watched Mike Coopland stand and, as ever, rest both hands on his lectern before asking his opening question.

'Tina, what was your occupation?'

'I didn't really 'ave a full-time job as such.'

'But you did earn money?'

'Yeah. You 'ave to, don' ya?'

'How did you earn money?'

'I worked in a local factory when I could. When there was no work there I 'ad 'ave sex.'

'And men paid you?'

'Yeah. 'Course. I've never done it with women. Ya couldn' pay me enough for tha.'

All of the women jurors and four of the men smiled.

'So you were a prostitute?'

'Part-time. My motto was always "factory first, fuckin' second". There was stuff I wouldn' do tho' - when it came to 'avin' sex, not in the factory. I'd do anythin' they asked in the factory.'

'Miss Smith,' Mulvenny interrupted the laughter. 'Control your language, please.'

'Sorry, sir.'

'Did you have a boyfriend?

'Yeah. Tha's why there was stuff I wouldn' do. 'E's moved on since then.'

'He knew you were a prostitute?'

'Yeah. I didn' 'ide anythin'.'

'How did he feel about it?'

'He was OK with it. I spent as much of the money I got on 'im as I did on maself, so why wouldn' 'e be?'

Mulvenny silenced another ripple of laughter. Mike watched most of the jurors warm to her. In his experience prostitutes were always great witnesses. They told the truth without hesitation or embarrassment. In many ways he respected them more than politicians.

'What did you buy for yourself?'

'Drugs mainly.' She looked at the jury. 'Stupid I know, but everyone did where I grew up. I jus' got caugh' up in it more than most. Tha's why I'm dyin'.'

Mike let the jury deal with that. More than one blinked back tears.

'Tina, did you encounter Ethan Hall?'

'Yeah. He was the wors' thing tha' ever 'appened t'me. 'E was worse even than the drugs.' Her eyes flickered in Ethan's direction. Her hands fidgeted in her lap.

'Why was he worse than drugs?'

'Becose they only kill ya. He did stuff to me, 'orrible stuff, made me do wha' I said I wouldn'. He kept doin' it.'

'What did he do to you?'

Tina Smith's pale skin paled even more. Mike was sure the jury could see it. He waited. Her sudden reticence was a Godsend. He willingly gave her as much time as she needed.

'He made me cum. Even tho' I told him I didn' want to. Tha' I wouldn'. Somehow he knew how t'do it.'

'Did he touch you?'

'No. He jus' talked t'me. He never stopped talkin'. It was like...' She hesitated again. 'This sounds stupid.'

'What does, Tina?'

'It was like his words were touchin' me, workin' on my skin and inside me. It was like I could feel them.'

'Tina,' he said her name softly, gently, drawing her and the jury in. 'he made you orgasm?'

'Yeah.'

'How many times?'

She blinked repeatedly. He prayed the jury recognised she was fighting back tears.

'Tina?'

'I don' know. It was so many times. He kept me there for two days. An' he didn' stop. He didn' need food or sleep or anythin'. He jus' kept talkin' an' my body kept doing wha' he told it to.'

In the dock, Ethan Hall watched the colours of her pain shooting out from her. He watched what he guessed to be sympathy colouring the air throughout the courtroom. The unusual feeling in the pit of his stomach stirred some more as Coopland asked his next question.

'How were you when he stopped?'

'It felt like I was nearly dead. An' I was a shitty mess.' She looked at the jury for a second time. 'Sorry if tha' sounds 'orrible, but it's the truth.'

'Why did he stop?'

'I dunno. Maybe he got bored. One minute he was doing it t'me, the next he stopped and left me alone.'

'What did you do?

'Nothin' t'start with. I couldn' move. When I could I got maself in the shower and washed everythin' away. Then I tried t'get enough energy back t'get out of there.'

'Were you able to?'

'Yeah. He'd disappeared.'

'Did you inform the police?'

'Tha's not what people like me do. Besides, who'd believe me?'

Mike looked pointedly at the jury.

'So why be a witness now?'

'Becos I read in the news that he was getting' away with everythin'. Becos tha' in't right. Ya can do the things I've done an' still know wha's right and wha's wrong.' Her hands fidgeted again. 'An' I'm doin' it becos I'm dyin' an' I need t'do something good before I go.'

'Tina, thank you.'

Mike sat down. He didn't have to perform. She had moved him as she had many in the courtroom. He just let it show.

The court-appointed advocate was from a local Chambers. His name was Andrew Norton. He was thirty four. Two years ago he had attended an Advocacy training day that Mike had run. He had not engaged well. As he rose to cross-examine he glanced down at the questions he had been told to ask.

'Miss Smith, by your own admission, you are a prostitute?'

Eight words, Mike told himself.

'Part-time. Yeah.'

'You sell your body for sex?'

'Most of it.'

More laughter. Mulvenny reinforced his authority.

'So why should we trust you?'

'Everybody in the room does something for money. You'd trust a gynaecologist an' he sticks 'is fingers into twenty women a day.'

Mulvenny had to work harder this time. Norton coughed. Ethan Hall felt his face begin to burn.

Eventually Norton said, 'Ethan Hall paid you for your services?'

'He didn' pay me for wha' he made me do. He turned me into a prisoner. Tha's against the law. Even I know tha'.'

Norton shot a look towards the dock.

Mike saw it and thought, Not even Ethan Hall can help you now.

'You are a drug addict, aren't you?' Norton asked.

'Yeah.'

'Are you a sex addict, too?'

'I like a good fuck - '

Mulvenny settled the room again and reminded the witness.

'Sorry, sir.' She said. 'I'm jus' bein' honest. An' the truth is I like sex as much as everyone else, but what he did t'me wasn' sex. It was violence. It was torture. Ethan Hall did worse t'me than the drugs ever 'ave – and I'll be dead soon 'cos of them.'

The mood in the courtroom shifted from humour to sympathy. And, in some quarters, a tearful admiration.

Mike Coopland knew that if he hadn't been at work he would have been crying too. But he was at work. And he had a job to do. So his next thought was, Anne-Marie Kline please be as good in the witness box as this prostitute.

CHAPTER 54

MONDAY - TRIAL DAY 6
3.19pm

Anne-Marie Wells, world famous photographer, took her seat in the witness box for the second time. She looked at the scene in front of her and blinked twice. First two photos taken, she told herself; context established, character studies to follow.

Mike Coopland rose and thanked her for returning. There was something about his wig she hadn't noticed before. It made her think of a Knight's shield.

Click!

Third photo taken and a title for the series popped into her mind.

Trials and Tribulations.

Mike Coopland got straight to the point. 'You remember Ethan Hall's visit clearly?'

'Yes. Like it was yesterday.'

'And he cured you of cancer?'

'I believe so.'

Ethan Hall heard the word she had so deliberately chosen and his anger burnt even more as the feeling in the pit of his stomach twisted and tugged. He wanted to scream, 'You *know* I cured you!' He wanted to make her orgasm. Here. Now. He wanted the world to see it.

Sitting to his right, handcuffed to him once again, Duncan felt the synesthete's increased tension.

Anne-Marie saw it.

Click!

'And then he left?' Mike Coopland asked.

'No.'

'What did he do?'

'He made me go upstairs, into our bedroom.'

'Why didn't you tell us before?'

'I was ashamed of what happened. And my husband has suffered enough because of...because of Ethan Hall.'

She heard herself say his name. She felt something in her mind release. It made her want to laugh, but she forced herself to continue.

'I didn't want my husband to know about this too. I know I was wrong, but I just wanted to carry the burden of it myself.'

'Did he force you upstairs?'

'In a manner of speaking. I didn't want to go. I just wanted him out of the house. But he had hypnotised me. I had no free will.'

'But you could hear him?'

'Yes.'

'And you could move unaided?'

'Yes.'

'What happened in the bedroom?'

'He made me lay on the bed.'

'Where was he?'

'Standing at the foot of the bed.'

'Were you clothed?'

'Yes.'

'What happened next?'

'He told me that I was going to orgasm for him, that he was going to make me.'

'Did you try to escape?'

'Yes, but I couldn't move off the bed. I was trapped inside my body and it was pinned down.'

'How did he achieve that?'

'By his words. He did everything with his words. He was talking all the time.'

'What effect did his words have?'

She looked at the jury; let them see her embarrassment and shame.

'They penetrated me. They made me orgasm. Repeatedly. Even though I begged him not to. He wouldn't stop.'

Those who could, returned her gaze. Some looked down. No one wrote.

Click!

'How long did this attack continue?'

Ethan Hall snorted. 'What I did wasn't an attack,' he said louder than he meant to. His stomach twisted and tugged some more. 'My attacks are so very different.' Both guards heard him. They adjusted their positions.

'I can't say for sure. It seemed to go on forever.'

'And he watched you throughout?'

'Yes. He couldn't take his eyes off me.'

'Bitch!' Ethan hissed. 'I only do whatever I choose! I was in control!'

'Was he attracted to you?'

'Yes. Obviously so. He had that look in his face. I could see he was aroused.'

Ethan growled. The feeling in his stomach spread outwards. His hands began to shake.

'Was he masturbating?'

'No. But I could tell that he wanted to. I expect he did afterwards. Once he was alone.'

She looked at the dock. Saw his fury. Killed him with a photo. Click!

She saw Mr Justice Mulvenny about to speak. She went on quickly.

'I'm sure Ethan Hall has masturbated because of it many times since. Alone somewhere.'

'You lying cunt!'

Ethan Hall jumped to his feet, his body shaking uncontrollably.

'You don't know anything about me! About what I can do!'

The guards reached for him. He shook and turned and snapped against them. Despite their size, they struggled to restrain him.

'I will destroy you all! I will fucking destroy you all!'

'Mr Hall!' Mulvenny roared, 'Calm yourself!'

'I haven't even started yet! D'you hear me? I don't need to be free! I don't need to touch them anymore! I will kill you and everything you believe in!'

'Mr Hall!'

'I'll kill everything - every fucking hope and belief, everything you take for granted – as easily as I killed the first three! Cunts! You are nothing to me! Nothing! I am Shiva! D'you hear me! Shiva!'

Anne-Marie Wells watched the guards adjust to his energy. She took her final photo just before they brought him down. She knew it was over.

CHAPTER 55

WEDNESDAY - TRIAL DAY 8
9.38pm

Less than forty eight hours after Ethan Hall's outburst the jury returned a guilty verdict. On all counts. It took them twenty seven minutes to reach their decision.

'Barely long enough,' as Mike said afterwards, 'for everyone to have their say.'

He had concluded the prosecution case that morning. Ethan Hall hadn't spoken again, but it was irrelevant; the jury had already made up their minds. Mike's closing speech had been a brilliant formality.

Mulvenny accepted the jury's verdict and thanked them. His deliberation had also been brief. He had passed sentence that afternoon.

A Whole Life Tariff.

Ethan Hall would die in prison.

Peter Jones insisted that the celebration party be held in The Cross Keys. They had all arrived by mid-afternoon. Marcus and Anne-Marie had booked a room in the Lace Market Hotel on High Pavement, close to the **Influence** offices. The others intended to rely on taxis. No one planned to be in a fit state to drive by the end of the evening. The plan was working perfectly.

Now, for some, the emotional high of victory was giving way to moments of reflection.

'Impossible not to feel sorry for Tina Smith,' Janet said to Kevin

McNeill, whilst the younger members of the team began another drinking game. 'Life dealt her an awful hand right from the very beginning.'

'And, despite that, she was still more willing to help than Campbell.'

'Yeah. It would be hard to warm to that guy.'

'A classic example of the silent majority, eh?' Kevin scowled. 'The sort who want everything to be perfect in their life, who are quick to point out what they have the right to expect from the rest of us, but who are never going to do the right thing when the situation demands it.'

'You're sounding bitter, DS McNeill.'

'I'm drinking bitter, DC Harris. And the cheapest whisky chaser I can buy.' He drained his pint glass. 'Do you want another wine?'

She checked her watch. 'No, it's time to go on to the vodka. Large, please. Tonic, no ice.'

Kevin grimaced. 'I timed that wrong.'

'If you're drinking cheap whisky, you can afford a large vodka. Simple economics.'

'I didn't know you were an economist,' Peter Jones joined in as Kevin ordered the drinks.

'I don't have a qualification, but I'm good with numbers.'

'Oh, I see.' Peter grinned. 'You know what they call an economist without a qualification, don't you?'

'No. What?'

His grin widened. 'I'll tell you when we're back at work. When I'm on safer ground.'

'You know what Boss, sometimes I've got no idea what you're talking about.'

'That's probably just as well.' Peter turned back to Mike Coopland and Brian Kaffee. For the last three hours they had both been ordering wine by the bottle, rather than the glass. Brian was slumped against the bar. Mike was standing with his feet further apart than usual. Peter pointed at the floor. 'Is it spinning yet?'

'Dear boy, I fucking well hope so. It's the Earth, for God's sake. It's essential that it's spinning.'

'Your brain's still racing, then?'

'At a hundred miles a minute. Don't think the drink's going to slow it.'

'I know what you mean. It's going to take a couple of days, eh?'

'For sure. That one was way too close for comfort.'

'I didn't notice.'

'And from what I heard, the armed unit also left it until the very last minute to bring down your would-be killer.'

'I didn't notice that either.'

'Of course you didn't.' Mike looked at the bottles lining the shelves behind the bar. 'We can just be extremely grateful that your CHIS came through with enough information for you to put a counter-plan in place.'

'And that, for the last couple of nights, I'd noticed what turned out to be Jolly's car parked near the house when I went for a walk.'

'You didn't have to put yourself in the line of fire, though, did you?'

'I was strongly advised to let one of the armed unit take my place.'

'You never were very good at taking advice.'

'It was me he was coming after, so it had to be me in front of him. I'm not a normal member of the public. I'm a copper. We don't hide behind others. We confront the bad guys.'

'For your birthday I'll buy you a Superman costume.'

'Says the man who wears a wig to work.'

'Steady! I love that wig.' Mike scratched his scalp. 'Any chance you'll be able to prove the hit was organised by Brent?'

'Highly unlikely. As I understand it, Mr Jolly's only comment to date has been "Fuck off".'

'Well he's certainly going to get fucked off to prison for an extended stay.'

'Yep.' Peter grinned. 'Good job for me his preferred tool was a knife and not a long-range rifle.'

'See, that's the thing. I can never decide whether you're the luckiest or the best copper alive.'

'What's luck got to do with it?'

'Tina Turner. 1984.' Kaffee pushed himself upright.

'What?'

'The song, "What's love got to do with it", it was a hit for Tina Turner in 1984.'

'Jesus Christ!' Peter feigned dismay. 'Anyway Mr Coopland, the question still stands. Where was the luck in this investigation?'

'Seriously?' Mike rolled his eyes. 'Just when we need it, in the nick of time, you come up with two new witnesses and pages of notes that could best be titled, *Diary of a Homicidal Maniac*. A document that our defendant never expected us to find and which absolutely helped to throw him off his game.'

'Sounds like good policing to me.'

'It sounds like luck.'

'How can you say that?'

'Because that's what it was! Listen – Brian you be the Judge – how did you find the very lovely Tina Smith?'

'She offered her services, in a manner of speaking.'

'Exactly. Nothing to do with you, just good luck. And how did you get Ethan Hall's notes?'

'From an informant.'

'Luck again!'

'No! It was the result of a brilliantly created and managed

relationship with a member of the criminal fraternity.'

'Bollocks.'

Peter put his hand on Kaffee's shoulder. 'Brian, you're the Judge. What do you say?'

'I need to piss.'

Mike raised his glass. 'Eloquent as ever, Mr Kaffee.'

Brian set off, staggering in the direction of the Gents.

Mike helped himself to wine from his Junior's bottle. 'We did good between us, Detective Chief Inspector,' he said quietly.

'We certainly did. We certainly did good.'

Marcus and Anne-Marie were sitting at a table in the corner. Peter joined them. Fatigue was etched across both their faces.

'A holiday might be a good idea,' he said.

'We've just been talking about it.' Anne-Marie sipped at her Sauvignon Blanc. 'We might go back to Malaysia.'

'Where you were married?'

'Yes. The East Coast. We're going to look into it over the next few days.' She pushed her glass away. 'How are you, now that you don't have to look after all of us anymore?'

'I always have to look after you. It's in my job description. It's what keeps me so young.'

'You need to buy glasses, my friend.' Marcus forced a smile. 'There's something that I need to tell you, if that's OK? Just to clear out the cupboard entirely, as it were.'

'Sure. But if it's about your meeting with Calvin Brent, you don't need to. I mean if you're going to tell me that you actually did what Brent asked and met with his man, I'd save your breath.'

Marcus gasped. 'How did you know?'

'Brent wouldn't have given you a choice. And you would have been foolish in the extreme to refuse him to his face, especially before any of us knew about it. Besides, on this very rare occasion

Brent wanted the same result as we did. So it follows that you'd want to help, even if you didn't like the way you were asked, even if it was impossible to make a difference.'

'You could have told me that in the first place.'

'Maybe.' Peter reached into his jacket pocket, felt his car keys. 'Listen, I've changed my mind. I'm not going to go home tonight; can't face the thought of a taxi. So I'm going to book myself into the hotel instead. Join you both for breakfast, if any of us are to able to face food first thing in the morning.'

'Sounds like a good idea.' Anne-Marie reached out and squeezed his hand. 'Tonight is not the night for being on your own.'

'True. I'm parked in there,' he nodded in the direction of The Lace Market car park. 'I'll just pop over and get my briefcase out of the car. I don't want to leave it overnight.'

'See you in a minute.'

Peter made his way across the crowded bar without Mike or McNeill or any of his team noticing. The ice-cold January air hit him as soon as he stepped outside.

'Jesus!'

The pavements were covered in thick frost. He nearly lost his balance twice as he made his way into the multi-storey. His car was as the top. Out in the open.

He had parked there deliberately, spending some time that afternoon looking out over the city, watching the occasional bird swoop past at eye-level, trying to find a sense of peace, before making his way into the pub.

He chose to take the stairs. Twelve levels. Moving as fast as he was able. By the time he reached his destination, his heart was thumping against his chest.

'I've really got to start doing some exercise.'

The frost was thicker up here. He trod carefully. His car was the only one he could see. Reverse-parked, boot against the wall.

A figure wearing a dark coat with a hood up around his head appeared suddenly from behind the far side of the car. Peter stopped walking and reached into his pocket for the keys, sliding them between his fingers as he clenched his hand into a fist.

'What are you doing?'

The figure ignored him and pulled himself up onto the wall.

'What do you think you're doing?'

The figure pushed himself into a standing position, his arms well out from his sides helping him to balance. He wobbled momentarily, then his left foot slipped on the ice and he almost fell forwards.

'Get down off there!' Peter moved slowly. 'I'm a police officer. You can talk to me. I can help you.'

The figure twisted awkwardly in his direction. Peter saw the face clearly for the first time. He sobered instantly.

'Oh dear God...'

CHAPTER 56

WEDNESDAY - TRIAL DAY 8
10.21pm

Peter Jones let go of the car keys and eased his hand out of his pocket. He took another two steps forwards.

Slowly.

Gently.

The figure tensed. 'Stop there! Don't come any closer!'

Peter stopped. The voice was not as he remembered it. The body had changed too. Even with the heavy clothing, it was clear he had lost weight. Peter began to shake as a whole mix of emotions threatened to overwhelm him. Then the DCI took over.

'Nic, we just need to talk. Right? You have been waiting for me, haven't you?'

'Yes.'

'I'm pleased you have.'

'He led me back. So I could show you something.'

'Andrew led you back?'

'Yes.'

'I'm pleased he did.'

'He knew the way.'

'I'm very glad.' Peter inched forwards. 'I'd like to be closer to you when we talk, if that's OK?'

'Why?'

'Because it will help me understand you better, and it will mean I can see clearly what you have to show me.'

'You don't have to be close to see that.'

'This must be important, though, or Andrew wouldn't have led you back. Am I right?'

'Yes. Of course. You were the clever man who was always right.' Nic wobbled again.

'No. I've made a lot of mistakes. Andrew will have told you that.'

'He's told me lots of things. And he's shown me things, too.'

'I'm sure he has. Can I come closer, please?'

Nic sighed. 'You're not really asking me. You never were. You always do what you decide. It doesn't matter now, though. I'm a flier. I know how to let go and take off. I told the man on the bridge that. He didn't believe me. Do you?'

'I want you to explain it to me. So I can understand. That's why you need to let me be close.'

'That's right!' Nic wiped a gloved hand across his face. 'I have to wait until you get to where you need to be. Just as I always did. And then you will tell me you are ready to listen. Just as you always did. And then I get the chance to talk. And you pretend that what I'm saying is important. You see, I remember the game and I can do play it one more time. But now I make the rule. And the rule is, you have to stand next to me.'

'Thank you.' Peter moved carefully, cautiously. Pulling himself onto the wall was tricky, standing upright harder still. The ice beneath his feet was slippery smooth. He refused to let his eyes look down. Instead he turned his head and looked at Nic. They were one arm's length apart.

'I feel free now,' Nic said. 'You can't imagine how that is.'

'Tell me. Please.'

'You won't understand. Even if you think you do. I'm different. I can just let go of everything. I can make my own choices. I can be *me*, the real me, not the pretend version that had to fit in with everyone else. I can be free like Andrew. Free as the sky.'

He giggled.

'They won't let you fly from the bridge. D'you know that? They put it up in the air – all the way up - and then have things in the way and yellow men who pretend they have interesting things to tell you, but are really there to keep you inside.'

'Tell me about tomorrow, please. Where is Andrew going to lead you tomorrow? Where is the next bridge you might visit?'

'It doesn't work like that when you're free, when you can fly. Let me show you - '

Peter saw Nic's knees bend as he prepared to leap and thrust his right arm out with as much force as he could muster, catching him in the chest, knocking him off the wall and back into the car park. He heard the thud as Nic's shoulders and head hit first and a groan as he lost consciousness.

Then his own right foot went from underneath him.

Peter forced his head back, in the direction of safety, knowing his body would follow if it possibly could. The momentum of his right foot, kicking out into the air, acted as a counterforce, threatening to take him over the edge. For a split second it felt as if the pull of his head was winning and then his left foot slipped and the air took him.

His arms splayed out as he fell. His eyes closed. His mind showed him birds taking flight, disturbed by the beaters. He heard the sound of guns. The loudest – and last – was inside his head.

CHAPTER 57

TEN DAYS LATER
5.08pm

The funeral had been everything she expected.

Cold.

Grey.

Ice-hard earth, with the frost still proclaiming its victory.

Grief so great that tears were left to run freely.

The sound of occasional laughter, hurting as the space between loss and shock was filled with dark police humour.

They were all there, apart from Nic. He had been placed as an in-patient at the Priory Hospital. He was receiving treatment for acute mental illness. They had all made a point of telling each other they didn't blame him for Peter's death.

Marcus, of course, had delivered a eulogy that only he could; creating in them all what he called a *memory-lane*, a way of taking their minds in the most positive of directions whenever they thought of Peter Jones. She watched him work with them individually as the wake progressed, the great influencer shielding himself from his own loss by doing what he did best.

Working.

He had been right, Anne-Marie reflected. That was the essential difference between him and Ethan Hall. Her husband was a worker for good. She was sure he would be even better at it now. Especially when he'd had time to work on himself, to find his new perspective.

He wasn't the only one who needed to do that, she considered.

Everything seemed to have changed fundamentally since Ethan Hall had gained prominence. Everything was becoming more extreme. The *Pass it on* killings had spread onto every continent. Governments were trying to decide if – and how – they might hold social media organisations accountable. She couldn't help but feel there was an increasing tolerance of what had been, until only recently, intolerable.

'I wonder what my photos will show in the coming years?'

Anne-Marie made no attempt to answer her own question. Not today. Not now.

She was standing in the bedroom, alone. She reached down and touched the bed, the one she had wanted to burn, the one she had continued to lie in because she had chosen to keep a secret.

It didn't hold those memories of Ethan Hall anymore. They had disappeared when she killed him with a photo. Now the bed was a space only. A space covered by colours and fabrics of her choosing.

Her memories were also her own creations, existing in the space she called *mind*. She could learn how to colour, cover or discard them, too. She could learn how to lay comfortably in her own thoughts and feelings. She could create her own memory-lanes.

Just as Marcus had said.

Anne-Marie looked out of the bedroom window. He was standing in the garden, staring into the valley. Standing there with his back to her and his face raised to the sky.

He was saying goodbye; she knew that. Tomorrow they were flying to Malaysia. When they returned they were going home – back to their old home in The Park.

It had come on the market suddenly. They had revisited, just to check their instinct was right. It was more than right. They had bought it back within an hour.

Anne-Marie moved her right hand to the windowpane; pressed her palm and fingers against the glass. 'Going back to go forwards,' she whispered. 'And together we'll build something even better than before.'

She had faith.

CHAPTER 58

Karl Brent is dead.

Stabbed seventeen times by an inmate he thought he controlled.

They all know I am responsible for his death. But they can do nothing.

I have the power.

They handed it to me. They thought that by locking me in here, they were protecting themselves – protecting you.

But I've told you, haven't I? You can't close the door and turn the key on influence. You can't keep it in.

So now I have a new herd. Only this one I can use. Just as I used the security guard and a prison officer to start the killings.

Freedom, the way you understand it, is a mirage. You all keep running towards it until you die, exhausted and desperate.

I have real freedom.

I have the freedom to change your world, because I know the greatest truth:

Every plague, every contagion, begins small.

So small you don't notice it. And then, when you eventually do, you identify it incorrectly. You misdiagnose it because your secret fears, your need to hang on to normality, blind you to the threat it brings. You look the other way and sing your stupid nursery rhymes until it is too late. And then you scream for help and blame everyone else.

I told you to sit on the sidelines and watch because that is what you do best. You are spectators in your own destruction.

And I have more for you to see.

Far more.

My message to you is simple:

The contagion I have unleashed is growing.

You will know Chaos.

Pass it on.

Chris Parker is a specialist in Communication and Influence. His fascination with the power of words and how they can be used to create intrapersonal and interpersonal change began in 1976. It became a lifelong study that has underpinned over four decades of work in a variety of professional roles and contexts.

A Master Practitioner of Neuro Linguistic Programming (NLP), Chris is a highly experienced management trainer, business consultant, lecturer and writer. He has provided Communication Skills and Influencing Performance training for a wide range of clients including blue-chip organisations, politicians, actors, sportsmen and women, LEAs, public and private leisure providers and healthcare professionals. He has taught on undergraduate and postgraduate programmes throughout the UK and Europe and worked with many individuals to help create personal and/or professional change.

Some of Chris's bestselling titles include *Campaign It!* with Alan Barnard, *The Brain Always Wins* with John Sullivan, the three Marcus Kline thrillers and two poetry volumes, *The City Fox* and *Debris*.

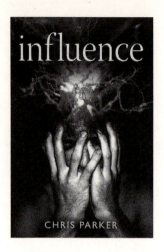

BOOK ONE IN THE MARCUS KLINE TRILOGY

Influence kills...Influence is the greatest force on earth. Influence equals power, the power to affect people and events. The most powerful people alive have the greatest influence. And they can use it for good or bad. Marcus Kline is the world's leading authority on communication and influence. He can tell what you are thinking. He can see inside you. He can step inside your mind. Yet when a series of murder victims bear the horrific hallmarks of an intelligent and remorseless serial killer, Detective Inspector Peter Jones turns to Marcus for help - and everything changes. As the killer sets a deadly pace, the invisible, irresistible and terrifying power of influence threatens friendships, reputations, and lives. When events appear to implicate the great Marcus Kline himself, everyone learns that the worst pain isn't physical...

BOOK TWO IN THE MARCUS KLINE TRILOGY

'I'm going to say a few words.'

That's the promise made by Ethan Hall, the serial killer and master hypnotist, when he recovers from his gunshot wounds and escapes from hospital. It's a promise that causes havoc, loss and unending pain. Using language to bend people to his will, influencing others to carry out the most destructive acts, Ethan Hall extracts his revenge on Marcus Kline and those closest to him in the most personal and savage ways.

Six months have passed since a series of horrific murders forced Marcus Kline, the world's leading authority on communication and influence, into a unique confrontation with Ethan - a battle of words like no other. Now Marcus is trying desperately to save his cancer-stricken wife and rebuild his life, his reputation and his shattered self-confidence. Only Ethan Hall has other plans.

Now, with Marcus Kline's self-belief at an all-time low, the struggle for survival, sanity and salvation teaches everyone involved that things can always get worse.

URBANE

Urbane Publications is dedicated to
developing new author voices, and publishing
fiction and non-fiction that challenges, thrills and
fascinates.

From page-turning novels to innovative
reference books, our goal is to publish what
YOU want to read.

Find out more at
urbanepublications.com